PROLOGUE

"How long has he been like that?"

"Ever since he got the news," Ashanti responded without bothering to look over his shoulder. He was standing in the doorway of Abel's bedroom.

Ashanti's eyes were fixed intently on the man sitting on the edge of the queen-sized bed. The man's back was to them, and his face turned towards the window, sad eyes staring out, yet seeing nothing. For as long as Ashanti had known his friend and mentor, he had always seemed invincible, courageous enough to stand against any and all odds, and determined enough to come out on top every time... or at least he had been. Since he had received the phone call a day before, he seemed a mere shell of his former self. Ashanti had never seem him that broken and it scared him.

"So he hasn't said anything since?" the visitor asked. "Oh, he's spoken, but only half of it was coherent. His rage was clear enough, though," Ashanti said, remembering Animal's first reaction after receiving Kahllah's call.

At first, he was too shocked to speak; instead only able to gasp for air and fight back sobs. But when he did find his voice, he roared. Animal went into a blind fury; salivating and trying to smash everything he could get his hands on, including their hostage, George. It took the combined efforts of Ashanti, Cain, Abel, and an injection of the same sedative they used to keep George quiet to still Animal.

Ashanti felt his homie's pain and wanted to kill George too, but he was the only bargaining chip they had. Acting off emotions and killing Lilith's son would do little to help them get Animal's children back or avenge the murder of his wife. When Animal finally woke from his drug-induced slumber, he was calmer, but he was also different. They had all tried to rouse him, in one way or another, but he was non-responsive. It was like his mind had folded in on itself and he was trapped somewhere inside.

"Damn, Blood, why am I just finding all this out? If there was trouble, I should've been one of the first to know about it," the visitor said angrily.

This time, Ashanti did look at the visitor. His eyes were hard and cold. They no longer held the glint of the mischievous kid he remembered, but those of a young man who had seen firsthand the worst the world had to offer. "Nobody knew you were out. It's not like you announced that you were home from prison, or even bothered to reach out to me. Had I not run into Nef I'd have still been thinking you was upstate."

"I had to get on my feet. You know my style; I didn't wanna come around niggas while I wasn't correct, looking like I wanted a hand out. I've always stood on my own, so I needed to get back right before I made my presence felt. Maybe if you visited more or wrote a nigga, I could've kept you abreast of current events," the visitor shot back.

Ashanti bristled at the truth in his words. "Yeah, maybe I could've done a better job at keeping in contact, but I sent

ANIMAL 4.5

LAST RITES

KWAN

ANIMAL IV: Last Rites

For information contact: Write2Eat2@gmail.com

🏵 Created with Vellum

you bread once a month like clockwork since you been down."

"Indeed you did, and I appreciated that, my nigga, but when you spend twenty-four hours a day looking at walls, and eating shit from the cops, sometimes it's nice to see a friendly face once in a while. But I ain't here to point fingers; I'm here to pay my respects to my best friend." The visitor glanced at Animal. He could feel the pain rolling off him in waves. He knew how much Animal loved Gucci and couldn't imagine what he must've been going through. Losing someone you loved could do irreparable damage, which is one of the reasons he refused to commit to a woman. There was no doubt in his mind that one day he would die in the streets, and he didn't want to inflict that on whoever was foolish enough to fall in love with him. "So, how you wanna play this?"

"I wish I knew," Ashanti said. "I'm a soldier. Animal has always been our general, so we fed off his lead, but as you can see, he isn't in much of a position to lead us right now. I've put a few things in motion, and Kahllah is handling the business with Gucci in California, but as far as a battle plan, the final call is on Animal. It's his woman who was killed, and his children who are kidnapped. This is a delicate decision and I wouldn't dare try and make it for him."

"Then I guess we need to hear it from the horse's mouth," the visitor said, entering the bedroom.

"Good luck with that. I told you he hasn't said anything since yesterday," Ashanti told him.

"That's because you're not speaking the right language." The visitor continued into the room. He shrugged out of his jacket and rolled up the sleeves of his shirt, showing off his muscular forearms. He had always been big, but spending the last few years in prison had turned him into a hulk.

"One last thing I need to get off my chest," Ashanti

called after him. The visitor paused. "Welcome home, Brasco."

Brasco took a couple cautious steps and came to stand within a few feet of Animal. He wasn't sure what frame of mind he was in, and didn't want to risk getting too close. He had seen Animal when his emotions took over and it wasn't a pretty sight.

"Animal," he called softly. Animal's eyes flickered, but beyond that, there was no response. Brasco moved to stand directly in Animal's line of vision, but Animal continued staring in the direction of the window as if he were looking through him. "Animal, first I'd like to offer my condolences for the loss of your wife. Gucci was a good woman and I'm sorry. Now, I know you're hurting, but I'm gonna need you to shake it off so we can decide what should be done next. Nobody wants to make any moves without your say-so."

Animal said nothing.

Brasco cast a glance to the doorway where Ashanti was standing. Ashanti shrugged his shoulders, as if to say, *I told you so.*

Brasco clapped his massive hands in front of Animal's face, making an almost thunderous sound. "Animal, are you in there?" Animal blinked, but that was the extent of his reaction. When Brasco went to rejoin Ashanti, his face was saddened. "I see the lights on, but ain't nobody home."

"I tried to tell you. Brasco, you might as well give it a rest. Animal will come around in his own time or he won't. It doesn't change the fact that we got shit to do," Ashanti said in a clipped tone. He hadn't meant to be so sharp with his friend, but his frustration was starting to bubble over. "Let's head back into the living room. I got a few more things I need to holla at you about while we still have the apartment to ourselves."

Brasco followed Ashanti into the hall, but stopped short, sparing Animal one last glance. It bewildered him to see a man who was once so full of fire, reduced to the shell sitting on the edge of the bed. "Damn, my nigga. Where are you?"

*

Animal was in a dark place. He was sitting alone, on the beach outside his house... or an apparition of it. He was mere feet away from the rolling ocean, yet he could not smell the salt carried on the sea. The full moon overhead was the only source of light, but instead of its normal soft white glow, it was blood red; as if the man in the moon had opened up a vein and was bleeding out into the night sky. The sand was a sickly shade of gray, and felt rough and jagged, like broken glass. Animal ran his bare feet through the sand, feeling the sharp grains cutting into his soles. He examined one of his feet, expecting it to be cut and bleeding, but it was smooth and unmarked. He dug his feet in again, this time deeper, letting the pain wash over him. Pain was his anchor to the dark, yet peaceful, place.

Water splashed on his bare feet, drawing his attention to the ocean. It looked all wrong. Instead of rolling blue waves, he found clashes of an inky blackness that could've just as easily passed for tar instead of water. Animal cringed, but it wasn't the sight of the black sea that disturbed him; it was what he saw when he looked deeper. Just beneath the surface, he saw faces, dozens of them... the faces of his victims. Those whom he had either killed, or caused their deaths, stared back at him from just beneath the surface. He knew each face, remembered each death, and each reason. Every face had a story. Animal felt no guilt or remorse about any of the poor souls dwelling in the murky water save for one: the one he couldn't bear to look at because of the pain it caused him. The one, of all of them, that he didn't see coming.

Gucci was his rock, his rider, his rib. She was the person who he had pledged to spend the rest of his life with, and she had earned it. Gucci had been with Animal through thick and thin, never turning her back on Animal, no matter what he had put her through. Losing Gucci was like someone sucking Animal's soul from his body, and leaving just an empty husk. He felt nothing, not compassion, not grief, not even his ever-faithful companion, rage, could be found within him. Animal was totally numb, floating in the dark limbo that was left of his life. Gucci had loved, honored, and obeyed her husband until death finally did them part; a death that he blamed himself for. Had he only taken a minute to think, instead of letting his sense of honor control his actions, maybe he wouldn't have followed Red Sonja so blindly, and Gucci would still be alive.

"I have failed you, my love," Animal whispered to his wife's ghost.

"A wise woman once told me: if you give people flowers when they're living, you need not be burdened by guilt when they pass. Kindness in life goes much further than it does in death, where it can't be appreciated," a familiar voice said from behind him.

Animal cocked his head to once side, but didn't turn around. He didn't need to see the speaker to know whose voice it was. He was yet another apparition in the dark place

Animal has banished himself to. It seemed all the people and reasons why he had hated himself resided there. "Be gone, specter, and leave me to my grieving," Animal grumbled.

"This isn't the inside of my head, it's yours. You're the architect of everything here, including me," the man stepped from the shadows and into the moonlight. He was tall with a shaved head and rough salt and pepper stubble covering both sides of his chiseled chin. Smoothing the folds of his robe, he took a seat in the sand next to Animal. "So, is this what it's come to, another round of you retreating in on yourself instead of standing up and facing life? Do you never tire of wallowing in your own self-pity?"

"They killed Gucci," Animal said in response to the question.

"As I warned you they would when you insisted on pursuing her." He scooped up a mound of sand with his right hand and let it trickle into his left. "A man cannot live in two worlds and not expect them to spill into each other," he said, watching the sand overflow from his palm and blow away on a phantom wind that seemed to have come from nowhere. "Have you not caused enough accidental deaths in your young life to know that by now?"

"Is that what you've come here for, to rub my shortcomings in my face?" Animal asked.

The man turned his head slightly to regard Animal, showing the black patch that covered one of his eyes. "Quite to the contrary, my bastard seed. I've come to resurrect you."

Animal gave a soft chuckle. "Even from the grave you're still my guardian angel, huh Priest?"

Priest shrugged. "A parent's work is never truly done, as this whole ordeal should've taught you." Priest laid his hand on Animal's shoulder, and bid him to stand. Priest looked at his son almost lovingly. "My heart weeps for what has happened to you tonight, my son. The devil has come into your home and left her taint on everything you hold dear. Now the question remains, what do you intend to do?"

Animal shook his head in frustration. "My head is just all over the place. Everything is fucked up and I'm the cause, as always. I've failed everyone who has ever depended on me to keep them safe. Father, for the first time in my life I don't know what to do."

"You do what comes naturally, murder your enemies," Priest said as if the answer should've been obvious. "Animal, I don't pretend to know your pain because after your mother I've never allowed another woman into my heart, but I do know what it's like to lose your children to circumstances beyond your control. Child, in your short life you have been violated in the most intimate of ways, but no offense you've suffered can compare to what has happened to your family. Every minute that those involved are allowed to breathe God's good air is a mockery to not only your pedigree as a harbinger of death, but it's an offense to the memory of every soldier who has laid down their life in the name of your survival."

Animal dropped to his knees and dug his fists in the sand. As Priest spoke, a slow fire began to build in Animal's gut. Kastro, Gladiator, Mimi, even Priest. They had all given their lives so that Animal could have the fairytale ending with a wife and a couple of kids. By not taking action, he was dishonoring their memories and he owed them more. When he looked up at his father, his eyes burned with hatred.

"I'm going to kill them, the men who touched my family." Animal's voice was laced with pain.

Priest placed a hand atop his son's mop of curls. "Not just those men, you will kill them all... mothers, fathers, brothers, sisters. Their entire bloodline must be extinguished."

"Yes, there will be blood," Animal agreed.

Priest smiled like the proud father that he was. "So it is said, so it shall be done." When he removed his hand from Animal's head, a spiked crown of thrones had appeared on it. "Take up your pistols, and cleanse the world in their vengeful fire."

PART 1

AWAKENINGS

CHAPTER 1

When Red Sonja returned to the apartment, she found Ashanti and an unfamiliar face huddled around the kitchen table locked in a deep conversation. When they noticed her standing there, the conversation abruptly stopped.

"You know when you enter a room and everybody stops talking, it gives the impression that you were the topic of conversation," Red Sonja said, setting the bags she was carrying on the counter. She had made a supply run while the men stayed behind to attend to Animal.

"Nah, you weren't the topic of conversation," Ashanti said. "At least not this one," the man she'd never met chimed in.

"The name is Brasco," he stood and extended his hand. "Sonja," she told him, but ignored his hand. This was her first time meeting Brasco but she'd heard more than a few stories about him from Animal. He probably talked about Brasco more than he did Ashanti, which irritated her. She had a natural dislike for anyone who represented any part of Animal's life prior to her.

"So, you're the infamous Red Sonja?" Brasco openly let his eyes roll over her. Sonja's fire engine red hair hung loosely around her tanned shoulders. The jeans she wore were so tight that he could see her cameltoe through the fabric. He had to admit, she was far prettier than he imagined her to be from Ashanti's stories.

"The way you're looking at me says you're either trying to imagine what my pussy tastes like or thinking about taking a swing at me."

"Maybe a bit of both," Brasco flashed a wicked grin.

"Knock it off, Brasco. We ain't got time for this shit," Ashanti cut in.

"Kick back, Blood. You know I would never push up on anything that belongs to the homie Animal," Brasco said.

"I'm not property to be owned, and you'd do well to remember that when speaking to me or about me," Red Sonja said seriously. "Ashanti, what is this knucklehead doing here?"

"Brasco is going to help us with our little problem. We're gonna need some solid cats with us on this and he's one of the most solid I know," Ashanti told her.

Sonja rolled her steel grey eyes. "Just what we need, another wannabe thug-ass nigga who's itching to shoot somebody."

"First of all, I ain't no wannabe nothing. My résumé speaks for itself. And furthermore, I ain't itching to shoot somebody; I'm itching to shoot any and everybody who had a hand in this," Brasco said with conviction.

"I hear you talking, tough guy," Sonja said sarcastically.

"You gonna hear my pistol too when the time comes for me to let that muthafucka bark."

"Well, now that the two of you are acquainted, can we get back to business?" Ashanti's voice betrayed his frustration.

Red Sonja gave Brasco one more dirty look for good measure before addressing Ashanti. "Any word from The Lotus?"

"The last time I spoke to her she was cleaning up the mess in California and then jumping on a plane to follow a lead into this Brotherhood angle," Ashanti told her.

A horrified expression crossed Red Sonja's face. "You mean clean up as in..."

"No, she would never desecrate Gucci's body like that. She's already in the city morgue, but Kahllah has a friend on the inside that is going to conveniently misplace her paperwork for a time so they can't identify her just yet."

"That's cool for a temporary solution, but how long do you think we'll be able to keep a corpse lost in the shuffle?" Sonja asked. "Eventually, it's going to come out that Gucci is dead and when that happens, it's going to play out like a Lifetime movie. A woman is brutally murdered, and her fiancé, who happens to have a history of violence, is nowhere to be found. Care to take a guess as to who the prime suspect will be?"

"That's bullshit. Animal would never hurt Gucci!" Brasco said assuredly.

"Don't matter what we know, all that's gonna matter is where the evidence points," Sonja said. "Gucci's death is something that's going to be impossible to hide, so at this point I think our best bet is to put together a story that's so airtight that it keeps Animal from the gas chamber and all of us from being mistaken as accessories. Turning our attention towards the more immediate problem, my father's wife has both our children and we need to get them back. The more time we waste, the more we risk Lilith hiding them away from us somewhere in her networks. I won't have my child fall victim to the Brotherhood and their brainwashing, or Gucci's son. I will bring those children home."

Brasco snorted. "If your dad's cartel is as heavy as you say it is, then we're probably gonna need a small army to have even the slimmest of chances of getting those kids out alive."

"Not an army," Ashanti spoke up. "Just a few good niggas who don't mind dying."

CHAPTER 2

S hai sat in his new office, located inside the Empire State Building, looking out at the skyline. The sun had recently set and the city was breathing its second wind, transforming from a collective of shiny glass towers to a complex pattern of bright lights and sounds. New York was a beautiful city during the day, but at night, it was like looking into the cosmos. It was a city full of possibilities and opportunities. Looking down from twenty stories above street level, Shai felt like he was the king of it all. And he was.

Aside from the few years he spent in college, Shai had lived in New York all of his life. He was the youngest son of who some said was the last of the old world gangsters, Poppa Clark. Poppa Clark had always strived to make sure that his children were afforded the best of everything from education to the way they lived. It had been his life's mission to build a world for his children where they wouldn't have to suffer through the same mistakes that he had made, but when he was killed, Shai found himself placed on the underworld throne by default. Like his father, Shai also had a vision of the world he wanted to build, one where he would reign as the undisputed king, and he was well on his way to seeing his dream come to fruition.

There was a soft knock on his office door.

"Come," Shai said, without bothering to turn away from the window.

A man who looked to be in his early to mid-thirties came into the room. He was dressed in a tan blazer, black shirt, and black jeans. On one side of his face, he bore a scar that had been gifted to him by a woman named Kastro before he cut her throat. "He's here."

"Thanks, Angelo. Show him in," Shai said, taking a minute to button the jacket of his gray suit and settle into the wing-backed chair behind his desk. He noticed Angelo still lingering in the doorway. "Is there something else?"

"Shai, are you sure about this? I mean, I'm not questioning your judgment or anything like that, but it's kind of beneath you to be taking a meeting with a solider, a foot soldier at that."

"Angelo, as I recall, back when you were a foot soldier, my father would talk to you all the time. He kicked it with all you guys whenever he got the chance," Shai told him.

"Yeah, but that was different. We were soldiers in Poppa's army. This kid ain't one of us. To top it off, he and his brother are fucking sociopaths," Angelo pointed out.

"As always, I thank you for your council, old friend, and I'll take your concerns into consideration during my meeting," Shai said dismissively.

"Whatever you say, boss," Angelo said, with a hint of sarcasm in his voice. He went to fetch the visitor.

Shai knew that he had offended Angelo, but it hadn't been intentional. He had been under a tremendous amount of stress lately. Being handed the throne was one thing, but holding it was proving to be something else. The crown was weighing heavily on his head and it was driving Shai further away from the man he was and instead making him the man he needed to be to ensure the future of his family and preserve his father's legacy.

A moment later, Angelo returned with a young man trailing him. Shai had never met him personally until then, but knew him by his reputation in the streets. He wore a Yankee fitted cap pulled low over his face, but not so low, where you couldn't see the scowl painted across it. Long braids spilled from beneath his cap and tickled his shoulders. As he ambled into the room, his pants sagged so low that Shai couldn't help but to wonder how he could walk with them like that. He looked around, openly admiring Shai's expansive office. His eyes landed on the double doors on the other side of the room and he hesitated for a moment, as if he were having second thoughts. After a brief mental debate, he continued towards the desk. Without waiting to be invited, Abel helped himself to the seat across from Shai.

"Feel free to make yourself at home," Shai said sarcastically.

It was then that Abel realized his error in etiquette. "My fault, Shai. It's not too often than a hood nigga like me sits with kings, so I don't know the rules." It wasn't a cop-out, just Abel being honest.

"I ain't no king, shorty. I'm a man, same as you and Angelo." Shai nodded to his friend, who was standing behind Abel as if he were expecting trouble out of the youngster.

"If you say so, Shai," Abel said with an easy smirk. "Dig, I know you're a busy man so I'm not going to take up too much of your time. First and foremost, thank you for agreeing to meet with me on behalf of my big homie. Ashanti says to tell you that he appreciates it."

"You're not sitting across that table because of Ashanti. Shai agreed to meet with you on the strength of Big Doc," Angelo corrected him. Big Doc was one of the O.G.'s in the organization. Apparently, he was doing time with someone Ashanti knew and owed them a favor so he reached out to ask Shai to spare a few minutes for the youngsters.

Abel looked at Angelo like he wanted to spit on him, but held his tongue. It wasn't the time or place to chin check the old-head. "However it went, we appreciate it. Now," he turned back to Shai, "as you may or may not have heard, we've recently suffered a tragedy."

"Yes, unfortunately I have," Shai shook his head sadly. "These are terrible times we're living in when a man's wife and family are no longer respected as off limits. Animal and I haven't had the smoothest relationship over the last few years, but my heart still goes out to him. As a husband and a parent myself, I can imagine what he's going through. Please offer him my condolences."

"Your condolences are appreciated, Shai, but I came hoping for your help," Abel told him.

"How so?"

"The people who have taken Animal's children are no slouches. They've got muscle and political connections. These are things we're a bit short on, but you have them in abundance," Abel said.

"Is that right?" He leaned back in his chair and steepled his fingers, looking at Abel as if he had lost his mind.

"Look, Shai, I know what you're thinking and I'm not here asking you to get involved directly, just to provide us with an umbrella. If the cartel thinks we're affiliated with the Clarks, they might be willing to listen to reason instead of taking this thing further than it's already gone. We ain't asking you for no money, and my crew busts their own guns. All we need is for you to keep everybody honest while we work this shit out."

Shai shook his head. "I'm empathetic to your problems, but I can't get involved, directly or indirectly. It could kick off an international drug war between us and Poppito's Cartel and I can't put my entire organization at risk for Animal's beef."

"It's Animal's beef now, but how soon do you think it'll be before it becomes your beef too?" Abel shot back. "Now that Lilith is calling the shots, the cartel is looking to expand. It's Puerto Rico and the south at the moment, but it won't be long before they're encroaching on the east coast cities you lay claim to."

"When and if the time comes where Poppito or Lilith forget their places, I'll remind them where the Clarks stand. Until such time, I can't get involved. But to show that I am not completely without compassion to your plight, I'll reach

out to some of my people in the F.B.I. and see if they can help get a line on Animal's kids."

Abel laughed. "Picture a man like Animal sitting around waiting for the law to bring back what belongs to him. You saw how he reacted when he thought you tried to kill Gucci, so can you imagine the wrath that's gonna be unleashed behind what them Puerto Ricans did?"

"That sounds like a nice way of saying he's about to start killing shit," Shai read between the lines.

"That's an understatement, chief. Like you said, Shai, you're a family man and a parent. How would you react if the shoe was on the other foot? Animal is going to go on a biblical rampage and carve out a path of bodies to get to Lilith, and that path is going to cut right through your backyard."

Shai's face became serious. "Now you listen to me. You boys are pissed, and rightfully so, but I'm not going to have Animal or anyone else come to New York and make it a war zone. Feelings aside, he needs to keep that shit in Cali, and out of my city."

Abel matched his seriousness. "I hate to burst your bubble, good king, but Animal is already in your city."

This caught Shai by surprise. "How is it that a natural disaster has blown into town and I wasn't made aware?" He was speaking to Abel, but the question was really directed at Angelo.

"Because, with all due respect, the Dog Pound answers to no one, not even kings," Abel said.

"For somebody who came in here looking for a hand out you sure are a cocky little fuck," Angelo said.

"There's a difference between being cocky and being honest, old head," Abel shot back. "Look I ain't saying nothing that everybody in this room doesn't already know. Regardless of whether the Clarks help us or not, people are going to die, we were just hoping to limit some of the casualties by reaching out to you, Shai."

Shai sighed. "And as I've already told you, I can't get in the middle of this. I've got a family and a city to run. Making an unnecessary enemy of the cartel would be..." he searched for the right words, "...bad for business."

"Oh, I get it. Lilith has got you in her pocket too, huh?" Abel accused. "You know, for all that king of kings shit you talk, I'm kind of surprised to see you follow a trend."

"You're treading on thin ice. I'd hate for you to fall into the deep end," Angelo warned.

Abel laughed. "Nigga, I'm already drowning," he said, standing up. "I understand your position, Shai. I can't say I respect it, but I understand. Before I go, let me give you some food for thought: tigers are gluttons. Even when they're full, they'll keep eating as long as there is fresh meat in front of them. When you hear them claws scratching at the walls of the city, I want you to remember that you turned your back on the best chance you had to put that bitch down." He turned to leave, but Angelo blocked his path.

"I don't recall you being dismissed," Angelo said.

Abel looked him up and down. "Homie, you must not have heard me when I said the Dog Pound don't answer to nobody. Now you can either let me pass, or grab your strap and get busy. I've got shit to do."

Angelo looked to Shai, who motioned for him to let Abel pass.

Abel stepped towards the door then stopped short. "You know, I once asked Ashanti why he or Animal never went after your family when they thought you'd shot Gucci intentionally."

"And what did he say?" Shai asked.

"He said because Animal wouldn't allow it. Even though your boys had done some fuck shit, he felt like you and he were honorable men, and honorable men respected the sanctity of families. I guess he was half right on that."

His words touched Shai, but he kept his demeanor neutral. "Abel, it may not count for much, but I am sorry that it has to be this way."

Abel smirked. "I seriously doubt that, but before it's all said and done you will be."

*

"You should've let me dust that lil nigga instead of letting him walk out," Angelo said once Abel had gone.

"Dust him for what, coming to try and help reunite a man with his kids? Where is the wrong in that? Am I not supposed to be the king of the city?" Shai got up and began pacing the room. Turning Abel away was a business decision, but that didn't help his conscience any. "Men who willingly play the game getting touched is something I can deal with, but families... " his words trailed off. "No matter what's going on women and children are supposed to be off limits, and Lilith has crossed that line. This isn't how the game is supposed to be played, Angelo. She's gone too far."

"In times of war there'll always be men who have to make the hard decisions. Those are usually the men who end up winning." Angelo pointed out.

The double doors on the other side of Shai's office swung open and in walked a man wearing a tailored black suit. He was dark-skinned with a clean-shaven head and eyes as green as jade. On his face, he wore an easy smile, one that he had spent years practicing to throw his enemies off. He was a master of espionage and misdirection.

Trailing him was a man who was slightly more handsome, but equally as dangerous. Instead of a suit, he wore baggy blue jeans and a long sleeve graphic t-shirt that hugged his muscular frame. His long black hair, which was usually braided into two Pocahontas ponytails, hung freely about his face. He had taken to wearing it like that to hide the small scar near his ear that ran along his jaw. He and his partner had been in the next room listening the whole time Shai was talking to Abel.

The two men represented a group of mercenaries who called themselves La Muerte Negra roughly translated to The Black Death. They had started out as a street crew in Harlem called the Road Dawgz until they took their game international. La Muerte Negra had changed the tides of war and the fortunes of kings and it was their unique skill set that had brought them stateside and into an uneasy partnership with Shai Clark.

"I take it you heard all that, K-Dawg?" Shai asked the man in the black suit.

"Indeed I did, and I expected no less. To be honest I'm glad to see my lil' dawg still has his fangs," K-Dawg said and invited himself to the seat Abel had vacated moments prior. His partner, Justice, remained standing.

"You say that like it's a good thing," Angelo said.

"It is, all depending on who the dog ends up biting." K-Dawg crossed one long leg over the other. "Overall, I'd say this was a pretty damn interesting turn of events," he chuckled. "Please tell me how the fuck you can find humor in a man's kids getting snatched? That ain't how the game is played!"

Shai said angrily. Being a parent, he empathized with Animal and what he was likely going through.

K-Dawg turned his green eyes to Shai. "I've been playing this game a lot longer than you, so please don't try and lecture me on the rules," he checked him. "In all honesty Shai, this kidnapping angle wasn't something I saw coming, but I'd be lying if I said I was overly broken up over of it. Animal was a piece on the chessboard that I had written off until he was recently put back in play. This kidnapping might've been a blessing in disguise."

Shai gave K-Dawg a disapproving look. "Spoken like a man who doesn't have kids."

K-Dawg stood and faced Shai. All traces of the businessman he presented himself as fell away and all that was left was the street nigga that he was. "While you're standing there trying to judge me, like I don't know the pain of loss, let me give you a little history lesson, my nigga. I am the product of the white man who raped my mother, and was raised by a man who hated me enough to try and kill me when I was barely old enough to read. I was a curse on my family and brought down everybody who was ever dumb enough to care about me, but my one moment of redemption came when it fell to me to raise my sister's kid. All I had to do was make sure that kid had at least a halfway decent shot at life to balance out everything I had ever done wrong, but I fucked that up because I just couldn't seem to keep my nose out of the life. My love of the game corrupted the one thing I was supposed to keep pure, and I had to watch from a distance as my nephew became everything I was supposed to protect him from."

"So what's your point?" Shai asked.

"My point is, a man can't live in both worlds and expect them to not overlap. For as long as we choose to play the game, no matter how hard we try and insulate the people and

things we love, eventually they all get sucked into our bullshit. We either hang up the hustle or ride out and take whoever along for the ride with us. There are no gray areas. Nobody is exempt from this simple fact, including kings, Shai. You'd do well to remember that moving forward."

"And you'd do well to remember the terms of our agreement," Shai shot back. "I'm in this to make money, not settle personal vendettas."

"Whoever made omelets without breaking eggs? Don't get so beside yourself that you forget who has made it possible for your plans to expand to come to fruition!" K-Dawg told him. "Look, Shai, I understand your concerns but it's all going to work out in the long run. Animal is as lethal as they come, but without the proper support his chances at succeeding Lilith are slim to none. He'll fight the good fight as he always does, but this is a battle he can't win."

"But what if he does?" Shai questioned. "Once he's done with Lilith what's to stop him from following the trail back to us and discovering our parts in this? If Animal comes at me again there won't be a reprieve this time. He's going down for the long nap. Is that going to be a problem?" He was speaking to K-Dawg, but looking at Justice.

K-Dawg looked from Shai to Justice. "What do you say, Jus? If it comes down to it, will Animal dying be a problem for you?"

Justice shrugged his shoulders. "It's like he said before he gave me this beauty mark," he pointed to the scar on his face. "We ain't brothers no more."

K-Dawg smiled. "See, just like I said, everything is going to work itself out. But if you're still afraid of the blow back from this, I'll make a phone call or two and see about getting these little niggas cleaned up. I think twenty-thousand per head should be enough to get every broke nigga in the streets to try and collect."

"We've tried to use hired killers on Animal in the past and it's never worked out well for them," Shai said, recalling the countless men he had sent after Animal over the years only to have them get sent back in bags or go missing.

"Of course hired help wouldn't be able to do much with Animal, which is why I'm putting the paper on the heads of his homies. Making Animal the target, would be the obvious choice, which is why we're not going to touch him... at least not yet. I'm going to target his support system, Ashanti, Brasco, the whole Dog Pound. All them little dirty niggas is about to get it. I'm going to cut Animal off from anyone who I know that would bust their guns for him. Let's see him go to war with no army."

Shai shook his head in marvel at K-Dawg's cunning. "You had to be a general in some past life," he said sarcastically.

"I've been a general in every life that I have or will ever live, including this one," K-Dawg matched his tone.

"Do what you gotta do, K-Dawg. Just make sure this shit doesn't come back on me or my family," Shai warned.

K-Dawg stood and gave a mock bow. "As you command, your highness. Let's blow this joint, Jus. It smells like sex in here and I don't want that stench getting in my suit," he looked Shai and Angelo up and down before strutting out of the office. Justice made to follow his friend, but stopped short and spared a glance at Shai and Angelo. There was a strange expression on his face, and he opened his mouth as if he were about to say something, but thought better of it and walked out. "I don't like them cats, especially that slimy muthafucka K-Dawg," Angelo said once they had gone.

"I'm not a big fan of K-Dawg either. He's sneaky, dangerous, and I can't trust him as far as I can throw him," Shai said.

"Then why continue to deal with him?" Angelo asked.

"Because right now, he's the lesser of two evils. We could've probably got the deal done on our own, but there are certain guarantees that he brings to the table that we couldn't get anywhere else."

Angelo shook his head. "I still don't like it or him. That dude is a grease ball and it'll only be a matter of time before he double crosses us."

Shai smiled. "I would expect nothing less from him. I know K-Dawg has a card up his sleeve that he hasn't played yet, but before it's all said and done, he'll find out he isn't the only one who knows how to deal from the bottom of the deck."

CHAPTER 3

The night was quiet... too quiet depending on who was listening. There was the usual hustle and bustle that came with living in New York City—too much traffic in the streets and seemingly too many people on the side-walks—but it felt like something was missing... something only a native New Yorker would be able to pick up on. There was an absence to the night that Alonzo aka Zo-Pound couldn't put his finger on, but it made him clutch the .357 jammed between the driver's seat and center console a little tighter.

Zo-Pound was a man who had learned early in life that it was always wise to be on point, no matter where you were, but he had always felt at ease in Harlem. It was the only home he had ever known and every time he stepped into a familiar neighborhood, it hugged him like a mother's embrace. He loved Harlem and for a long time could never imagine being anywhere else, but that had all changed over the course of the last year.

The crew he ran with was led by his biological brother

Lakim and a man who he loved like a brother, King James. They were an ode to the throwback gangsters of the eighties and were fast on the come up. For the last couple of years, they had been locked in a turf war with New York's resident king, Shai Clark. There were heavy casualties on both sides and Zo was happy when they were finally able to put the conflict to bed and got back to making money. King James became known as the man who had stood against a tyrant and lived to tell about it. It made their crew notorious seemingly overnight, which turned out to be both a good and bad thing. They were able to open their lanes up and see some real paper, but with more money came more problems. It seemed like every time they turned around there was another upstart crew looking to come at them and trying to mimic what they had been able to do against the Clarks. The crowns Zo and his team wore were getting heavy, but six months prior, they became down right back-breaking. Unbeknownst to them, they weren't only on the radar of other crews, but also of the police. It was like they couldn't go a week without somebody getting locked up or killed. Zo could feel the fire getting close, but it actually burned him when they lost Dee.

Dee was a stand-up young dude who had been running with their crew. Zo had known Dee since he was a little dude on the block slinging nickel bags of crack. Over time, he had gotten his weight up and became a part of King James's inner circle. When Ashanti started pulling away from their team to pursue other ventures with Kahllah, it had been Dee who stepped up to fill the void he'd left in not only their crew, but as Zo's right hand man. All Dee wanted to do was fuck bitches and get money, but sometimes men aspiring to reach certain heights were called on to do more. A dude Dee had met through a friend had been buying ounces from them over a span of a few weeks and decided he wanted to step his order up to a half-bird.

Zo and Dee were supposed to go and close the deal and bring the money back, but in a strange twist of fate, Zo had gotten into a car accident on his way to pick Dee up for the exchange and ended up spending the night in the emergency room. Zo urged Dee to reschedule, but Dee wanted to prove that he could carry his own weight and went to do the deal without Zo. As it turned out, the dude who wanted the coke was really a stick-up kid and had been lining Dee up the whole time. Dee walked into an ambush and when the smoke cleared, two people were dead and Dee ended up sitting on sixty years for the bodies.

Losing Dee hurt, not just because he was a part of the team and Zo's friend, but also because he was a young man who had just been stripped of the rest of his youth over some bullshit. Getting into that car accident was a blessing in disguise for Zo-Pound. Had he been with Dee instead of in the emergency room, he'd likely be occupying a cell next to his friend or a plot in a cemetery. That was the second bullet Alonzo had dodged, and he didn't intend to test fate for a third time. When the game he'd played all his life started coming with more risks than rewards, it was time to switch hustles. This is what had him sitting in his car on 148th and Riverside Drive in the middle of the night.

When Zo's cell phone rang, he was hopeful, thinking it might be the person he'd been waiting on for the last twenty minutes. He looked at the face of his stereo and saw "Boo" lit up in digital letters. Wifey was calling to check in with him, no doubt wondering where he was since he'd promised to be home by then. After letting it ring a few times, Zo finally hit the answer button and activated the car's Bluetooth.

"Nothing, waiting on you," Porsha's voice came through the speakers.

"I know, and that's my fault. This shit is just taking a little longer than I expected," Zo said apologetically.

"Obviously," Porsha said with a hint of irritation in her voice. "I still don't see why they couldn't come fix the lift in the morning during normal business hours."

"Because I'm not a normal businessman," Zo reminded her. "Listen, baby, if I wait until the morning to get this done I'm gonna lose money. I own a garage and people wanna get their cars in early so they can be out early. I ain't got time to slow this money up. Besides, these Mexican niggas are gonna fix the lift for me at half cost of what most of the other places wanted to charge. So if being at the shop after hours is gonna save us a few dollars, I gotta do what I gotta do. I hope you can understand that?"

"You know I do, but I guess I'm just missing you. Since you retired from the block you've gotten me spoiled on you being here at night."

Zo smiled as if she could see him. "Yeah, I can't front, I dig being home at night with you too. You know at first I was skeptical about going back to this nine-to-five shit, but the transition wasn't as hard as I thought."

"That's because you're an owner now and not a worker," Porsha said proudly.

"True indeed, baby, and I have you to thank for giving me the push I needed," Zo said sincerely. When Zo first stared contemplating retiring from the drug game, he wasn't entirely sure what he would do for money. It had been Porsha who pushed him to invest some of the money he stacked into a business. She thought they should open a store or boutique, but Zo had something else in mind. There was an old timer he knew that owned an auto body shop in the neighborhood that was swimming in debt. Zo paid off a large chunk of what the old head owed in exchange for a majority stake in the auto body shop. Zo didn't make what he would've from selling drugs through the auto body shop, but it brought in enough money for him and his lady to live comfortably. More importantly, he owned something that was worth something for the first time in his life.

"That's what a good woman is supposed to do; push her man to be great. Now how much longer do you think you're going to be?" she asked.

"Shouldn't be too long at all," Zo told her. His eyes were fixed on the rearview mirror, and the white Maserati that had just parked two car spaces back. In that neighborhood, the car stuck out like a sore thumb. "I'll hit you when I'm on my way home to see if you need anything."

"Okay, love you babe."

"Love you too," he replied and ended the call. He hated lying to Porsha, but he didn't feel like hearing her mouth that night. Since Zo stopped hustling on the block, their relationship had been going great. She didn't have to worry about late night phone calls telling her he was dead or in jail and she no longer had to be ashamed when people asked her what her man did for a living. As far as she knew Zo was now completely legit, but it wasn't entirely true. He was no longer on the block, but he was still hustling harder than ever. The difference between his new hustle and his old one was if he got caught he wouldn't get state time, he was going to straight to the Feds.

Zo grabbed the manila envelope from the passenger seat and got out. At the exact moment, he was exiting his Audi, the Maserati driver was easing out from his vehicle. In his hand, he carried a Barney's bag that looked like it was carrying more weight than it was meant to. He was a young light-skinned man who wore his hair in a wavy fade.

A diamond studded chain hung down over his white V-neck t-shirt that played tricks with the streetlights. His jeans sagged slightly, showing off his Ralph Lauren boxers and cuffed at the bottom to lay perfectly over his Ferragamo high tops. To those who didn't know him, Ocho could've easily been mistaken for a dope boy, but he had put street level crimes behind him when he hooked up with Zo- Pound and traded in his iron and lead for paper and plastic.

"What up wit'it my nigga?" Ocho greeted Zo. "Waiting for your slow ass," Zo gave him dap. "You

know I hate to be kept waiting."

"My fault, big bro. I had some shit that demanded my attention, feel me?" Ocho said in a serious tone.

"Everything good?"

"Yeah, some niggas tried to burn my lil' mans and them on some paper they owed for some numbers and I had to step up and let them know just what type of animals they were dealing with," Ocho patted his waist where he had his gun stashed.

"Be cool out there, Ocho. Don't let that street shit get in the way of this money," Zo warned.

"I feel you on that, my G. The money we been getting off them numbers is way sweeter than what I was seeing on the block, but beneath these fancy clothes and cars still beats the heart of a goon. Ain't no nigga living will ever be able to say they took something of mine," Ocho boasted. "Again, my apologies for making you wait, Zo, but I came bearing compensation."

He held the Barney's bag out to Zo, who took the bag and peeked inside. There were three boxes inside: the one on the top contained a pair of women's boots and the two on the bottom were brimming over with cash. The money was what had added the additional weight to the bag.

"Nice," he nodded in approval. "How did you know Porsha wanted these?"

"When we double-dated last week I remember hearing her telling Lauren how bad she wanted them, but her size was on backorder everywhere she looked. I had the Pop-Out-Babies on the lookout for them, so you know when they came through we booked 'em," Ocho said proudly. When he saw the apprehensive look on Zo's face, he realized his mistake. "Yo, my fault Zo. I should've probably cleared it with you first. I didn't mean any disrespect."

"It's all good my G. When you know better you do better," Zo said nonchalantly. He knew Ocho hadn't meant any harm, but it still didn't stop him from being quietly irritated. He wanted to be the one who tracked the boots down for Porsha. "Nice ride," he turned his attention to the Maserati.

Ocho shrugged. "This shit fly, but it's a temporary arrangement. I got some white boys poppin' out with us. I had them rent three of these from that exotic car place that caters to the celebrities when they're in town. Between that pale skin and them clean credit card numbers they never gave my boys a second look when they came down to pick them up."

"That's where that white privilege comes into play. You know they would've put one of us through all kinds of bull-shit if we had tried to roll in there to grab something."

"Word up!" Ocho agreed. "Them white dudes wanna be down so bad that they're ready to fuck up a life that most of us would kill to have, just to hang in the slums and be able to claim a set. By the time the car place realizes the cars ain't coming back, we'll already have them whacked up, put back together, and re-sold."

"Y'all be careful with that. These ain't some Honda

Civics y'all ripped off; they're luxury cars. I wouldn't be surprised if they had low-jacks on them," Zo warned.

"Man we got all that shit covered," Ocho said dismissively. "I know some El Salvadorians out in Queens who'll disable all that shit for a few dollars."

Zo was impressed by his foresight. "You little muthafuckas cover all bases when you steal, huh?"

"Not at all. If you gonna do, you gotta do it right. See, that's why a lot of these niggas wanna run with us, but they ain't built for it. They pop out, but they ain't really poppin' out. We the original Pop-Out-Babies," Ocho said proudly.

The Pop-Out-Babies were the larcenous band of young thieves he held sway over. They were a collective of the best boosters, scammers, and con artists in the city. The young crew had the swag of Hollywood players but criminal minds worthy of the I.D. Channel. When Zo first hooked up with them, they were pulling credit card scams and boosting things to re-sell in the hood, but he taught them to refine their hustle. They excelled at identity theft and could clone credit cards better than anyone he had ever seen. The best part was that Zo didn't have to deal with them directly unless he wanted to. The Pop-Out-Babies answered to Ocho and Ocho answered to Zo. For all everyone on the outside knew, Zo was just the part-owner in a garage, but it was his business with Ocho that allowed him and his lady to live a cut above everyone else. Porsha wasn't dumb, she knew what Zo and Ocho were into, but she had no idea of the level at which they were playing.

"Y'all just make sure you don't hold onto them cars for too long, O. Have your fun, but don't be stupid about it," Zo said.

"C'mon, you know me better than that. We're supposed to drive them out to Queens tomorrow night and that'll be the last time you see them," Ocho assured him. "You know, it'd be a lot easier if you let us bring them through your shop to get the body work done. The money we giving them Queens niggas we could be kicking to you."

"You must've lost your damn mind. I told you before; I ain't mixing no dirty paper with this clean shit. If it ever goes down the garage is one of the few things the government won't be able to seize because it's totally legit. I ain't trying to fuck that up for no punk ass few dollars."

Ocho raised his hands in surrender. "Hey man, it was just a suggestion."

"Well, suggest it to somebody who don't mind going to federal prison," Zo told him. "Oh, while I'm thinking about it, I got some fresh numbers for y'all to get to work on," he handed Ocho the manila envelope he had been carrying.

Ocho peeked inside the envelope. "How long do you think we have?"

"I don't know. I just came up on them earlier, so I'd say you got a couple of days. Still, you might not wanna wait that long to burn them out. Don't blow them on stupid shit like Ubers and Jordans; tear down those electronic stores. It's almost tax season so you know niggas gonna be on the hunt for them flat screens and shit. Grab a few of them GPS systems too. We got more than enough lost niggas in the world who could use some direction."

"Kind of like how you came along and started giving us direction, huh?" Ocho asked.

"I don't know if I'd say I gave y'all direction, more like I helped you get organized."

"That's why I fucks with you, Zo, because you're humble as hell. You got all these young niggas working under you, but you still carrying on like you're one of the soldiers."

"That's because I am," Zo said. "Regardless of whether

I'm calling the shots or not, I'm still going to be a soldier. That's just how I was raised."

"Right, right." Ocho nodded. "Yo, speaking of soldiers, I gotta show you this new chopper I just copped," he started back towards the Maserati. "I got a home girl who lives down in N.C. Her baby daddy is stationed at a marine base and he be getting his hands on all the high powered shit."

"Word? Let me check it out," Zo said excitedly. He was a gun enthusiast.

"I got it right here in the trunk," Ocho hit the lock. "You know police be all over the place out here so I couldn't ride with it inside the car. Go ahead and check it out," he stepped to the side to allow Zo access to the trunk.

Zo leaned into the trunk and looked around, but didn't see anything other than a plastic tire cover. "O, fuck is you talking about? I don't see no gun."

"It's right here," Ocho pressed his pistol against the back of Zo's head.

Zo was dumbstruck. "Ocho, what the fuck you doing?" he asked trying to remain as still as possible so he didn't get popped on accident.

"Getting in where I fit in, big homie," Ocho replied. "I guess you've been spending so much time in the house up under your girl that your ear hasn't been to the streets lately. Word is that there's a price on your head."

"A price on my head?" Zo asked in surprise. He hadn't run afoul of anyone in a long time so he had no clue who it could be that wanted him dead.

"When a nigga offers you twenty stacks for some light work, you don't ask too many unnecessary questions."

"This is some sucka shit, Ocho. We supposed to be partners," Zo said.

"Yeah, we supposed to be, but there's been a change in the business arrangement," Ocho spat. "I know twenty bands ain't a lot to somebody who's seen hundreds of thousands hustling with King James but to a nigga like me, who ain't never seen that much money at one time that I didn't have to split, it is. Don't feel no way about it, Zo. I genuinely fucks with you, but this is about business."

"And this is personal," a voice cried out.

Zo's eyes instinctively snapped shut just before Ocho's head exploded, coating Zo's face and the trunk with blood and brain bits. There were two more quick shots, followed by the sound of a body hitting the ground. Zo raised his head slowly and saw a man with a mutilated face and holding a smoking gun standing over Ocho's body. One side was handsome and brown while the other resembled something out of a horror movie. It was as if someone had taken a blowtorch to it, leaving behind charred skin and a milky white eye.

"Cain?" Zo asked in surprise.

Cain was the fraternal twin brother of Abel, and the polar opposite of his brother. Whereas Abel was the bark, Cain was most certainly the bite of the dog. Unlike his boisterous and fun-loving brother, Cain was a quiet young man who mostly kept to himself, but once you crossed him or someone he loved, all bets were off. Zo had seen Cain commit some ungodly acts and never bat an eye. His fierce sense of loyalty and homicidal temper reminded Zo of Animal in many ways, except Cain had no conscience. He was every bit of the killer as the biblical figure he'd been named after.

Cain nodded, as if confirming his identity. "Been a long time, homie, and from the looks of things, the reunion couldn't have come sooner," he looked down at the corpse at his feet.

"You saved my life, man. I can't believe after all I've done for this little nigga his ass was gonna cross me for a few dollars over some shit I'm clueless about," Zo kicked Ocho's dead body.

"You should know by now that you can't trust nobody, but family. That's kind of why I'm here. I'm afraid I don't come bearing good news." His face darkened.

"What's wrong? Is the crew whole?" Zo asked, fearing the worst.

He shook his head. "No, we're not."

"Who did we lose?"

"Gucci."

Zo was so stunned that he had to lean against the Maserati for fear that his legs would give out. He'd expected it to be one of the soldiers: Ashanti, maybe Abel, possibly even Animal. They all dealt in the game of death and as such were subject to its rewards and consequences, but Gucci wasn't of that life. Her only connection to the game had been falling in love with the card dealer. "Damn, how's Animal?"

"Inconsolable," Cain said. "Animal loved that girl more than life and I'm afraid losing her has broken him in ways we can't even begin to fix."

"How did it happen?"

"Murdered in their home in front of their son, and Animal's daughter," Cain informed him.

"His what?" Zo asked in shock. He knew Animal and Gucci had a son together, but this was his first time hearing about a little girl.

"It's a long story, but the short version is the people responsible for killing Animal's wife have also taken his

children. Zo, I know you ain't in the life anymore, but we could sure use your pistols on this one."

Zo stood there, in quiet contemplation of what Cain had just laid at his feet. It had been a long time since he had been about that murder game. When he got out of the life, he promised Porsha that he was done for good. It was a promise he had planned to keep until that night. Zo took his cell phone out and hit the last number dialed. "Baby, I'm sorry but it looks like it's going to be a longer night than I expected."

CHAPTER 4

"I dig the way you think, lil' bro." Brasco nodded in approval after Ashanti had finished running down the suggested line-up of desperados to ride out with them. "I don't think I've ever had the pleasure of meeting ya man Zo-Pound, but his name was ringing off in the penitentiary. Correct me if I'm wrong, but I heard he retired his guns?"

"He did, but I'm sure Zo will pick them back up for this," Ashanti said confidently. "Every man we've called on for this owes Animal a debt in one way or another, and we need to collect."

"Do you think King James will lend a few soldiers too? I heard his crew is real heavy in the streets these days," Brasco said.

"Yeah, King James has gotten his weight up and he's got plenty of shooters to spare, but I didn't reach out to him," Ashanti admitted.

This surprised Brasco. "Why the hell not? I heard what Animal did for him, putting that beef to bed, so I'd think he'd be the first one to offer support."

"At a different time under different circumstances I'd have called on him, but shit ain't been the same between us lately. Me and King James have had some... differences, for lack of a better word," Ashanti said.

Sonja snorted and pursed her lips as if she was about to say something slick, but a sharp look from Ashanti silenced her.

The relationship between King James and Ashanti had become somewhat of a sensitive issue. They used to be good friends, but lately they rarely spoke other than to be cordial when their paths or business dealings happened to cross. The problem that existed between them wasn't that serious, and could've likely been fixed with a conversation, but both of them were too stubborn to be the first to reach out and admit their wrongs.

After their last adventure and Animal left to begin serving his prison sentence, Ashanti found himself back on the block with King James. Tensions remained between he and King James's second in command, Lakim, because he felt like Ashanti was being given too much say in the crew, but there was no denying the value Ashanti brought to the table. He had been instrumental in putting an end to the beef with Shai Clark as well as their expansion into new territories. Things were good for Ashanti but he couldn't help but wonder if they could be better. For the most part, Ashanti had never been out of the hood until he'd met

Kahllah and the small sample of the world outside the projects he'd tasted made his young soul long for more. When the opportunity presented itself for him to travel and study under the infamous Black Lotus, he took it without a second thought.

Kahllah had opened Ashanti's eyes to a great many things, including the money to be made by breaking international laws. With her, he could make more money for one job than he could from selling drugs in an entire month. In between the contract killings, and rigorous training she put him through, Ashanti was afforded the chance to travel the world and behold some truly marvelous things, things that he would have never been able to see or experience if he'd limited himself to just hustling on the block. Some within King James's crew took Ashanti's hiatus from the drug game as him turning his back on his roots, but it was really a young man wanting to grow.

"Whatever the differences between you and King are, I suggest you put them to the side. The few of us are a tough bunch, but it's gonna take more than a few shooters to go against the cartel," Brasco said.

"And that's why I sent Abel to speak with Shai. He has the soldiers and the connections," Ashanti told him.

Brasco frowned. "Homie, I ain't trying to bust your bubble or nothing, but I can't see that nigga throwing us no assist on this. I know y'all done made nice but let's not forget that The Dog Pound and the Clarks have spent the better part of a decade trying to kill each other."

"A lot has changed since you've been gone, Brasco," Ashanti told him.

"Except for the fact that Shai still hates all you little hood boogers," Sonja added her two cents. "You and Animal forced Shai into that little truce so don't go thinking you guys are all chummy-chummy just because bullets aren't flying anymore. You guys have embarrassed him more times than I care to count, and men like that have memories like elephants. If by some strange twist of the universe he does agree to help, it'll probably be to so he can double-cross you the first chance he gets. Shai Clark is a snake and I wouldn't trust him."

"For as much as I hate to admit it, I'm with Red on this one," Brasco said.

Ashanti had considered all this before sending out his messenger. They were at peace with the Clarks, but the bad blood that had been built between them over the years still lingered. The twins had been the most animate about wanting to reach out to the Clarks, so much so that Cain had refused to go when Ashanti asked, which is why he sent Abel instead. Bringing Shai in to help might've been a long shot, but considering what they were up against, Ashanti had to explore all options, and that meant taking a helping hand wherever he could get one, even if it came from a former enemy.

"Look, there are no easy answers to any of this. All I know is that Animal has never abandoned me, or any of us for that matter, during times of need. I'm in this with him to the end, even if it turns out to be just the two of us taking on Lilith and her whole fucking army," Ashanti said in frustration.

"Say that shit, Blood!" Brasco pounded his fist. "You know I'm with y'all. It wouldn't be the first time we went against impossible odds, and I don't plan to make it the last. Be we three or three hundred, we gonna ride for Animal."

"How touching," Sonja said sarcastically.

Ashanti turned to her angrily. "You know, it amazes me how you can sit idly by talking shit like you didn't bring all of this down on us. Since you've been here all you've done was tell us what we're doing wrong. If you've got a better idea as to how to go about this I'd love to hear it."

"'ve got more than an idea, I've got an edge," Sonja said with a smirk. "Before I escaped from the compound I hacked into Lilith's computer and stole a bunch of files and downloaded them to a flash drive. There's a shit load of information about my father's cartel on those files; names, dates, stash house locations, cartel associates, etc."

"You've been sitting on this information all this time and are just now saying something?" Ashanti asked heatedly.

Sonja rolled her eyes. "I didn't say anything because I didn't know what was in the files until we got to New York and I was able to look through them. In case you hadn't noticed, I've been running for my damn life for the last few weeks."

"I'm sure we can find something in those files to use against the cartel," Brasco said what everyone else was thinking. "Sonja, go get the flash drive while I try and rouse Animal. Maybe this bit of news will snap him out of his funk."

Brasco and Red Sonja went off to handle their respective tasks while leaving Ashanti in the kitchen and to his thoughts. Sonja revealing that she had the flash drive was the first bit of positive news he'd heard in what felt like forever, and it had come right on time. He'd been down on himself for not being able to do more to help Animal. He would never admit it for fear of looking weak, but Ashanti was starting to become desperate. Ashanti was an excellent field commander, but he was no general. Animal had always been the problem solver of the crew, and now that the mantel of leadership had been passed to him, he was staring to feel the weight that came with it.

Red Sonja and Brasco arrived back in the kitchen nearly at the same time. They both wore grim expressions.

"What's wrong?" Ashanti asked.

"The flash drive is gone," Sonja said holding up her laptop.

"And so is Animal," Brasco added.

"What the fuck do you mean he's gone?" Ashanti asked, as if he couldn't comprehend what Brasco was saying.

"Blood, I searched every room in the house and the only sign of him is this," Brasco held up the soiled thermal shirt Animal had been wearing.

"This doesn't make any sense. Less than an hour ago, you guys said you couldn't even get a response out of him, let alone get him to move! I gotta hit the streets and find him," Ashanti said.

"I'll go with you," Sonja offered.

"No, you wait here in case the others show up. I can cover more ground alone and without you talking shit in my ear the whole time." Ashanti grabbed his jacket and left before she could protest.

Sonja hated being told what to do, and the irritation was apparent on her face. Animal slipping off to do God only knew what could potentially ruin everything. She had schemed too hard and come too far to have her plans derailed because he couldn't keep his emotions in check. It was partially her fault. She knew what kind of man Animal was, and what he was capable of when pushed. She just hoped that Ashanti found him before he killed someone before she wanted him to do so.

Brasco had made himself right at home, raiding the fridge and helping himself to some lunchmeat and a beer. He settled himself in a chair and began flipping through channels on the television mounted above the refrigerator.

"What the hell are you doing? We're in the middle of a crisis and all you can think to do is stuff your face and watch television?" she asked angrily.

"A man can't kill on an empty stomach," Brasco told her in between bites of the lunchmeat. "And if you must know, I'm not watching television, I'm looking for the twenty-four hour news network."

"What good is watching the news going to do us?"

"It's simple. If Animal is anything like I remember, he'll make his whereabouts known soon enough, and when he does you can bet your pretty red ass that it'll be newsworthy."

PART 2

BLOOD & CONCRETE

CHAPTER 5

L arry stood at his post, outside Pesto's restaurant, blowing into his hands trying to warm them. The temperature had dropped considerably that night. He stomped his feet to try and keep the circulation going in them while rocking from side to side. Standing there trying to keep from freezing reminded him of the many winter days he'd spent walking the prison yard of Attica Correctional Facility, where he had made his home for the last decade. Upstate New York winters were brutal, especially when you had little other than an army jacket and thermals to fight them off. Those were dark times for Larry, but it was the cost he paid for his actions while he was on the streets.

In his pre-prison days, Larry had been a heavy hitter in the hood, known for his violent temper and quick trigger finger. In his mind, when he was released from prison, he would hook up with his old crew and things would go back to business as usual, but it was not to be. Things had changed in New York and the balance of power had shifted. Everyone he had known was either dead or in prison. His dreams of going back to the top were dashed and replaced with a job his parole officer had gotten for him as a dishwasher at a diner. Larry hated that job more than anything, but he couldn't quit. Staying gainfully employed was a condition of his parole. Dishpan hands were a small price to pay if it meant keeping him out of prison. What Larry had become after his release was disheartening, but he held onto the hope that one day he would find an opportunity to come up and reclaim some of his former glory. That opportunity came when a friend of a friend introduced him to a lawyer named Stein who was in need of a man with Larry's particular skill set.

Stein was a prime example of what was wrong with the legal system. He was rude, had a closet drug problem, and cared more about money than he did the clients who he bilked for their money. Stein was a piece of shit and Larry detested him, but for all his faults, he kept money in Larry's pocket and his parole officer off his back. In return, all Larry had to do was make sure nobody fucked with the lawyer, which proved to be harder than it should have been. Stein had a fascination with the underworld and loved to play the role of a gangster, which kept him in messes that Larry was called on to clean up. Had this been a few years ago, Stein would've been one of Larry's victims, but as it stood, he was his meal ticket.

Stein was having dinner at Pesto's, which he did at least three to four nights per week. It was one of his favorite restaurants. Larry had eaten there once or twice and wasn't impressed with the food, but Stein loved it. Normally Stein dined alone or with a business associate, but that night he was one of a party of six. It was a special occasion, the birthday of one of the young chippies Stein had been keeping time with, so the restaurant was closed to the public for a few hours while Stein and a few of his associates wined and dined the young girl and one of her friends.

On the way there, when Larry heard the young girl tell her friend how it was the best night of her life, he almost felt bad for her. He had seen how Stein and his friends liked to play, so he knew what was in store for the young girls once the lawyer had gotten them thoroughly drunk and drugged up. They'd likely wake up the next morning in some strange motel room, naked with only broken memories of the night before. To men like Stein, the young black girls were little more than playthings to be discarded once they'd had their fun with them.

Larry was pulled from his revolting thoughts of the lawyer and their unwitting young victims when he spotted someone coming down the street. He was a young man dressed in all black with a hood pulled over his head. A red bandana hung from his right pants pocket, flapping on the night breeze like a blazing battle flag while Converse the color of blood burned like neon lights across the cold concrete. As he neared the entrance of Pesto's, where Larry stood guard, one of his hands dipped into his pocket. Larry's hand inched closer to the gun tucked in his pants. If the young man made any sudden moves, Larry was going to give him the business end of his .45. When the man's hand came out of his pocket, holding a pack of cigarettes, Larry relaxed a bit. The young man tapped one of the cigarettes out of the pack and put it between his lips.

"You got a light, Blood?" he asked getting closer. His head was lowered so Larry couldn't see his face.

Larry kept his eyes on the man while he fished for the lighter in his pocket. "Here," he handed it to him.

The man lit his cigarette. "Much obliged," he exhaled a cloud of toxic smoke and extended the lighter back to Larry.

When Larry reached for the lighter, the young man let it drop to the ground. Instinctively, Larry bent to pick it up, and when he felt the press of cold steel against the side of his head, he realized his mistake. Larry's eyes slowly moved up and for the first time he saw the man's face. It was familiar, but Larry couldn't place where he had seen it before until the young man's lips parted into a sneer and revealed a mouth full of gold-plated teeth, sprinkled with diamond cuts. It was then that Larry realized where he had seen the face before. It was two years prior when he had been in the day room at Attica and the news ran a segment about a serial killer who had been dubbed the Animal.

"Wrong place, wrong time," Animal told him in an almost apologetic tone before blowing Larry's brains all over the concrete. Before Larry's body hit the ground, Animal had already disappeared inside Pesto's.

*

Richie Stein was a man who liked to indulge in the finer things in life: fine food, fine women, and fine drugs. That night he had helped himself to a healthy portion of all three. He was seated at a private table in the back of Pesto's Italian restaurant with several of his associates and his current flavor of the month, a young chocolate stallion by the name of Lisa. He'd met her when she came into his office looking for a lawyer to get her drug dealing baby daddy Scooter out of a jam he'd gotten himself into.

During a routine traffic stop, Scooter got busted with an ounce of cocaine and an illegal firearm. With his prior record, his best bet was probably to take the seven to ten year plea agreement the D.A. was offering, but Stein had convinced him that he had a good chance at beating the charge. He didn't advise Scooter to take it to trial because he really felt he could win, but because he knew Scooter had a shitload of dirty money tucked away. By the end of the trial, Stein had bled Scooter of his entire stash, and the judge sentenced him to twenty years when he blew the trial.

Lisa was devastated when Scooter was sent away. She was left a single mother with no job, no man, and no prospects. Lisa found herself in desperate need of a shoulder to cry on and Stein was right there. It wasn't long before he went from consoling her in her time of need to knocking the lining out of her pussy. Lisa was a true freak and did things to Stein that made his eyes pop. Stein convinced Lisa that he really liked her and had even dangled the prospect of moving her into his condo, but it was all bullshit. As soon as Stein got bored with Lisa, she'd be cast off like the rest. But in the meantime, he was in the mood for a little fun.

"Sweetie, how about you bring us another bottle of Dom," Stein told the waitress when she came to their table to see if they needed anything else.

"Right away, sir," the waitress said and scurried off to do as she was told. Stein was a big tipper and she liked to keep him happy.

"That'll be the third bottle in less than two hours, Richie. If you don't slow down on that champagne, you're going to be too drunk to drive home," Harvey warned. He was an older man, who wore horn-rimmed glasses that always seemed to slide down on his nose. Harvey served as Stein's personal assistant and errand boy, but he doted on him like a mother hen.

"That's what I've got you for, Harv." Stein laughed. "Stop being such a killjoy. These young ladies came out to have a good time and I intend to make sure that they do. In fact, I should've ordered two more bottles instead of one!"

"Damn, you wasn't lying when you said you knew some ballers, Lisa," Claudette said, downing the last of the champagne in her glass so she could get first dibs when the fresh bottle was brought out. She was one of Lisa's hood rat friends who she'd brought along to her birthday dinner.

"I told you that my boo was about that life," Lisa boasted. She loved to show off for her friends and that night Stein made sure her stunt game was on one thousand. She was so into herself that she didn't even notice the sneaky glances that had been passing back and forth between Stein and Claudette all night.

"So, do you ladies come here often or is this your first time?" Joseph Levy asked. He was one of Stein's associates, a data analyst from a company called NYAK. Stein represented them when their employees needed legal help, which lately seemed to be often.

"Shit, I can't afford this place. It's my first and will probably be my last time," Claudette said.

"Bitch, you better stop playing. I told you Richie said I can have my official birthday party here tomorrow night, and you know I need my girls in the building," Lisa bragged.

"No disrespect, honey, but you must have one awesome shot of pussy if this cheap bastard is going to throw you a party here." This was Lou, a low-level button man for a local crime family. Lou's father, Big Lou, was a client of Stein's. The lawyer didn't really care for Lou, but he kept him around because he always had a line on drugs and parties.

"Why don't you watch that gutter mouth of yours?" Stein scolded him. "I'm not cheap, I'm frugal. Besides, nothing is too good for my girl," he threw his arm around Lisa, but purposely let his fingers brush Claudette's shoulders.

Claudette flashed him a knowing look that sealed the deal. After Stein dropped Lisa off, he planned on doubling back and trying his luck with her friend.

Stein's scheming was interrupted when an unfamiliar face walked into Pesto's. "Who the fuck is this?" Stein asked with a sour expression on his face. From the way he was dressed, Stein could tell that he wasn't a regular customer because Pesto's enforced a strict dress code. More importantly, he wondered how the intruder had gotten in because he'd left specific instructions with both Larry and the manager that no one was to be allowed in without his approval during the celebration. Heads would roll for his orders not being followed.

"Don't worry, I got this," Lou wiped his mouth with a napkin and got up from the table. He ambled across the room and blocked the young man's path. "This is a private party, dipshit. Why don't you take a walk to the Chicken Shack down the street?"

In response to his insult, Lou received a bullet to the face.

The sound of gunshots and the body in the middle of the floor caused a panic inside the restaurant. The waitress who had been sent to get a fresh bottle was on her way out of the back and when she saw the gunman, she dropped the bottle

and took off back the way she had come. A few seconds later, two brutish men came out wearing off-the-rack suits. They were the muscle for Pesto's, but their muscles did little to help them against Animal's bullets. They had barely cleared the doors when Animal riddled them with bullets.

Levy was the first one at the table to try and make a run for it. He leapt from his seat and made a break for the side door. Animal let him reach it before he put a bullet through the back of his head and flipped him forward. Animal advanced on the table, where the rest of the party sat, too terrified to move. The man called Harvey threw his hands up in surrender.

"I'm just an assistant," Harvey blurted out.

"Then consider yourself fired," Animal told him before putting two in Harvey's chest. He turned his hard eyes to the girls. "I need a word with the counselor. Get gone or get dead." Lisa and Claudette wasted no time scrambling out of the restaurant and leaving Stein to his fate. Animal pulled up a chair and sat across from the terrified lawyer. "I presume you're Richie Stein." It was more of a statement than a question.

Stein swallowed hard. "Yes, I'm Richie Stein, but I don't know what this is about," his voice trembled. If it weren't

for the fact that he was wearing a three-thousand-dollar suit, he might've pissed himself.

"This is about your other life, and your connection to the cartel."

"I'm sorry, but I don't know what you're talking about," Stein lied.

Animal placed his gun on the table, facing Stein. "I'm going to act like you didn't just piss on my head and try to tell me it's raining. You've represented several members of Poppito Suarez's cartel over the years. You're one of Tiger Lily's whores, but I'm not interested in your pussy; I wanna see what that mouth do. I need information on a man named Luther Graham."

"Who?" Stein faked ignorance.

Animal fired a shot, nearly missing Stein's head and knocking him off the chair he was sitting on. "Don't play me, you fucking snake. I'm talking about your little pet project. See I did some digging before I came in here and shot up your little party, and found out a few interesting things about you and Luther Graham. It seems you two have been spending quite a bit of time together lately. Just as recently as two weeks ago you cleaned up a solicitation charge for him."

"Well... ah, my firm has been very successful so sometimes we like to pay our blessings back by doing pro-bono work. Giving back to the community and such, you know?"

Animal reached across the table, grabbing Stein by the tie and dragging him through abandoned platters of pasta and champagne glasses. He dumped Stein on the floor and placed his foot on his throat, cutting off his oxygen.

"Bitch nigga, do I look stupid to you? Muthafuckas like you don't do shit for poor communities but bleed them, so miss me with that I care about the ghetto shit. You're a four hundred dollar an hour lawyer who makes his money off the suffering of rich folks, so don't think for a minute that I'll believe you actually give a shit about a guy who works as a messenger whose biggest accomplishment is supporting a hundred dollar per day drug habit on a minimum wage salary. Two weeks ago, you cleaned up the solicitation, but three months before that you got him off on possession and the year before that you stood with him on an assault charge. Ain't that much pro-bono in the world. This ain't no casual sex, y'all are in a relationship."

"Okay, yeah. So maybe I did represent the guy, but I don't see why that has you waving a gun in my face," Stein said.

Animal leaned forward. "It's got everything to do with me waving this gun in your face," he brandished the gun for emphasis. "And it might be the deciding factor as to whether you walk out of here or get carried out. It's obvious to a duck that Graham didn't pay all those legal fees, so I wanna know who his guardian angel is?"

"I'm bound to my clients by confidentiality!" Stein gasped.

Animal pointed his gun at the lawyer's face.

"These bullets are about to bind you to the afterlife."

Stein weighed his options. If he talked then nine times out of ten, he was dead, but if he didn't talk then death was a guarantee. He decided to take his chances. "I handle all the criminal law cases for NYAK. They're the ones who wanted me to get Graham out."

NYAK stuck a cord in Animal's head. In addition to Graham, and Stein's names, he'd also seen NYAK mentioned in the files he'd stolen from Sonja. According to what he'd learned from a Google search on the name, NYAK was supposed to be a biochemical company that specialized in clean energy. "Why the fuck would a multi-million corporation care if a low life like Graham went to jail or not?"

"On my mother's eyes, I don't know."

"Then your mother must be a blind bitch, because I think you're lying." Animal yanked Stein to his feet, and hurled him through a nearby wine rack, shattering several of the bottles. Stein was just struggling to his feet when Animal grabbed one of the shards of broken glass and jabbed it into Stein's leg, causing a fountain of blood to squirt out.

"Oh my God, I think you hit an artery!" Stein yelled, clutching his thigh, trying futilely to stop the flow of blood.

"I'm no doctor, but from the way you're leaking, I'd say I did. Now we can play this little game all night, but you'll bleed out long before I get tired of fucking you up. Why did NYAK want Graham released?"

"Okay, look... all I know is that it was important to someone on NYAK's board of directors that I get Graham out. Other than what his charges were and how much I was being paid, I didn't ask a lot of questions."

"Typical of a lawyer, all cash, and no care." Animal shook his head sadly. "Where can I find Graham? You're his lawyer so I know you know how to reach him."

Stein considered lying, but thought better of it. "I don't know where Luther lays his head these days. The only time I see him is when he's made a mess that I have to clean up. The last few times I had to see him in person he'd come to my office or we'd meet at Original Sin. He's been spending a lot of time with a broad who works there named Momo. She's an Asian chick who's got an ass like a Black girl and Graham is crazy about her. If anybody can tell you where to find him, it's her."

Animal was familiar with Original Sin. It was a Member's Only club where you could indulge in just about every vice imaginable. It was also a viper's nest, and getting in to press Momo about Graham wouldn't be an easy task. They didn't fuck around in Original Sin and if you got caught wrong, they didn't call the police, they buried you.

"Since you've been inside you must be a member. Set that card out, Blood," he snapped his fingers to hurry him along.

Keeping one hand on his wound, Stein reached into his pocket and handed Animal his wallet.

Inside the wallet, Animal found the membership card, which resembled a hotel key. On the front of it was the club's logo, a snake swallowing its tail. There was also a few hundred dollars, which Animal helped himself to. "Spending money and such," he said sarcastically before tossing the wallet at Stein's face.

"Do you know how long I was on the waiting list to get that card?" Stein asked, suddenly more worried about his exclusive membership than his bleeding thigh.

"Probably longer than you've got to live," Animal ejected the clip from his gun and slapped a fresh one in.

Stein's eyes widened. He thought because he'd played nice and crossed Luther, he'd be allowed to live, but it wasn't to be. "Wait, I told you what you wanted to know and you're still going to kill me? Kid, I don't know who you are but you don't want to do this."

"You're right. I don't, but I've been robbed of most of my choices," Animal chambered a round and pointed his pistol at Stein's face. "As far as who I am, I'll happily tell you; I am the broken dreams of a man who only wanted better, the sobs of a murdered lover as she took her last breaths. I am the bastard child of a man who served the devil and called it God's work and the last thing you'll ever see before you leave this world," he told him before he opened fire and pushed the lawyer from this life, never to swindle again.

CHAPTER 6

Original Sin wasn't hard to find. It was a popular watering hole for criminals and misfits who handled heavy paper. The establishment was located in a privately owned house deep in Brooklyn on a nondescript block. They tried to keep it low, but the spot stuck out like a sore thumb because of all the luxury cars lining the block and in the adjacent parking lot next to the house. They only reason the police didn't come snooping around is because the people who owned it paid them a hefty sum to look the other way.

The man guarding the door was a beefy cat, who was known on the streets as a killer. He was a no-nonsense dude called Devil who had been putting dudes to sleep for more than a decade, and even though he was getting on in years, he was still quite lethal. He had recently come into the employ of Original Sin when things started going sour with his regular job, which was providing security for rappers. He had sometimes complained about it, but standing outside like a bookend, he found himself missing those long nights in warm smoke-filled studios and even the discomfort of being inside a packed club trying to keep screaming fans away from his charges. Those days were becoming further and further between, and the gigs coming less. That's how he found himself in his current position, one of the Gate Keepers at the infamous Original Sin.

Had you told Devil six months ago that he'd have to start moonlighting doing security gigs for extra money, he'd have laughed at you. He was the personal bodyguard of one of the biggest rappers in the game, Don B., and head of security at a multimillion-dollar record label, Big Dawg Entertainment. When Devil was running with Big Dawg in their heyday, the world was their playground and money flowed in rivers. They were kings riding a wave that at the time seemed endless until the bottom fell out.

Devil's employer, Don B.'s, shady business practices had come back to bite him on the ass and the lawsuits started flying like singles at a strip club. All it took was for one artist to force him to open the books and it opened a floodgate. Big Dawg still sold a huge amount of records, but between the IRS, lawsuits, and back royalties he was forced to pay off, money started going out faster than it was coming in. Everybody at Big Dawg had to tighten their belts. Those who were smart enough to plan for rainy days were able to weather the storm, but the ones like Devil who spent money like there was no tomorrow found themselves in bad shape. Devil hated what he had been reduced to, but he hated being dead broke more so he did what he had to do to keep his head over water.

When Devil looked up and saw Animal coming in his direction he had to do a double take to make sure his eyes weren't playing tricks on him. He had heard a million stories about what had become of the notorious assassin, from him being dead to serving life in prison, but as he beheld him in the flesh, he realized that none of them were true. Men like Animal were like roach infestations; no matter what you did to get rid of them, they just kept coming back.

"Sup, Red Devil?" Animal greeted him by his full street name.

"Out here trying to make a dollar like everybody else," Devil told him. "I'd heard they buried you in a dark hole for all time."

"You know they can't keep a good man down."

"I don't know if I'd call you a good man, but you are a resilient little fuck," Devil chuckled. Animal's face remained stone serious. "C'mon, man, lighten up. I know you didn't come here to press me about that shit between you and Don B.?" Animal had been one of the artists Big Dawg Entertainment had to pay as a result of the lawsuit over missing money.

"Nah, man. My bank account is actually looking real good about now, probably better than some of y'all nigga's," Animal mocked him.

"Then what the fuck you want? Me and you ain't got no problems," Devil said.

"Me and you ain't got no problem, D, but I might have a problem with somebody inside this establishment you're protecting. I need a word with one of the girls," Animal told him.

"I ain't never known you to be no lady killer, unless you was murdering the pussy," Devil said. He was familiar enough with Animal to know when he was out for blood, which his face said he was that night.

"Never said I was gonna kill her... never said I wasn't either. I'd be worried more about my own life than the life of some whore if I was you," Animal told him, flashing the gun in his pants. "Now if them coins they throwing you to play watch-dog are worth it, then by all means stick around and take your rightful place in tomorrow's headlines. But if you're still the wise O.G. that I remember, you'll take the rest of the night off."

Devil looked into Animal's eyes and saw something that made him cringe... total emptiness. He was no fool; he knew Animal and his pedigree and no amount of money was worth him trying his hand against the young killer if he didn't have to. Devil coughed dramatically. "You know what? I ain't feeling so hot. I think I'm gonna take the rest of the night off." He started down the block. He stopped short and called out to Animal. "Does this mean you're back in the life?"

Animal weighed the question. "Nah, I'm just passing through," he told him before disappearing inside.

*

When Animal passed through the door that Devil had been guarding, he found himself standing in a dimly lit hallway with another door at the other end. His red Converse squeaked beneath him as he moved across the hardwood floor.

Stein turning him onto Original Sin was the first solid lead he'd had since he'd set out earlier that evening with the flash drive. It pissed him off to know that the mother of his daughter had been sitting on the information the whole time and hadn't said anything and he intended to call her out on it, but first he had to get to Momo and find out where he could put his hands on Luther. He still wasn't sure how Graham or NYAK connected to the cartel, but Lilith wouldn't have kept files on them if he didn't play some sort of role in the grand scheme of things.

As Animal neared the door, a slot opened near the top

and a pair of eyes studied him. He stood there trying his best not to look like it was his first time, while whoever was behind the door sized him up. He held up the card key Stein had given him for the person behind the door to see and held his breath. For all he knew he could very well be walking into a set up, but he had come too far to turn back. He could hear a series of locks being undone on the other side before the heavy door was pulled open and he was allowed to enter.

The inside of Original Sin was nothing like Animal had thought it would be. Based on the name and what he knew went on inside, he had expected it to be some seedy dive but it wasn't. The large room, which was a common area, was tastefully decorated in very modern-looking furniture and fitted with flat screen televisions on the walls. There was also a large bar, and several sofas where you could enjoy a drink or make your selection from Original Sin's unique menu of vices. Women walked around in expensive-looking lingerie, showing their wares to the respective men who may have been interested in paying for their services.

Keeping his head down, Animal made his way to the bar to order a drink and observe. He sat on a stool near the end, which gave him a clear view of the entire room through the mirror that covered most of the wall behind the bar. A scantily clad barmaid made her way up and down the bar taking the orders of the patrons on the benches. Animal tried to get her attention and she held her finger up asking that he give her a minute.

While he waited for the bar maid, Animal busied himself discreetly surveying the room. What made Original Sin different than most establishments of that nature was they only hosted the most exclusive clientele. From politicians and businessmen to thieves and killers, Original Sin would cater to them all, and they'd do so indiscriminately so long as they were members.

There was all kind of money floating around Original Sin that night, from the clean to the dirty. Animal even recognized a few of the faces from his days in the music business, but fortunately, they didn't recognize him. Had this been a few years ago, Animal could see him and Tech running up in the spot and making everybody turn their pockets out, but that was a different time and he was a different man on a different mission.

"What can I get for you?" the barmaid startled Animal. She was a pretty redbone with thick lips and gorgeous eyes. Animal hadn't even noticed her walk up. He was focusing so hard on what was behind him that he wasn't paying attention to what was in front of him. That was starting to be the story of his life.

"Hennessy, neat," Animal told her.

"Coming right up," the barmaid said and went about the task of making his drink.

Animal watched her as her fingers glided expertly across the bottles on the shelf, stopping at a bottle of Hennessy. As she cracked the bottle and searched for a nozzle to fit it with, Animal admired how her shape filled out the tight black dress she was wearing. She had a small waist that let out into a heart shaped ass and well-defined legs. Animal couldn't help but to wonder if drinks were all she served at Original Sin.

"Here you go, sweetie," the barmaid placed a napkin on the bar in front of Animal before sitting his drink on it.

"Good looking out, baby," Animal pulled his money out and was about to pay for his drink when she stopped him.

"That's not how things work in Original Sin. Alcohol is probably the only thing that you can get for free in this place. Everything else you pay for. Didn't anybody explain the rules to you before you became a member?" she asked suspiciously.

"I must've slept through that part at orientation." Animal cracked a smile. "Consider it a tip," he slid a hundred dollar bill across the bar.

The barmaid picked up the bill and held it in the light to make sure it was real. "I like your style, New Fish," she snapped the bill and stuffed it into her bra. "So, what's your vice?"

"My vice?"

"Yes, your vice. People don't just come here because they enjoy the décor, everyone has a vice," she rested her elbows on the bar and looked Animal in the eyes. "You're eyes are too alert for you to be a drug addict, and you're too pretty to have to pay for pussy, so I'd say you're a gambler."

Animal nodded in approval at her assessment. "In a manner of speaking, yes. I am a man who has been known to go all in depending on the hand I'm dealt."

"I knew it!" she said proudly. "You don't work in a place like this for as long as I have and not pick up a few things. I've been working here so long that I've learned to read men well enough to know what they want before they ask for it."

"That's quite a talent," Animal said, sliding a cigarette from his pack and placing it between his lips.

The bar maid produced a long grill lighter and lit his cigarette for him. "One of many," she said suggestively. "Working at Original Sin requires you know how to multitask."

"And what else does working here require you to know how to do?" Animal asked.

"I take my dinner break at ten. If you're still around I wouldn't mind showing you," the barmaid said.

Animal looked at her with predatory eyes and spoke in

a sultry tone. "Normally I would eat your yellow ass alive, baby girl, tonight I'm craving a different flavor. Maybe another night though."

"They say it's always the pretty ones who break your heart," the barmaid sighed. "Sin has got 'em all from the old and sophisticated to the young and ratchet. Pick your poison."

"I was thinking something a little more on the exotic side, like foreign. Y'all got any Asian girls working tonight?" Animal asked. "My homie told me about this Chinese chick he rocked out with that had a body like a Black girl."

The bar maid rolled her eyes. "You must be talking about Momo, and she's Japanese," she corrected him.

"Yeah, I think that was her name. She around?"

"Momo is here, but she's up in the penthouse with her regular Thursday night client," she told him.

"Penthouse?" Animal wasn't familiar.

"The penthouse, as in the three private rooms on the top floor where you can take some of our more elite girls, if your pockets can stand the extra hit. You can't get up to the penthouse unless you're spending at least a stack," the barmaid explained. "Damn, how is it that you're a member of this club yet you don't seem to know anything about how it works?"

"I told you, I didn't pay much attention when my homeboy was giving me the run down," Animal lied.

The barmaid gave him a disbelieving look "And who is your homeboy again?"

"Black... his name is Black," Animal lied. He couldn't very well say Stein for fear of raising uncomfortable questions about his relationship to the lawyer, but he could pull off Black. There was a dude named Black in every hood.

"Which Black?" the barmaid asked suspiciously. "What you mean? I just told you his name is Black,"

Animal stalled. Of all the barmaids behind the bar he could've ordered from, he had to get the nosey one.

"I mean, which Black as in Black from Harlem or you talking about Black from Red Hook?" she asked.

Animal hadn't expected there to be more than one. This would be tricky. Animal knew he had to choose his reply wisely, because if he answered wrong, his ruse would be exposed and security would be on him in a heartbeat. He leaned in and said with a sneer. "You and I both know that the only Black who's a member of this club is from Brooklyn. Now if you insist upon playing games, we can get one of your bosses out here and you can let them tell me why I'm being hassled when I pay my membership dues like everybody else." Animal was taking a gamble, but fortunately, it paid off

"Take it easy, pretty boy. I was just testing you. Better me then security, because they'd have probably taken you somewhere and whipped your ass for being in here feeling around like a newly blinded man. They don't take kindly to perpetrators at Original Sin," the barmaid told him.

"I'll keep that in mind for future reference," Animal said, throwing his drink back then slamming the empty glass on

the table and motioned for her to pour him another. "Now if you're done jerking me off, how about you tell me how a man would go about getting a date with this Momo?"

The bar maid refilled his glass. "I told you she's doing her Thursday Night Special, which means she's occupied with one client for most of the night," she explained. "Don't stress yourself out about it, pretty boy. There are plenty of girls in here who are just as bad as Momo. Why don't you grab one of them and visit one of the romp rooms. The penthouse ain't for everybody."

Animal downed his drink and slid the glass back to the barmaid. "Like I said earlier, I'm a man who likes to go all in. Thanks for the yak," he slid off the stool.

"Say pretty boy!" the barmaid called after him. "I never caught your name."

"That's because I never threw it," Animal capped and walked off.

The barmaid continued to watch Animal as he moved through the room, checking out some of the girls and watching some of the guys intently. Something about him didn't feel right and she knew her gut never lied.

CHAPTER 7

Talking to the barmaid confirmed what Animal had learned from Stein, that the girl Momo indeed worked at Original Sin. For a while, he was concerned that he'd been fed bad information and Stein had sent him off to chase another empty lead, but Stein's information was on point. It was almost a shame that he killed him, but there was nothing he could do to change that now, nor would he if he could. Lilith and everybody connected to her were meat.

The barmaid had said that Momo was with her regular Thursday night client and he couldn't help but to wonder if the client might've been Graham. If it was, then he'd be able to kill two birds with one stone. The more digging Animal did, the more he felt like Graham played a bigger role in the cartel's operation than he had originally thought. What was more interesting was the fact that a company as big as NYAK would've gone through so much trouble to keep him out of harm's way. There was a connection between the company and the cartel, and Luther was the missing piece. He needed to talk to the mystery man, but first, he had to find a way upstairs.

Animal worked his way around the room, checking out the ladies. There was no shortage of women trying to be selected for the night. The barmaid wasn't lying when she said Original Sin had just about every kind of woman under the sun to choose from. A few approached Animal to see if he was ready to cash in his card, but they didn't do it for him. To their credit, they were all fine, but he was looking for more than fine. He needed a girl of a high enough quality to get him upstairs to the penthouse. After nearly a half-hour of trolling, he found her.

She was a natural five-nine, but inched closer to six feet in the gold stiletto thigh high boots she was wearing. The green sheer sarong did little to hide her body, which was something out of a young man's dream. From the way her ass jiggled when she walked, it appeared to be all natural. Her skin was so rich and so dark that it seemed to drink up the light in the room. She walked through the room, oozing confidence, swinging her incredibly long weave. As sexy as she was, it was her smile that made Animal's breath catch in his chest. He had never seen her a day in his life, yet his heart ached for her. The woman was nothing short of a goddess, and she would be his ticket into the penthouse.

Animal watched as both men and women alike threw themselves at this midnight goddess. A few dudes were on her with their Mack-rap, and heavy jewelry, but she side-stepped them like they were piles of shit. A young brother Animal recognized as a wide receiver from the New York Jets stepped out into her path. He said something slick to her, which Animal couldn't hear, before popping open the knapsack he was carrying and flashing his money. It was some of the thirstiest shit Animal had ever seen, but it's what passed for game those days. Animal thought for sure she would bite, and the baller would ruin his best shot at getting up to the penthouse, but to his surprise, she threw her head back and laughed. She said something to the wide receiver that he clearly didn't like and kept it moving, leaving him there to pick up his face. It was then that Animal understood it wasn't money that moved her, but something else entirely.

Animal slid into one of the armchairs at an unoccupied table that would put him in the path of the goddess when she walked by. He threw his sunglasses on and adjusted his chain before making himself comfortable. He shut out the music and listened for the clicking of her heels on the hardwood floors as she drew near him. Animal let her get halfway past him then made his play. "Say baby, when you make it back this way why don't you bring me a bottle of Henny?" Animal capped without bothering to look up at her. It was a sucker's bet, and the sure money was on her ignoring him and continuing on her way, but his luck had held yet again and he heard her heels stop.

"Excuse you?" the goddess sounded offended.

Animal tilted his head back to look up at her. "I asked if you can bring me back a bottle of yak, when you swing this way again," he repeated his statement.

The goddess moved to stand in front of him and looked down. "What do you think, I'm one of the waitresses?"she glared down at him defiantly.

Animal removed his shades. It was important that she saw his eyes so that there was no misunderstanding about him. "No, I think you're the woman I've chosen to share a bottle with for the night."

The goddess was taken aback. "That's mighty presumptuous of you. What makes you think that I don't have better things to do tonight than listen to your ass talk shit?"

"The fact that you're still here entertaining this conversation instead of brushing me off. Time is precious and real hustlers don't waste it unless they got it to spare," Animal shot back.

"You got a real slick mouth, youngster," the goddess said with a smirk.

"That ain't the only thing slick about me. Why don't you go grab that bottle and come on back here so I can read you some quotes from The Diary of a Real Nigga," it was a request, but came across as a command.

"The ride you're looking to go on ain't gonna be a cheap one."She told him.

Animal gave her a stone-faced look. "Baby, if I was a nigga worried about money, I'd have never even opened my mouth to you. Now why don't you go get that bottle and clear your schedule for the next couple of hours," he said confidently and turned his attention to one of the flat screens. He could feel the goddess staring at him, but he refused to acknowledge her until she did as he asked.

As Animal listened to her heels click away, he had no idea whether she would actually come back or not, but he was hopeful. A few minutes later when the goddess had returned with the bottle of Hennessy, he knew he had been right in his assessment of her. Unlike some of the other girls, the goddess wasn't moved by how much money a man could spend, but how strong his will was. She was used to men folding and bending according to her whims and the fact that Animal had dared speak to her as if she were just an average broad intrigued her.

Animal looked up at the goddess, standing there with the bottle of liquor and two glasses. "You gonna just stand there gawking, or you gonna sit down so we can break bread?"

He hooked his foot around the leg of a chair across from him and pulled it closer.

"You're a cocky muthafucka, ain't you?" the goddess accepted the seat he offered and placed the bottle and glasses on the table.

"Not cocky, love, just observant. You don't strike me as a woman who isn't much in the way of playing games, so I figure laying my cards on the table was the best play," Animal said in a smooth drawl.

"And what if I'd told you to go fuck yourself instead of entertaining you?" she asked.

Animal shrugged. "Wouldn't be the first time I'd be rejected by a beautiful woman. It might've stung a taste, but I think I'd have lived," he took the bottle and cracked the seal. "What's your name, beautiful?" he poured two short shots.

"They call me Kat, and you are?"

"These days I go by Red, at least until we're a little better acquainted," Animal capped.

Kat looked from his red Converse to the red bandana that was hanging from his right pocket. "What are you, some kind of Blood, or something?"

"Or something is closer to the truth. It's a pleasure to make your acquaintance, Kat," Animal raised his glass.

"Likewise, Red," she toasted him, before throwing her liquor back. "Well you're on the clock now, so what's your pleasure?"

"I'm trying to go around the world and back again," Animal said, openly admiring her.

"That's an expensive ride." She returned his hungry look. "Like I told you when I came in," he pulled a roll of money from his pocket and sat it on the table, "I ain't stunting the cost as long as the ride is worth it."

Kat picked up the roll and eyed it greedily. Without discussing price, she slipped the whole roll into her halter-top. "If you're spending all this I'm going to take you on a ride you'll never forget, honey. Let's move this party to the penthouse." Kat stood up and extended her hand.

Kat led Animal through the room by the hand, drawing more than a few scorned stares from the men who had missed out on her company for the night. Many of them were clearly wealthier or more powerful than the young hooligan in the red sneakers, but the fact that he was skating off with Kat meant he had something that their money couldn't purchase... swag.

Just beyond the bar were the stairs that went to the upper levels. Guarding them was a gargantuan man who bore a striking resemblance to a gorilla. He stared at Animal with hard eyes, while Kat whispered something in his ear. He nodded then stepped to the side to let them through. On each landing of each floor that they passed, there was at least one bouncer assigned to guard that level. One bouncer on each floor seemed hardly enough to provide adequate security for a place that did that business in such high volumes, which told Animal there were likely reinforcements hiding in the cut, waiting for the signal to roll out and bust some heads. He filed that bit of information away in case he needed to call it up later.

When they finally reached the top floor, there was another member of the security team. This one was a burly young man wearing thick black glasses. Instead of standing at attention like the others, he lounged lazily in a chair thumbing through a newspaper. He finally looked up from his reading when he noticed Kat and Animal, adjusting his frames.

"Sup, Boogie?" Kat greeted him.

"Ain't shit, Kat. I didn't know you were working tonight," Boogie said.

"Shit, I'm working whenever there's money in the building," Kat replied. "I'm gonna need a room for a couple of hours."

Boogie glanced over his shoulder to the upper level and took a quick survey of open vs. closed doors. "Go ahead, you good. Only one room is in use so you can take your pick of the other two."

"Okay, thanks, baby." Kat stepped past Boogie, headed for the upper level.

When Animal made to follow her, Boogie stopped him. "Hold on, Slick. You gotta pay the toll to cross the bridge," he held one of his meaty palms out.

"I got it, Boogie," Kat reached in her top and pulled out the bankroll she'd taken from Animal. She peeled a few bills off the top and handed them to Boogie. "I'll settle the balance when we're done," she pulled Animal along up the stairs.

"Make sure you don't forget me, Kat. You take care of me and I'll take care of you!" Boogie called after them as they went down the hall to select a room. He continued to watch Kat's phat ass sway back and forth, touching himself.

"She gots to let me taste that!" he said more to himself than anyone else.

Animal surveyed the infamous penthouse. There were three rooms on the top floor, two along the left wall and one down at the end of the hall. Kat had selected the room down the hall to entertain Animal. Just as Boogie had said, there was only one other occupied room on the floor at the time. That had to be the room Momo was in. He looked over his shoulder to gage the distance between the staircase landing that Boogie occupied and the room his target was in. It would be close, but not impossible.

The inside of the room reminded Animal of some of the hotels he had stayed in over the years. There was a king sized bed, two chairs, and a writing desk with a lamp and an iPod dock on it.

"Make yourself comfortable, Red. I'll be back in a second." Kat slipped into the small bathroom inside the room.

As soon as Kat was out of sight, Animal got up and began surveying the room. In addition to the bathroom, there was also a door that opened up into a small closet, which was empty save for a few rolls of tissue and a half empty case of soap. He next searched the drawers to make sure there weren't any concealed weapons. After checking the room for hidden cameras, he moved to the window. It overlooked the parking lot in the back of the building. He tried to open it, but as he suspected, it was locked. That ruled it out as a potential exit, at least a painless one.

Animal had just sat on the bed when Kat reappeared from the bathroom. She had shed the sarong and was now wearing only a G-string and two floral pasties over her nipples. He couldn't help but to watch her big ass as it sashayed over to the writing desk. She pulled her phone from the small sequined bag she was carrying and began scrolling through it. Once she found the desired playlist, she hit play and sauntered back over to stand in front of Animal. She pulled him to his feet, pressing her body against him.

"So you want it straight up, or do you have something else in mind?" Kat asked.

"Actually, I do have something else in mind. That is if you're up to it?" Animal said suggestively. He draped his arms around Kat.

"And what's that, baby?"

"Sleep," Animal hissed, before spinning Kat around and putting her in a reverse chokehold. She struggled against Animal in an attempt to free herself. "Don't fight it, baby.

Just go to sleep," he added a touch more pressure. Eventually Kat's struggling ceased. Animal laid her gently on the bed and checked her pulse. He didn't want her dead, just out of the way. Animal dug in her bag and lifted the money he'd given her before slipping out of the room.

Once in the hallway, Animal pressed himself firmly against the wall to avoid detection. From where Boogie was standing on the landing, he couldn't see that far down the hall unless he came up the few steps to the floor. Animal slid along the wall until he reached the room where he knew Momo and Luther were. He pressed his ear to the door and heard the sounds of rough sex. There was also something else, a scent Animal couldn't quite place. It didn't smell like any of the usual suspects; cigarettes, weed, crack, or even angel dust. Whatever it was they were smoking had a foul edge to it.

After sparing a glance down the hall to make sure the coast was still clear, Animal set about the task of gaining entry into the room. Thankfully, the locks weren't magnetic; they were regular keyholes with tumblers. He had been breaking and entering with Brasco and his uncles since he was a kid, so he was able to make short work of it. He took a minute to screw the silencer to the end of the gun he was carrying before going inside.

The room was dark, and Animal had been worried that they'd notice the light from the hall when he slipped into the room, but they were so busy going at it that someone could've let off a bomb in the room and he doubted they'd have even blinked, let alone stopped fucking. Momo sat atop Luther, bucking back and forth his lap. Her body was illuminated by the soft glow of streetlight outside the window. You could tell that her supple ass and erect breasts had been surgically enhanced, but whoever had done the work was gifted enough to where the implants looked almost natural. Watching Momo ride Luther like a cowgirl at a rodeo, Animal was able to understand why men so willingly paid top dollar to be with her.

Animal was inching across the room, towards the bed, but he froze when he saw Momo's body shift. She had turned almost to the point where he would've been in her line of vision, then leaned over and reached for something on the nightstand. There was the flash of a lighter and Animal was able to see the glass cylinder between her lips as she touched the flame to it. She took a deep hit, held in the smoke, and leaned in to release it into Luther's nose. Smelling it in the hallway was one thing, but being in a closed space with the stench made Animal want to retch. When Animal decided he had seen enough, he decided to make his presence felt and flicked on the light.

"What the fuck?" Luther jumped up, knocking Momo off his lap in the process. He was a light-skinned man with a slight build, and a mouth that looked like it was too big for his face.

"How you doing Luther?"Animal stepped closer to the bed, keeping his gun trained on him.

"Do we know each other?" Luther asked.

"Not yet, but I suspect before it's all said and done I'm going to know you and your secrets very intimately." Animal stepped closer. In the light, he could see both of their faces and it was obvious that they were both high as kites, but Momo looked like she was on another planet. She looked at the gun in his hand and seemed more curious about it than afraid of it. Whatever they were smoking must've been some heavy shit.

"Fuck this about?" Luther asked. From the tightness of his mouth when he spoke you could tell the drugs had numbed it.

"This is about why a broke nigga like you is so popular

amongst the rich lately. You're so popular, and how I can use that popularity to my advantage."

"Dude, I don't know who you think I am, but you're wrong. I'm just the manager of a messenger service."

Animal's open hand slapped Luther so hard that he fell off the bed. He was so high he probably didn't feel it, but it got his attention. "The last nigga who tried to play me for a fool tonight ended up dead. Now shoot straight or you gonna feel some real fire," he brandished his gun.

"Are you a demon?" Momo looked at Animal with an almost child-like innocence. She was kneeling on the bed, rocking back and forth. "Mama told me bad spirits come to take loose young girls to hell to pay for their whorishness. Have you come to take me to hell?"

"Well, sweeties, that'll all depend on how helpful your friend is." Animal played on her delusion.

"Tell the demon what he wants to know so I don't have to go to hell. I don't wanna go to hell, I wanna play some more," she crawled across the bed and pawed at Luther's manhood.

"You heard her, Luther. Tell the big bad demon what he wants to know or else when he goes home he'll be bringing company for dinner," Animal said sinisterly. "I already spoke to your lawyer so I know about NYAK. I also know that you're connected to Tiger Lily and her cartel in some way, so I'm trying to figure out the connection. Is NYAK laundering money for the cartel?"

Luther chuckled. "Dude, not only are you clueless but you're barking up a tree you really don't want to climb. If you already know I'm connected to the cartel then you realize I've got important friends... friends who'll take everything you love if something happens to me."

Animal clocked Luther with the butt of his gun, opening a gash in his head before snatching him to his feet and shoving his gun under his chin. "Tiger Lily and the cartel have already taken everything I love, so there isn't much more they can do to me. I got nothing else to lose, can you say the same?"

"If you shoot me, you'll never get the information you're looking for," Luther warned.

"Yeah, I had thought about that," Animal tucked his gun and pulled a knife from his back pocket. "This is why I came prepared to start hacking off pieces of you until you tell me what I need to know."

"Okay, okay," Luther relented. The threat of his impending death seemed to sober him up. "Look, I'm just a courier. I sometimes take important things from point A to point B and get well compensated for it," he admitted.

"Whatever you're transporting back and forth must be extremely important for someone to make sure you've got one of the best lawyers in the city on-call for when you fuck up. What do you deliver and who do you deliver it to?"

"C'mon, man. You know who I'm dealing with so you know what they'll do to me if I talk," Luther pleaded with Animal.

Animal patted the blade against Luther's cheek. "And obviously you have no idea what I'll do to you if you don't." Luther looked into the eyes of the wild haired young man who had intruded on his freak session and saw no signs that he'd be able to reason or negotiate with him. He was already in the crosshairs of the cartel for his recent fuck ups and his lawyer, Stein, had advised him to lay low until they worked things out, but Luther wouldn't listen. His brain whirled, desperately searching for a way to buy himself some time to figure a way out of the mess he was in. It was either remain silent and die right there, or talk and die later. Neither prospect was appealing. He opened his mouth to fire off his best lie, but Momo saved him the trouble.

"To hell! To hell! The demons have come to take us to hell but I ain't going!" Momo shouted before leaping from the bed and charging. Her attack caught him off guard, and she managed to knock him into the wall, dislodging the knife from his hand.

Animal intercepted Momo's wrists just as her long acrylic nails tried to claw his eyes out. For a girl her size, Momo was stronger than Animal expected. In fact, she was a little too strong. Trying to wrestle her down was like trying to pin a three-hundred-pound man. When Momo grabbed him by the legs and Animal felt his feet leaving the ground, he knew it was time to take drastic measures. He punched Momo square in the mouth with everything he had. Her lip split, sending blood running down her chin. The blow was supposed to crumple Momo, but it only seemed to intensify her attack.

"I ain't gonna let you take me, demon! You hear me? I ain't gonna let you take me!" Momo screamed in his face then started strangling him.

Just beyond Momo, Animal saw Luther slip his pants on and grab his messenger bag from the floor. He was trying to use the distraction she had caused for his window of escape. If Animal lost him then he was sure he wouldn't be able to find him a second time, and it would also alert Lilith to what he was attempting to do. He had to end things with Momo and quickly. Animal raised his foot and kicked Momo in the stomach, sending her tumbling over the bed. It allowed him a second to catch his breath so he could deal with his next

dilemma, which was Momo coming up from the floor holding his knife.

Momo sprang across the room, madness dancing in her

eyes and every intention on gutting Animal. She had backed him into a corner. Animal drew his gun and shot Momo once in the thigh. She stumbled, but kept charging. He shot her again, this time in the stomach, slowing her down but her insanity carried her on. Animal had a code against killing women or children, but he was no longer dealing with a woman. Whatever Momo was on had turned her into something else. Animal grabbed a pillow from the bed to muffle the sound, and shot Momo twice in the chest, finally dropping her.

By then Luther was streaking across the room to the door. He had just managed to get it open when Animal kicked it closed again, almost lopping off one of Luther's fingers in the process. Luther swung the messenger bag at Animal's head, but the move was slow and awkward. Animal countered with a combination to the stomach, and tagged him on his chin one time for good measure. Luther's arms went flailing and the bag flew in the air, sending the contents flying. Luther made one last desperate attempt to grab for the documents on the floor, but Animal brining his pistol around stopped him.

ANIMAL IV: LAST RITES

"Stay down, stupid, before I smoke you," Animal warned.

"Don't matter. I was dead the minute you came in here asking questions about the cartel," Luther pulled himself to his feet. Animal thought he might've been ready to launch another attack, but instead he sat on the edge of the bed, shoulders sagging in defeat.

"I would think you would be more worried about the man holding a gun on you than some bitch that's a half a world away," Animal said.

"You think distance matters to someone like Lilith? If she wants you dead, you're dead, and it don't matter how far you run or where you hide. But you'll find that out on your own soon enough."

"Not if I kill her first," Animal countered.

A smirk formed on Luther's face. "You have no idea who or what you're dealing with, do you? Tiger Lily is an enemy you don't want."

"Why don't you let me be the judge of that? You think Tiger Lily is the first organized crime boss that I've gone against? No matter how big or bad they are, they all bleed the same."

"Lilith isn't just some boss; she's the mother of Satan!" Luther insisted. "Regardless of what happens to me today, it won't stop her plans. She's going to crack open the gates of hell and usher in the end of days."

"Unless I put a bullet in her head," Animal countered.

Luther laughed. "Man, where are you from, Mars? How are you gonna stop what's already in motion? At this point, there's nothing any of us can do except ride the wave and hope we don't crash on the rocks. You wanna find out what Lilith is up to? Do it your fucking self," he sprang from the bed and threw himself out the window.

Animal peered through the broken glass at what was left of Luther. He lay on the ground, three stories below, with his body twisted at an awkward angle. Blood pooled beneath his half-crushed skull and his memories leaked out into the concrete. Staring down at Luther he found himself feeling somewhere between shocked and disgusted. He was so afraid of Tiger Lily that he would rather have taken his own life than cross her. The fact that his adversary was able to instill that type of fear in a man gave Animal a new respect for her. Tiger Lily was something he hadn't been up against in a long time, a real gangster.

He had come to Original Sin looking for answers, but

instead ended up with even more questions and blood on his hands, which seemed to be the story of his life. Luther killing himself before Animal could extract any useful information only further complicated an already complex problem, but there wasn't too much he could do about it at that point except move on and hope he could pick up another useful lead from Sonja's flash drive.

As Animal was about to leave when he remembered the messenger bag and its contents. He knelt down and began gathering the papers up, thumbing through them to see what Luther carried that was so important that it earned him a get-out-of-jail-free card. The first thing he came across was a sheet of notebook paper with numbers and letters scribbled on them. It reminded Animal of the periodic table of elements his high school science teacher had pinned to the wall of his class. He set that aside and continued shuffling through the contents of the bag. He came across several bank statements and some other legal documents baring the name L. Angelino, who was listed as a minority shareholder in NYAK. Animal then understood why Luther found his accusations of NYAK laundering money for the cartel laughable. You didn't need to hire someone to wash your cash when you owned a stake in the laundromat. Angelino was Lilith's maiden name. He recalled Sonja mentioning it in one of their conversations. By getting Luther out of jail, Lilith was protecting her interests. Now the connections all made sense.

A smile crossed Animal's face. As it turned out, popping in on Luther hadn't been a total loss after all. Tying Lilith to NYAK might be just what he needed to leverage against her. If word were to get out about their connection, it would raise all kinds of uncomfortable questions that she, nor NYAK, were prepared to answer. She would likely do anything in her power to keep the secret from getting out; even return his children.

He sifted through the rest of the papers to see what else he could find. Most of it was junk, with little value to him or his cause, but he did find something that gave him pause. It was a shipping manifest for a boat called La Viuda Roja. He recognized the name from his time in Old San Juan. It had been painted on the side of one of the cargo ships that came in and out of the harbor, which the cartel controlled. Poppito had christened it with the nickname the soldiers had given his daughter Sonja, La Viuda Roja, The Red Widow. According to the manifest, the ship was supposed to be carrying rum and canned fish from Puerto Rico to New York, but Animal was no fool. He had a hunch that if he tracked down that ship the only thing he'd find on it was cocaine. He had just discovered how the cartel was getting their drugs in and out of the city. If he could intercept their shipment, it would be a crippling blow to the cartel. Of course, it was a long shot, but he had been beating the odds all his life.

"Looks like Christmas has come early this year," Animal said, packing the documents back into the messenger bag to take with him. He couldn't wait to cross-reference the information with what Sonja had on the flash drive. For the first time since it had all started, he could actually see a light at the end of the dark ass tunnel.

Animal surveyed the bloody room, taking stock of the mess and the dead body that now occupied and it filled him with something he hadn't felt in a long time, hunger. It was like those first pangs when you woke up in the morning and your body told you it was time to have break-fast. The emptiness had returned, the same emptiness he had spent so many years using death and violence trying to fill. Sitting on the sidelines for so long had dulled his taste for blood, but the small sampling that night had brought the thirst back. He wanted more and he would have it.

On his way out, he spotted the pipe Momo had been smoking on the floor near the bed. He knelt and picked it up to examine it. When he put it to his nose and sniffed, he recoiled at the foul smell. It was packed with small blue crystals, which looked like rock candy, but rock candy didn't turn hundred and forty-pound strippers into raging bulls. Whatever the drug was, it was like nothing he'd ever encountered in his years on the streets. He thought back on Luther's last words about Tiger Lily opening the gates of hell and wondered if the contents of the pipe were the key.

With the messenger bag slung across his back, Animal slipped into the hall and made his way back towards the steps. Things were as still as they were when he'd come so he gathered all the noise downstairs had muffled the sounds of breaking glass when Luther jumped from the third floor window. No matter. It wouldn't be long before they found the body, which meant he only had a precious few moments to escape Original Sin with the information he'd collected and his life. When he reached the stairs, he noticed several brutish looking men in black t-shirts making their way up. Leading them was the barmaid who had chatted him up when he was downstairs.

"That's the guy I was telling you about right there!" She pointed her finger accusingly at Animal.

"Is there a problem?" Animal asked as if he didn't already know what was going on.

The lead bouncer stepped forward. "Yeah, this is a member's only club. I'm going to need to see your credentials or have to ask you to leave."

"No problem. I was on my way out anyhow," Animal said, stepping past him. He was almost clear when a half-dressed stripper, who looked frightened out of her mind, appeared at the bottom of the stairs.

"There's a dead body in the parking lot!" the stripper shrieked.

His precious few moments were up.

A strong hand clasped Animal's shoulder from behind. He spun, drawing his gun with his free hand and pumped two slugs into the gut of the man who had grabbed him. Without missing a beat, he put a bullet in the forehead of the barmaid. She wasn't a threat, but it was what she got for snitching on him. One member of the security team tried to play hero and leapt into Animal's path. The young killer never broke his stride when he put a bullet between his eyes. His bulky body rolled down the stairs, knocking people over like bowling pins and clearing a path for Animal.

The sounds of gunshots threw the entire club into chaos, with everyone scrambling to get out of the way of the wild haired gunman. Animal zigzagged across the floor, dodging enemy gunfire. Seeing the exit in front of him, he willed his legs to pump faster. He had almost reached the door when several men popped out of nowhere and cut him off. Animal was sure he could take a few of them out, but he didn't have enough bullets left to go to war with the entire security team. He was trapped.

A thick stripper who had been trying to escape the gunfire wandered into Animal's path and it gave him an idea. He grabbed the girl and hoisted her onto his shoulder. She was heavy as hell, but adrenaline and fear gave him the strength to run with her across the room to the large picture window. He fired off the remaining bullets in his clip, weakening the glass before using the stripper as a battering ram and dove through the window to freedom. By the time, the security team made it over, all that was left to mark Animal's passing was some broken glass and a dazed stripper.

*

Animal half-ran, half-limped through an alley, fleeing the crime scene. He had banged himself up pretty bad when he jumped out the window, but a few cuts and bruises beat a bullet to the head any day. It wasn't until he was five blocks away that he finally stopped to catch his breath.

He checked the time on his watch and realized that it was almost midnight. He hadn't even realized that he had been gone so long. By then Ashanti and the others had no doubt realized that he was gone and were surely combing the streets looking for him, but he wasn't quite ready to be found yet. There were still a few things he needed to do before he headed back to share his discovery with his comrades.

Part of him felt bad about his abrupt departure. After all, they had laid on the line for him, disappearing without a word was inconsiderate on his part, but he was all out of words and overflowing with rage. The vision he'd had earlier had put him on the path and he now understood what he needed to do. The only reason Animal hadn't jumped on the first thing smoking to Old San Juan and blown Lilith's head off was because he didn't want to put his children in unnecessary jeopardy. Animal knew enough about the ways of the Brotherhood to know that his kids weren't in any immediate danger for two reasons; one was it went against the oldest codes of that order to harm a child and two they were also holding one of Lilith's sons, George. For as much shit as she talked about George being a soldier, she was still his mother. As a parent himself, Animal understood the unfading love of a parent for their child, but he also understood a parent's wrath if their children were put in harm's way. As long as George was kept alive, so would his children, but he still needed a solid plan to get them back.

The others wanted to negotiate with Lilith, and Animal wasn't opposed to, but he knew that when dealing with a tyrant like Lilith, you needed additional leverage to get them to play fair, which is why he had set out on his little solo mission of destruction. There was no way in hell he was going into the serpent's lair; he had to draw her out and that's exactly what he intended to do with what he had found in the messenger bag. Tiger Lily was sure to be livid when she found out Animal uncovered her secret, but she would certainly shit a brick when she found out what he had in store for her drug shipment. That would be the final slap in the face to spur her to action, but in order to put it in play; he still needed to find the Red Widow.

Luther had gone to his grave with the location of the freighter, and none of what he found in the messenger bag gave him so much as clue either. This was something he would need help with, and he knew just who to turn to. The only problem was that after the way they had parted the last time, he wasn't sure if his unexpected arrival would be received with open arms or a loaded gun.

CHAPTER 8

Twenty minutes after Animal's great escape, Original Sin found itself thrown into chaos. There were police cruisers and ambulances lining both sides of the block, and a wall of yellow tape had been erected to keep the onlookers from contaminating the crime scene. The once quiet block had been turned into a circus, and rightfully so. It wasn't every day that one of the biggest houses of prostitution and gambling in the city got busted. Some of the girls and a few of the higher profile clients had managed to slip out at the first signs of trouble, but the ones who weren't found themselves having to answer some very uncomfortable questions.

A brown Buick pulled to such an abrupt stop at the curb that one of the uniformed officers had to jump onto the curb to keep from being run over. As if they had been synchronized to do so, both the driver and the passenger doors came open at the same time. From behind the wheel, slid a tall, handsome, Hispanic man. Dressed in a tailored suit that was the color of a cloudy summer day, he looked more like a fashion model than a law enforcement agent.

With him, looks could be deceiving, but with his partner, not so much.

The second man who climbed from the car was Black... of a caramel complexion to be exact. He too wore a suit, but his was a dull shade of brown and fit him like he'd gotten it off the rack. He had a hard face, and wore his hair in a tapered afro that was at least ten years past its curfew. Unlike his partner, who could blend in pretty much anywhere, his whole aura screamed cop.

They were Detectives Alvarez and Brown, known amongst the criminal element on the streets as The Minority Report. They were notorious hard asses who abused their authority every chance they got and weren't above stepping outside the law to make a case stick.

"Detectives Brown, Alvarez," one of the uniformed officers greeted them.

"What do we have?" Brown asked in his gruff voice. The man seemed to be angry twenty-four hours a day.

"Well it seems to be some type of illegal gambling house. Busted a few whores working the joint too. As near as... "

"I know what Original Sin is, numb nuts," Brown cut him off. "I mean what happened?"

"Oh," the uniformed officer turned red from embarrassment. "Ah, according to witness reports, some guy came in and shot the place up. We've got several dead inside and at least a dozen wounded, in addition to a body in the parking lot. This place is a mess," he filled the detectives in.

"Employees or patrons?" Alvarez asked.

"For the most part, the casualties were all employees of this place but there was one who wasn't," the cop referred to his note pad. "A man by the name of Luther Graham."

The name tugged at Detective Brown's memory. "Where do I know that name from?"

"We found his wallet in his back pocket," the officer held up a clear plastic bag containing a black leather wallet. "He's a manager at a messenger service based in lower Manhattan."

"That's why his name sounded so familiar," Brown snapped his fingers as his memory kicked in. "His name has been buzzing downtown lately. Apparently, Mr. Graham has been arrested several times in the last few months, but we can't seem to get anything to stick to him. From what I hear he's a petty crook, so it raises the question as to how he ended up in a whore house full of long money gangsters."

"I think the better question is why would someone want to kill him?" Alvarez countered.

"Ah, actually he wasn't killed by the shooter. From what the medical examiner on scene says, Mr. Graham's wound was self-inflicted. He jumped out the window," the uniformed officer revealed.

"And the plot thickens," Detective Alvarez said absently. "Do we have the person responsible for shooting all those people or did the locals get to him first?" Alvarez asked, knowing how Original Sin dealt with troublemakers. He'd never admit it in a court of law, but he was a card-carrying member of the establishment.

"Neither. The shooter escaped before security could apprehend him," the uniformed officer said, much to Detective Alvarez's surprise. One thing he knew about Original Sin was that violators might've been able to get in, but they never got out.

"How did he manage that?" Alvarez asked. "Through there," the uniformed pointed to the busted first floor window.

Detective Brown looked from the window back to the uniformed officer. "You mean to tell me that somebody came into this joint, scared Graham into killing himself, took out half the security team and then jumped through the window to get away?" he asked in a disbelieving tone.

"I know it sounds crazy, Detective Brown, but all the witness accounts match up," the officer explained.

"That'll be all, thanks Officer," Detective Alvarez dismissed him.

"You hear this muthafucka? Flying men carrying guns!" Detective Brown snorted in disbelief.

"Stranger things have happened, Brown," Alvarez reminded him. In their time together, they had worked on cases that ranged from unusual to completely unexplainable, so he always kept an open mind no matter how farfetched the story sounded. "The officer has laid some interesting things on the table, but we need to speak with an eyewitness to fill in the blanks."

As if in answer to his prayers, several uniformed officers came out of the building, leading a group of men and women in handcuffs. Detective Brown happened to recognize one of them, a husky man wearing thick glasses. "How about a four-eyed witness?" Brown asked his partner and walked over. A quick chat with one of the officers revealed the charges they had him on; possession of an illegal firearm and marijuana. They charges weren't too heavy, but with his track record they were heavy enough for the detectives to bargain with. "We'll take this one off your hands," he pulled the man with the glasses from the line of prisoners. The two detectives walked him off to the side, where Brown shoved him against a wall. "My main man, Boogie Blind," he slapped Boogie on the back harder than he needed to.

"Good evening Detectives," Boogie flashed them a sarcastic grin.

"From the looks of it, this hasn't been a good evening for

any of us, especially you," Detective Brown said. "They caught you with a pistol and chronic," he shook his head in disappointment. "You're slipping, Boogie." Brown and Alvarez had had more than a few run-ins with Boogie over the years. He was a member of a small band of outlaws who dabbled in a bit of everything, but specialized in murder.

"They planted that gun on me and the weed was for my glaucoma," Boogie protested.

"That's bullshit and you know it!" Alvarez shot back. "Just face the fact that you finally got caught with your hand in the cookie jar. This is gonna go bad for you, Boogie."

Boogie sucked his teeth. "Fuck outta here. You can save those scare tactics for some novice nigga who ain't never been in the cage. This shit is a bullshit case and my lawyer is gonna eat it!"

"That's probably true," Brown agreed. "That old Jew you boys keep on retainer is more than likely going to find a way to get you out of this with little to no jail time at all, but it's going to put you in the radar and bring some unwanted attention to your little crew. How do you think Christian is going to take it when he finds out the reason his organization is being looked into is because your fat ass got greedy and went against his rule about moonlighting?"

At the mention of Christian's name, Boogie got silent. Christian was the leader of the crew Boogie ran with. Outside of the fact that he was a club promoter and ran girls, the police knew very little about him. The reason for this was because Christian was an extremely cautious man, and demanded the members of his team moved just as carefully. This is why he didn't like them taking side jobs. When freelance work went wrong for one of them, it brought unnecessary heat to the entire organization by association, such was the case with Boogie getting arrested while working security at Original Sin.

"Don't get all quiet on me now, Boogie," Detective Brown continued.

"This is about me and a bullshit case. It doesn't have anything to do with Christian," Boogie argued.

"That's until we make it have everything to do with Christian," Detective Alvarez added. "Christian dodged a bullet when all that shit happened with Chancellor. King's monarchy was torn apart, and he was smart to lay low after it, but situations like the one we have here tonight tend to re-open old wounds. When we get to sniffing Christian because of this petty shit you got caught up in, he's gonna tap dance all over your ass in them designer shoes he's so fond of."

"Man, y'all ain't about to go through all that over something as small as this," Boogie capped.

Detective Brown bounced him off the wall and grabbed him by the throat. "Try me, muthafucka! You and I both know that me and my partner are the kings of doing petty shit, so if you don't think we'll make it our personal mission to smear you and that cock-lover you work for, you'd better think again."

Boogie weighed his options. Christian had warned him against taking side jobs, but Boogie didn't listen. He made a nice piece of change working security at Original Sin and got all the free pussy he could handle. It was a sweet job, but hardly worth him fucking up his primary source of income and potentially winding up dead over a few dollars.

"What y'all want from me, man?" Boogie finally gave in. Detective Alvarez smiled. "Just a little information."

"I ain't no fucking rat!" Boogie spat.

"C'mon, man. You know I know that and I'd never disrespect you by asking you to tell on your fellow man, but this wasn't your fellow man that came in there and shot this place up. Hell, you're lucky you didn't wind up getting wheeled out on one of those gurneys tonight. All you gotta do is tell us who did this and we'll cut you loose and make sure the gun and your charges disappear," Detective Alvarez promised.

Boogie looked at the two detectives. Brown and Alvarez were a lot of things, but they weren't liars. If they promised to cut him loose and make the case go away, they would. "I don't know his name," he sighed.

"Did you get a look at him?" Detective Brown asked. "Briefly, before he started smoking muthafuckas. He was a young dude, dark skinned, handy as hell with a gun. I swear this nigga moved so fast that I didn't even know he had a piece on him until the first body dropped."

"Would you say he was a pro?" Detective Alvarez asked, jotting down notes on his pad.

"I'd say so. If he isn't then he should be. That boy was a lethal piece of work," Boogie said seriously.

"Anything else you remember about him? Maybe he had some tattoos or any other distinguishing marks?" Detective Alvarez asked.

"Yeah, his hair. He had this bushy ass fro that looked like it hadn't seen a comb in weeks."

"I guess we can knock barbershops off our lists of places to search," Alvarez snickered.

"Shut up, J," Detective Brown scolded him. "Is that it, Boogie?"

Boogie tapped his chin trying to think of anything else, and then he remembered a very important detail. "His teeth!"

Alvarez looked up from his scribbling. "What about them? Were they rotten, missing, what?"

"Nah, man, I mean shiny. He was grilled up like one of them down south niggas," Boogie explained.

At the mention of the grills, a troubled look passed between Detectives Alvarez and Brown. They were both thinking the same thing, but neither one of them wanted to speak it into existence.

"What?" Boogie looked back and forth at the stunned facial expressions on the detective's faces. "Why y'all looking at each other like you seen a ghost?"

"Thanks, you've been real helpful, Boogie." Alvarez ignored the question. "Officer," he waved one of the uniforms over to take possession of Boogie.

"What the fuck is this? Y'all said you'd spring me!" Boogie reminded them.

"And we will, but we can't very well let you walk away from the crime scene," Detective Alvarez told him. "We'll swing by the precinct in an hour or so and take care of everything," he promised before letting the uniformed officer take Boogie away.

"You hear that description?" Brown asked his partner, beating him to the punch.

Alvarez nodded. "I know what you're thinking, but it's impossible. The last I heard he'd gotten rich off some lawsuit and retired to a house on the beach in California when he got out of the joint."

"One man, a bunch of bodies, and a movie-worthy escape... it definitely fits his M.O," Detective Brown pointed out.

"I can't argue with you there, but it doesn't make sense. He did something nobody before him had been able to; beat the system. He retired to a wife, a big house, and a big ass bank account. If that were me there's nothing I can think of that would make me risk all that unless... "

"... Somebody was looking to fuck with your happiness," Detective Brown finished his sentence for him.

Detective Alvarez gave his partner a hard look. "Okay, let's say for the sake of argument that I entertain this fairy-tale of yours and somebody was actually dumb enough to wake the beast, he ain't gonna go back into his cage willingly."

"If this is who I think it is, I'm not looking to put him in a cage so he can get another early walk from a sympathetic judge. I'm looking to put him in the ground."

*

Detectives Brown and Alvarez bumped their way through the crowd on the way back to their car. Brown collided with a man wearing a Cincinnati Reds hat with so much force that he almost knocked him off his feet, and didn't even so much as look back to say excuse me. It was probably for the best because if he had, he'd probably have recognized him from their many years of playing cat and mouse in the hood and there was no telling what type of confrontation that would've led to. For as much as he loved a good fight, he was there as an observer that night. There would be time to settle old scores later.

After the detectives had gone and Original Sin had been officially shut down, most of the crowd had disbursed but

the man in the Reds cap remained a few moments longer. He looked on with neutral eyes as the coroners wheeled out yet another body under a bloody sheet. Death was nothing new to him as he had seen many men die in his thirty something years of life, but he felt a personal connection to the crime scene. Not a connection with the victims, but with the killer. He had seen his handiwork before and knew that the few bodies dropped at Original Sin were only the beginning.

When he felt he'd seen enough, he slipped away from the crowd and pulled out his cell phone. "Yeah, it's me," he said watching the coroner close the doors of the meat-wagon while he listened on his phone. "He's definitely passed this way."

PART 3

BROKEN FLOWERS

CHAPTER 9

Two hours after Ashanti had left the apartment there was still no sign of Animal. He had searched all their old haunts, but no one had seen or heard from Animal. In fact, a few of the people who he'd asked were surprised to hear that he was even still alive. It was as if Animal had vanished from the face of the earth.

Adding to his irritation were the phone calls he had gotten from the twins. Zo was in, as he knew he would be, but Shai had rejected them. Ashanti had expected as much, but he had hoped the young king went the other way. His reason for reaching out to Shai had been two fold. He actually did need help, in the worst way, but it was also a test. Shai and the cartel were in the same business so that meant they ran in the same circles and had access to the same networks. Ashanti doubted that Abel telling Shai what happened to Animal came as a surprise, but it opened the door for the real conversation and a test of Shai's character.

Abel telling Shai that Lilith had designs on his territory was a bullshit lie that Ashanti had fed him. In truth, he had no idea what Lilith's end game was, but he needed to truly see where Shai's head was at. In all the years Ashanti had known him, Shai had always been territorial. He hated anyone to get too close to what he laid claim to, so when he seemed unbothered by the threat of a major drug cartel encroaching on his turf, Ashanti knew there could be only one reason for his laid back stance; he had a stake in whatever the cartel was planning.

Ashanti was disappointed in Shai, but more disappointed in himself for thinking that Shai would rise to the occasion. It seemed like every time he gave the youngest Clark male the benefit of the doubt, he did some greasy shit that reminded Ashanti why Animal had stopped fucking with him in the first place. He'd always smelled the foulness in Shai; it was just too bad the rest of them didn't see his true colors before Tech was murdered.

Tech had been the original alpha of the Dog Pound. It was he who had taken Animal under his wing, and Animal who had done the same for Ashanti when the time came. This was back when they were all still associates of the Clark family, young attack dogs that would kill or maim on command. Tech was a good dude, but also a wild card. He was a true outlaw, beholden to no rules except those of the jungle; the weak are food for the strong. The fact that Shai couldn't control Tech never went over well with the other bosses whose toes he sometimes stepped on, and they began to put pressure on the young king to muzzle his dog. He warned Tech about his antics and the problems they were causing, but Tech continued to do as he pleased without care or concern for how Shai felt. The time eventually came when Tech had gone too far and Shai made an example out of him by having Tech gunned down.

The rest of the Pound wanted blood for what Shai had done, but Animal granted him a stay of execution. At the time, Ashanti was too young understand why he did it, and did hold some resentment over Animal's decision, but when he got older and more seasoned, he understood why Animal had done it.

They were babies, barely able to shoot straight, talking about going against an army of trained killers. By making them stand down, Animal had saved the young lambs from the slaughter. In hindsight, after all the grief Shai would cause them over the years it kind of made Ashanti wish they'd taken their chances and tried to kill him.

After hours of driving around looking for him, Ashanti figured that wherever Animal was, he wasn't ready to be found. There was nothing more for him to do but wait until the big homie revealed himself and what he'd been up to. Since Ashanti now had some time to kill, he decided to turn his attention to something he had been neglecting, his lady.

He and Fatima had been on the outs lately and it was his fault. Lately they had been clashing over how much time he spent on the road with Kahllah and how little time he was spending at home. Since things had gotten serious between Ashanti and Fatima, they decided to move in together. Ashanti secured them a nice apartment in downtown Brooklyn. He'd hit Fatima with some paper and let her decorate the place however she wanted. She made a quaint little home for her and Ashanti, but the problem was that he was never in it for more than a day or so at a time. Fatima understood that when Ashanti was with Kahllah it was about getting money. Her man was seeing more paper than he ever did on the block, and she made a fair piece of change at her legit job, so they were able to stack quite a bit of bread, but it felt like the more he got, the harder he went. After a while, she began to wonder if he was really out chasing the money, or simply the thrill of the kill.

Right before his last excursion to the west coast with Kahllah, Fatima had laid her feelings on the table. She let it be known that things had to change between her and Ashanti or she was leaving. He understood and promised that after they came back from California he was going to take some time off to stay home and work on being a better man to her. That was right before they went to visit Animal

and the shit hit the fan. Fatima was pissed that he was going to be away longer than promised, but she knew how Ashanti felt when it came to Animal so she accepted it. What hurt her was when he came back to New York and hadn't bothered to tell her. She had to hear through the grapevine that her lover was back in town. Ashanti hadn't done it to slight her, but there had been so much going on so fast that he hadn't had a minute to think since he got off the plane. That wasn't a good enough excuse for Fatima. He had finally gone too far and she washed her hands of him.

After some begging and pleading, she finally agreed to meet with Ashanti. She told him to come by her job when she took her break. She didn't make him any promises, but she would at least hear him out. It was all Ashanti could ask for at that point, and he planned to plead a very convincing case in the hopes she'd take him back. Fatima was the best thing that had ever happened to him and he told her every chance he got, but now it was time to show her.

Fatima worked as a security guard at Barclay's Center, which wasn't too far from their apartment. Ashanti had been against her getting a job, arguing that he made enough money to support them, but Fatima wasn't trying to hear it. She had learned from what happened to her father, Cutty, that street money didn't last forever and she refused to end up one of those dumb broads who ended up broke and flat on their asses when their men were taken from them. Besides that, Fatima had always been independent, either working or hustling for what she needed. She loved the fact that Ashanti had been willing to take care of her, but she needed her own.

There was a game going on that night, so traffic was a mess and parking was a nightmare. Ashanti had to park several blocks away and walk to the arena. As he was getting out of the car, he remembered the metal detectors he'd have to pass through to get inside, which meant he couldn't take his gun with him. Ashanti hated to go anywhere without a ratchet, it made him feel naked. When you lived as he did, death could come at any time so he prided himself on always being prepared. Barclay's wasn't too far and the streets were crawling with police, so he figured he should be okay. He planned to go in, say what he needed to say to Fatima, and get up out of there.

It was Ashanti's first time in Barclay's Center, and he had to admit he was impressed by the modernized arena. It didn't have the storied history, or feel of Madison Square Garden, but they had done a great job with it. He took his place at the end of the line, waiting like everyone else to go through the metal detector. Just beyond it, he spotted

Fatima. Her hair was freshly braided up, and the gray security slacks she wore hugged her ass nicely. It felt like a lifetime since he had seen the love of his life and a broad smile crossed his face as he thought of scooping her in his arms as she planted kisses all over his face. The smile faded when he got closer and noticed she was chatting it up with some dude. He too was wearing a security uniform so it could've very well been an innocent conversation between co-workers, but Ashanti's gut told him it wasn't. There was something about the guy that made Ashanti angry. He had been around enough creeps to know larceny when he saw it in someone's eyes.

Ashanti had been so fixed on Fatima and her co-worker that he hadn't even realized he'd made it to the front of the line. A skinny security guard, holding what looked like a price scanner in his hands, was giving Ashanti an annoyed look like he was waiting for something and Ashanti was holding him up.

"Sir, I asked to see your ticket," the security guard repeated for the third time.

"My bad," Ashanti said apologetically. "I don't have a ticket because—"

"No ticket, no entry," the security guard cut Ashanti off before he could finish his sentence.

"Listen, Blood, I'm just trying to explain to you that I'm not here to see the game; I'm visiting an employee," Ashanti said, trying to keep his cool.

"I ain't yo muthafucking Blood, nigga, so watch that shit, cuz," the security guard replied angrily.

Ashanti couldn't figure out what all the hostility was about until he noticed the tattoo on the security guard's neck, peeking out from the collar of his white shirt. He was from a Crip set. "Listen," he softened his tone. "I didn't come here off no bullshit. I'm just trying to see who I came to see and go on my way."

Seeing there was some type of disturbance, two more security guards came over to back up the skinny one. Now having numbers on his side, he decided to really get brazen. "You ain't about to see nothing, but the lights on the outside of the arena if you ain't got no ticket. Move on or get moved," he warned.

Ashanti took stock of the situation. He knew that as soon as he made his move he'd have the full force of the arena's security on his ass and might even end up getting arrested, but it would all be worth it if he got to break the jaw of the skinny Crip in front of him before it all went down.

"Ashanti!" Fatima's voice snapped him to attention, like a parent who had just caught their kid about to do something

wrong. At the mention of his name, a look of recognition passed across the skinny security guard's face, but Ashanti never saw it. He was focused on Fatima, who stood just behind the metal detector with her arms folded and glaring at him angrily. "He's with me," she told them and the security guards stood down.

As Ashanti stepped past the skinny security guard, he gave him a little bump with his shoulder. He wondered if the security guard knew how close he had come to getting put on medical leave from his job.

"Why are you coming to my place of employment starting shit?" Fatima greeted him with an attitude. Though she hadn't been working there long, she liked her job and didn't want to lose it over someone else's mess.

"Your staff here needs to be a little more courteous," Ashanti said, looking back at the skinny guard who had accosted him. After the incident, he had been removed from his post and was now standing near one of the concession stands talking to the dude who had been chatting it up with Fatima. It looked like he was being reprimanded, so the other one must've been their supervisor. "But fuck all that clown shit, I'm glad to see you." He leaned in to kiss her on the lips, but she turned her head and gave him her cheek.

"Damn, it's like that?"

"How is it supposed to be when I had to find out my man was back in New York on a post some chicken head made on Facebook?"

"Fuck is you talking about?" Ashanti was confused.

Unlike everyone else, he refused to ride the social media wave. He didn't own a computer and refused to allow any apps on his phone.

"I'm talking about this," Fatima held up her phone so he could see the post in question. As it turned out, some random chick had taken a selfie in the club he, Animal, and Abel had the shootout in, and Ashanti just happened to get caught in the background of her picture. He didn't know the girl and had no clue the picture even existed, but made a mental note to himself to track her down the first chance he got. That's why he didn't fuck with social media, because the things posted on it could get you indicted. "I heard there was a shootout at the club that same night and I hope you weren't involved."

He could've lied to her, but he knew Fatima would see right through whatever story he came up with. Being able to tell when he was lying was one of her gifts. Instead, he just lowered his head in shame.

Fatima rolled her eyes. "I can't believe you! Didn't we have a long discussion about shitting where you lived? We agreed that after you got out of the last mess that almost cost you your freedom that you would be more mindful about what you did in the city."

She was speaking about a close call that Ashanti had a few months prior. Kahllah had been paid to take out a target in New York, but she had her hands full chasing an arms dealer across Connecticut. Ashanti had offered to take on the job by himself, but Kahllah had been against it. She hadn't had time to assess the situation yet, and wanted Ashanti to wait. He figured she was just being paranoid and dropped the dude anyhow. As it turned out, he was a police informant who had been under surveillance. Ashanti hadn't realized how well-known his name and face were in New York City until less than an hour after he killed the snitch, he found himself in handcuffs. Luckily, for him, the arresting detective had been a man named Wolf who owed Kahllah a favor. Ashanti had avoided spending the rest of his life in prison by the skin of his teeth and it was agreed on by all parties that Ashanti wouldn't do anymore local jobs.

"This was different. The fools who got dropped were connected to the people who took Animal's kids," Ashanti explained.

At the mention of the kidnapping, Fatima's demeanor softened. "That is some sad shit, and my prayers are with Animal right now. Have y'all gotten any closer to finding the people who did it?"

"We know where the muthafuckas who did it are, it's Animal who we can't find," Ashanti admitted and went on to tell Fatima what had happened over the last few hours.

A terrified expression crossed Fatima's face. She'd seen what Animal was capable of when Gucci got shot, and didn't even want to think about what kind of horror show he was going to put on over his babies. "Ashanti, I know that's your friend and all, but I'm worried about what kind of fall out can come of this. Those cartels don't fuck around and they won't hesitate to kill entire families. What if they come for us because of your affiliation with Animal?"

"Baby, I promise I'm going to keep you as far away from this as possible. I saw how it tore Gucci up when we all thought Animal was dead, and I see how broken Animal is over her and I won't subject us to that. I'm a survivor, you ain't gotta worry."

"Ashanti, when I said us I don't mean as in me and you, I mean as in me and this life that's growing inside me," Fatima touched her stomach.

"What did you just say?" Ashanti's knees felt weak.

"I said that I'm pregnant. I only found out last week and

wanted to surprise you. That's why I got so upset when you stayed in California longer than expected," Fatima explained.

Ashanti was speechless. All he could do was stare at her stomach in shock. He had noticed she had been putting on weight, but chalked it up to the fact that they had been eating better than ever. The fact that she might be pregnant had never entered his mind.

"Aren't you going to say something?" Fatima asked. "I... I guess I'm just a little shocked," he stuttered. "That's not quite the response I was looking for," Fatima snapped.

She had been nervous about telling Ashanti since she found out and his response was the reason why. They were both young, but Ashanti was still very immature and more fascinated with the streets than anything. She didn't want him to feel like she was trying to lock him down. "Look, Ashanti, I know this was unexpected and this probably isn't the best time, but—"

"Don't... just don't say anything else," Ashanti cut her off. His face was serious as he tried to find the words. "Fatima, I told you how it was for me growing up; no father and a mother who pawned me and my sister off to settle a drug debt. I got to see firsthand how fucked up this world and the people in it are, and the last thing I ever wanted was to curse a child to this madness."

Fatima's heart sank. "I know, Ashanti, and I understand. This was unexpected for both of us and I know that with everything you've got on your plate this is just an added worry. I can do this on my own if I have to."

Ashanti looked at her as if she had lost it. "Fatima, are you out of your mind? If you'd let me finish, what I was about to say was, even though neither one of us come from the most stable backgrounds, it doesn't mean we can't build a solid foundation for our baby. Now I might not know a damn thing about being a good parent, but I know plenty about being a bad one and I'm going to use that as a blue-print as what not to do to my kid."

"So you're not mad?"

"Mad? Hell no! This is the best news of my life!" Ashanti scooped her about the waist and spun her around, drawing more than a few stares. "Fatima, when I said I loved you and would stick with you through anything, I meant that shit. You are my moon, and this child will be my stars."

"Ah... Fatima?" her supervisor was back.

"Sorry," Fatima said apologetically and motioned for Ashanti to put her down. She could only imagine how

unprofessional the scene must've looked, but she wasn't sweating it. If her supervisor could experience even a frac-tion of the joy she felt at that moment, he'd understand.

"Baby, I gotta get back to work, but we can talk about this some more at home tonight, okay?"

Ashanti's face darkened and the mood was killed. "You aren't coming home tonight, are you?" Fatima asked in a disappointed tone.

"You know my heart, Fatima. It won't let me rest until Animal's kids are safe," Ashanti said honestly.

"I figured as much." She was hoping that she had been wrong, but Fatima knew her man. He would be loyal to the end. That was something she both loved and hated about Ashanti. "I understand that you gotta do what you gotta do, but I need you to make me a promise first. Promise me that you're going to come home. I'm not saying it has to be tonight or tomorrow night, just as long as you tell me that you'll make it home so you can be a father to this baby."

"I'd die one thousand deaths before I let my baby be an orphan or leave my wife a widow," Ashanti promised.

Fatima chuckled. "Boy you crazy. You mean your baby

mama because we ain't married. Hell we're not even engaged."

"You're right, and we need to do something about that." Ashanti fished around in his pocket and came up holding his car keys. He pulled the ring free of the keys and squeezed it until it caved to a size slightly larger to the size of her finger. Ashanti took Fatima's hand in his and got down on one knee in the middle of the Barclay's lobby. "I don't want you to be my baby mama and I don't want to be your baby daddy. Let's do this the right way," he slipped the key ring over her finger. "Will you be my wife?"

Fatima looked around at the spectators who had gathered at the sight of Ashanti on one knee, including her supervisor. "Ashanti, are you serious? I didn't tell you this to try and force you into marrying me."

"I'm as serious as a heart attack. You and I both know that there's nobody short of God who can force me to do anything I don't want to do. Now say yes so I can get up off this damn floor and these people can stop staring at us."

"Yes, of course I'll marry you!" she declared with tears welling in her eyes.

Ashanti stood and pulled Fatima into a deep kiss, which got him a standing ovation from the crowd that had gathered during the proposal. "Me and you against the world. Never forget that."

"You just remember your promise to come home to me, baby daddy," Fatima teased.

"Fatima!" the supervisor was clearly in his feelings now. Ashanti cut his eyes at the supervisor and he shrank back. "Ma, let me get out of here before I fuck one of these niggas up and you have to find another job. I'll call you in a few and let you know what's popping," he gave her one last peck then made his way out of the arena. As he was leaving he passed the skinny security guard, who was now outside and chatting with someone on his cell phone. He gave Ashanti a dirty look, but the new father-to-be ignored him and kept walking. He was flying high and wouldn't let anybody or anything bring him down.

The skinny security guard continued to watch Ashanti as he crossed the street and walked past Tony Roma's Steak House. "Cuz, I'm telling you I'm looking at the nigga right now. I heard his bitch call him by name so I'm sure it's him! Hurry the fuck up before we miss out on this paper," he barked then ended the call.

*

Ashanti walked up Atlantic Avenue in a daze. It was as if everything that had happened over the last few days had fallen away and all that remained was Fatima's revelation. He still couldn't believe that he was going to be a father. He couldn't wait to tell Animal the good news, but then remembered T.J. and Celeste and felt fucked up. Here he was thinking about celebrating the upcoming birth of his first child, while Animal was still fighting to recover the two he'd lost. No, he would wait until all was resolved before breaking the news.

As Ashanti crossed Carlton Avenue, he spied a group of young men emerging from the block. They were young dudes dressed in baggy clothes, and one of them sported a blue bandana hanging from his belt. Ashanti wouldn't have paid them any attention had they not turned the corner and fell in step behind him.

"What up though, cuz? You just coming from the game?" One of them called behind Ashanti. Ashanti ignored him and kept walking. He knew trouble when he saw it coming. "Cuz, we just trying to find out who winning," the young man shouted.

Ashanti added pep to his step, and heard their footfalls speed up too. They were obviously out looking for a victim to start trouble with and thought they had found one in Ashanti, but he would show them different once he made it to his car and his gun. He had successfully made it to

Claremont Ave and Atlantic, where his car was parked in the middle of the block, closest to Fulton Street. He turned the corner, intent on making the mad dash to his weapon when something cold and solid hit him in the face. The world spun and Ashanti crashed hard to the ground on his back. He didn't have to touch his head to know there was a serious knot forming on it. When he looked up, he saw another young dude standing over him wielding a lead pipe.

"Where you in such a rush to get to, cuz?" the young man who had hit him with the pipe taunted. By then, the other boys who had been following him had caught up and Ashanti was surrounded. In one of their hands, he could see a large handgun.

"Fellas, y'all are about to make a bad decision," Ashanti said, attempting to push himself to his feet before one of the young boys kicked him in the mouth, busting his lip. Seeing his blood leak from his mouth onto the concrete filled Ashanti with rage, but he couldn't' make any sudden moves. The boys were obviously pussies, but they were armed and he wasn't.

"Hurry up and shoot this dude so we can get our paper," the young man with the lead pipe told the one holding the gun.

Paper? What did he mean by paper? Someone must've place a contract on Ashanti. His laundry list of enemies who hated him enough to want him dead was so long he'd have been out there all night trying to go through it. If he had to guess, he'd say it was Tiger Lily who had dropped the bag. If there was a price on his head then there were very likely prices on the heads of his whole team. Animal was lost in the streets somewhere, but Brasco and the others were sitting ducks back at the apartment. He had to get out of there so he could warn them.

"Shorty, this is your last warning. Take that cap gun and your friends and beat it before I change my mind about letting y'all live," Ashanti warned, trying to buy himself some time.

"You hear this nigga?" another one of the young boys spoke up. This was the one with the blue bandana hanging from his pants. "We got the drop on this fool and he's still talking like he's about that life. You should shoot him in his big ass mouth before you give him one to the dome," he laughed.

Ashanti made eye contact with the young man holding the gun. He could tell that he wasn't a killer, but peer pressure and a firearm could turn even the most sheepish men into something they really weren't. The young man with the gun pointed it at Ashanti, but he seemed hesitant. Behind his eyes, Ashanti could see the moral conflict raging between his fear and the pressure from his friends. He knew how this was going to go down, and his timing would dictate the success or failure of what he was planning.

"Shoot!" one of the boys shouted.

At the same time the young man with the gun pulled the trigger, Ashanti sprang forward. The bullet missed him, but grazed his leg, opening a gash in his thigh. He grabbed the gun and the young man's wrist just as he fired the second shot, which struck the ground harmlessly. The boys swarmed on Ashanti while he struggled with their friend for the gun. They struck him in his head and face over and over. They were beating the hell out of him, but Ashanti's will to live and be there for his child kept him from letting go of the gun. He managed to maintain his grip up to the point where the lead pipe landed on the back of his head dropping him to his hands and knees.

Blood poured from Ashanti's head and stung his eyes making it hard for him to see. "Put this nigga to sleep!" he heard one of them yell. Ashanti managed to clear enough of the blood from his eyes to see the young man who had the gun advancing on him. This time he saw no fear in his eyes, only determination. Of all the ways Ashanti imagined he would go out, at the hands of a pussy nigga on a Brooklyn street hadn't been one of them.

There was a faint chirping sound, followed by the young man with the gun abruptly falling to the ground. In the middle of his forehead, Ashanti could see a red dot, leaking blood onto the ground. There was another chirping sound, followed by the pipe wielder's chest exploding. By now, the boys realized they were under attack and they took off running. Ashanti watched as one by one they each fell. The last of them had made it halfway down the block before dropping out of sight between two parked cars.

Ashanti slowly got to his feet, still slightly shaken. He had come close to death before, but never quite that close. He wasn't sure who had intervened on his part, but he couldn't wait to thank them. A shadowy figure moved towards Ashanti. At first, he thought it was a man, but when they got closer, he could see his savior was a female. It wasn't just any female, it was the same girl he had squared off with in the club the night they snatched George.

She was dressed in black jeans, boots, and a black long sleeve t-shirt. Her long dread locks were pulled back into a ponytail allowing Ashanti to get a good look at her face... a face that looked much like his. He hadn't been sure if she was who he thought the night they'd fought, but now he was. There was no mistaking that it was the sister he'd long thought dead.

Angela was Ashanti's older sister. They had grown up in the same house under the same worthless addict of a mother. Both the kids had it bad, but Angela had it worse because she was a girl. It wasn't unheard of for their mother to force Angela to turn tricks with grown men in exchange for drugs, which was how they ended up getting split. Ashanti's mother had owed some dealers some money and when she couldn't pay, she offered her kids as collateral until the debt was settled.

Ashanti was never sure if their mother knew or even cared that the men planned to kidnap them and flee New York City. The men forced the children into the sex trade and for a while, they bounced from city to city peddling their wares. The brother and sister were kept together for a while before Angela was sold off to someone else. Ashanti managed to escape and eventually made it back to New York, but Angela hadn't been seen or heard from again until that night at the club.

"Angela," he called out softly.

"My name is Ophelia!" she snapped, using both hands to steady the gun. In her eyes, he could see the conflict raging.

"What has that crazy old broad Lilith done to you?" Ashanti asked sadly. It was like she was brainwashed to believe she was someone she wasn't.

"She's shown me the light... she's shown me the way!"

"No, she hasn't, she's filled your head with a bunch of bullshit. Look at me... look at my face," he urged.

She snapped her eyes closed as if the sight of him pained her. "You're trying to confuse me like my mother warned me you would. You're an enemy of the Brotherhood and enemies of my order must die!"

"Angela that woman is not your mother. Our mother died years ago in a dope house. If you shoot me, you'll be killing the only family you got left in this world. Just put the gun down so we can talk, please," Ashanti pleaded. She lowered her gun slightly and for a minute, it seemed like Ashanti was getting through to her.

"What's going on down there?" A uniformed police officer rounded the corner.

She spun and fired on the cop, hitting him in the shoulder. She was such a good shot that she could've hit him between the eyes at that range if she so chose, but she didn't want to kill him, just back him off long enough to finish the job that she had come to do. She had expected Ashanti to be on the move when she turned back to him, but he was still standing in the same spot. There was such sincerity in his eyes that she almost wondered if there was any truth to what he claimed.

In the distance, they heard sirens. A knowing look passed between them. They both knew how it would play out if they lingered. She tucked her gun back into the holster under her arm. "The next time we meet I won't hesitate to take your life," she hissed before disappearing into the shadows of the block.

Ashanti wanted to go after her, but he was in no condition to give chase. His whole body ached from the beating he took and the police were on the way. He limped back to his car and was able to get off the block just before the first police cruiser bent the corner. He pounded the steering wheel in frustration thinking how close he had come to being reunited with the sister he had been in search of for so many years. Seeing how Lilith had brainwashed his last surviving relative gave him a whole new reason to hate her. He vowed that no matter how things played out, he would get his sister back, even if he had to singlehandedly murder the entire cartel to do it.

*

Not long after Ashanti had fled the scene Detectives Brown and Alvarez showed up. They were just wrapping up at Original Sin, which wasn't too far away, when the call came in about the shooting near the Barclay's.

As usual, they were too late to catch anything except the aftermath of what had gone down. There were several dead bodies and no suspects, which seemed to be the reoccurring theme of their night. From what they'd learned from speaking to the medical examiner and the first officers on the scene, the dead youths had been murdered by a single shooter. They found multiple shell casings on the ground, but only one gun, the one belonging to the boys. The casings from the missing gun were different than the caliber of gun used at Original Sin, but the M.O. fit.

While Detective Alvarez spoke with the uniformed officers, trying to see if there was anything they might have missed, Detective Brown surveyed the crime scene. He shone his flashlight on the ground looking for anything that might've given him some insight as to who the other shooter might've been. He reached into his pocket and grabbed his pack of cigarettes, tapping it on the back of his hand to get one out. He tapped a bit too hard and the cigarette fell on the floor. When he shone his light down to see where his cigarette had gone, he found something. Focusing his

flashlight on the spot, he knelt down to get a better look. He couldn't be sure, but it looked like drops of blood.

"Over here!" Detective Brown called out, never taking his eyes off the spots.

"You find something?" Detective Alvarez approached. He was followed by the medical examiner.

"I sure hope so," Detective Brown said. "Is this blood?" he asked the medical examiner.

She fished around in the small case she carried and pulled out a black light. When she shone it on the spot the detective was pointing at, the drops were illuminated under the light. "Looks like it to me."

"Maybe it's from one of the victims," Detective Alvarez suggested.

"It's possible, but I doubt it. It's too far away from where the victims were found to be splatter," she explained.

"Is it enough for you to get a useable sample?" Detective Brown asked hopefully.

"It should be."

"Good, tag it and bag it," Detective Brown stood and brushed his knees off. "If we're lucky, maybe our shooter has been convicted of a violent crime and we've got their DNA in the system."

"That's a big if, and you know neither one of us has been big on luck lately," Detective Alvarez said.

"I know, Jay, but right now that's all we have left to go on."

CHAPTER 10

By the time Kahllah got off the long flight from LAX to Dulles International Airport, she was tired... more tired than she could ever recall being. Not just physically tired, but mentally too. The events of the last few days had her drained and there was still so much to do. She prayed to the creator to give her the strength she would need to carry her through to the end.

She'd tried to get some sleep during the flight, but found no rest. Every time she closed her eyes, she saw the bloody images from the house. Since she was a little girl, Kahllah's heart and mind had been hardened to the sight of death and destruction. It was all a part of the necessary cycle of life, but there were those rare instances when things hit too close to home and she couldn't help but to feel it, such as when she had found Gucci's body.

Kahllah and Gucci had only known each other a few short years, but the circumstances that brought them together helped to form what would grow into a sisterly bond. Gucci had proven to Kahllah that she genuinely loved her brother and would do whatever it took to protect him, just as he would for her. Often they'd speak of the risks that came with being with a man like Animal, and while Gucci

acknowledged the danger, she never budged from his side. They were soulmates and only death could part them... so it did. The sound that came from her brother when she broke the news to him about Gucci was like nothing she had ever heard. It was like the baying of a dozen hounds howling at a blood moon. Something had died inside him, but something had also been awakened. There was no doubt in Kahllah's mind how Animal would react to his wife being killed and his children kidnapped; he would follow the trail of blood to its source and attempt to take his vengeance against those who had wronged him, even if it meant fighting a war he had no hopes of winning. For what they had done to Gucci, he would gladly walk into the fires of hell and spit in the devil's face, and that's exactly what he was doing by going against the cartel and the woman who now led them.

To most, she was known as Lilith, wife of the drug chieftain Poppito and the one now pulling the strings of the cartel, but Kahllah knew her by a different name. Many years ago, she had been called Tiger Lily, one of the most highly successful assassins within the Brotherhood of Blood and Kahllah's instructor. Tiger Lily had been renowned for both her ruthlessness and her skill with blades, especially the uniquely crafted tiger claws that she used to dispatch her victims. It had been more than ten years since Kahllah had laid eyes on her old teacher and she had thought her to be dead until she found her sitting at the head of the Puerto Rican drug cartel. The moment Kahllah had found out the true identity of Animal's enemy, she made to warn him what they were really up against, but by then it was too late. A blood feud had been initiated and

Kahllah had to do what she could to stop it, before she lost anyone else close to her. This is what carried her across the country in the middle of the night.

Normally Kahllah would've flown into Regan National, where her contacts in the Brotherhood of Blood would've allowed her to travel with her weapons, but the last thing she wanted at that moment was to alert the Brotherhood to her presence. Members of the order she had served faithfully since she was a young girl had now deemed her a threat and wanted her dead. From what she had gathered so far, a man named Kahn had been responsible. Kahn was the commander of the Black Hand, a sect of the Brotherhood that was entrusted to enforce and dispatch its justice. Kahn was an ambitious man and had his own agenda for the direction he thought the Brotherhood should be going in and Kahllah, as a member of their inner council, could've represented a problem. This is the reason he'd used his influence within the Brotherhood to move against her.

It was also no coincidence that Kahn made his move at the same time Tiger Lily had resurfaced. They appeared to have two different agendas, but both seemed to involve Animal and Kahllah. If she could figure out what the connection was and expose it, she might be able to save her loved ones and restore her name to the place of honor where it belonged. To accomplish this, she would need answers and the only place she knew of to get them was from the old men under the mountain.

Getting an audience with the elders of their order was difficult for those in good standing so it would be damn near impossible for someone who had been branded rogue, such as Kahllah. She couldn't go through normal channels so she would have to be resourceful. The only problem with that was she now had very little resources to work with. The agents of the Brotherhood had already frozen her bank accounts and had her name and known aliases on a half-dozen watch lists.

Thankfully, they weren't familiar with all her false identities and she found one that had allowed her to make it from Los Angeles to Washington D.C. without incident. That was the easy part. Now the real task would begin.

She bumped through the airport making her way towards the area where they kept the lockers. For a few dollars, you could rent one of the small boxes to store things for extended periods of time. From inside the locker she retrieved a duffel bag. Inside the bag were cash, a car key, some bogus credit cards, a knife, and a small silver key. After collecting her belongings, she headed for the long term parking garage where she had a car waiting. Kahllah kept cars in the long term parking garages at several major airports and a few of the smaller ones too, in case of an emergency. She paid the bills every month and the parking attendants made sure the batteries were always charged. She did this in case of extreme circumstances where rental cars were too risky and she needed to make a quick getaway, such as her current situation.

It didn't take her long to find her car in the lot. It was a late model tan Honda Accord. It was a reliable vehicle and plain enough looking to where it could easily blend into traffic. From the film of dust on the outside of the car you could tell that it hadn't been driven in a while, but it started right up when she turned the key. She popped the trunk, then retrieved the knife and small silver key from her duffle bag and walked around the back of the car. She snatched the spare tire out of the trunk, exposing the moldy looking carpet beneath. With a flick of her knife, she sliced the rug open and revealed the false bottom. It was a steel plate with a key hole so small you'd likely miss it unless you were looking for it. Kahllah used the silver key to undo the lock and pulled the plate back to reveal the hidden treasure it concealed, several blades, a few small guns, and one of her signature black masks. She picked the mask up and ran her finger across the lotus flower carved into the metal. Now she was ready to play.

*

Kahllah felt better once she was armed. The few blades and handguns weren't quite the usual arsenal she carried around, but they'd have to do for the moment. Kahllah's final destination would be Virginia, but she would set up a temporary base of operations in D.C. Staying at one of the Brotherhood safe houses in D.C. was out of the question, and checking into a hotel would be too risky. The Brotherhood had agents everywhere. She drove to South East and checked into a seedy motel that she had become familiar with while once on a job down that way. The place was a complete dump and a rest haven for drug addicts. It was the last place anyone would expect to find an international assassin.

After checking into the room, Kahllah secured the locks on the door and flopped across the bed. The mattress was lumpy, and the sheets smelled like a combination of stale beer and sex, but it was the first time Kahllah had been able to lay still in days. For all intents and purposes, the room was a real shithole, but Kahllah had endured worse. When she was a little girl, she had been the property of slavers who forced her and the other girls to sleep in a small alcove they had carved out in the side of a mountain. There was barely enough room to stand up straight and at night the rats would make appetizers of the girls. If Kahllah could survive living under those conditions for all the years she was held captive, she could survive the motel for a night.

Kahllah's stomach growled fiercely reminding her that it hadn't eaten anything more than the peanuts they served on the flight in the last couple of days. There wasn't much more she could do that night that could help her or Animal, so she decided to grab something to eat and get some rest. After a quick shower, she threw on some fresh clothes, black jeans, a black shirt, and combat boots. She left the harness containing her blades, but did tuck one of the handguns into the back of her pants before leaving the room.

When she had arrived at the motel, she recalled seeing a McDonalds a block or so away, so that's where she was headed. Kahllah hated to put anything into her body that was less than natural but she didn't have the time or the energy to be picky. Between the shower and the cool night air hitting her, Kahllah was starting to feel more like herself. Her senses were alive and in tune with everything around her. The drug addicts and pushers on the block wisely gave her a wide berth as she passed them. The fact that she was a female walking through that neighborhood at that hour of the night and didn't look nervous said that she was prepared for whatever they might've been thinking.

She was in and out of McDonalds in less than five minutes. Kahllah was so hungry that she couldn't wait until she got back to her room, so she began eating her food on the walk back to the motel. She had just devoured a Fillet-O-Fish and was about to start working on her nuggets when she felt the hairs stand on the back of her neck. Years of combat training kicked in and Kahllah was immediately on high alert. Without making it obvious, she scanned the block for signs of potential danger. She spotted a green

SUV coasting down the same side of the street she was walking on. It was a gaudy monstrosity with a chromed out grill and rims that had to be at least twenty-eight inches. The car paced her and Kahllah's hand instinctively went to her gun, but she didn't draw. Behind the wheel of the SUV, smiling out at her, was a young man wearing a huge gold chain. He was obviously some sort of drug dealer or pimp, either way; she wasn't in the mood.

"Baby, you know you're way too fine to be out here walking, right?" the young man called out the window. Kahllah ignored him and kept walking. "C'mon, slim. Don't act like that; I'm just trying to be friendly." When Kahllah continued to ignore him, he parked the car at the curb and jumped out. "Why don't you slow down for a minute?" he jogged up beside her.

"Whatever you're selling, I'm not buying," Kahllah said in a less than friendly tone. She hoped he'd take the hint, but somehow she knew that he wouldn't.

"Damn, you're a cold blooded one, huh? Maybe I could help warm you up," he reached for her, but Kahllah slapped his hand away.

"Listen, I've tried to be nice about it but you're about as sharp as a roll of tissue. Get the fuck away from me and leave me alone!" she snapped. She tried to walk away, but he stepped into her path.

"Bitch, who the fuck do you think you're talking to?" the young man's eyes flashed anger. A small knife had appeared in his hand.

"Someone who is about to have a very bad night."

As soon as she saw the muscles in his shoulder twitch, Kahllah was in motion. She grabbed his arm and gave him a light tap on the elbow, causing his arm to involuntarily bend. Before the young man even realized what was going on, Kahllah had him pinned against a wall, with his arm twisted so that he was holding the knife against his own throat.

"I should kill you just for disrespecting me by pulling that little ass knife. You couldn't hurt anybody but yourself with that thing." She applied just enough pressure to where he nicked himself and a small tickle of blood ran down the blade. To her surprise, a smile spread across the young man's lips.

"It was never about hurting you. All I was paid to do was keep you distracted."

Kahllah threw herself out of the way just as the first spray of bullets slammed into the wall, cutting the young man down. She rolled to her feet just in time to see several figures dressed in all black and wearing masks surging towards her. They'd found her! Even with all the precautions she had taken, the Brotherhood had still managed to track her down.

Using a passing bus to her advantage, Kahllah bolted for the street. A second spray of gunfire erupted and lit up the bus, hitting the driver and several passengers. From their sloppy execution, she could tell the assassins were initiates and not seasoned members of their order, which she planned to use to her advantage.

Just as she had expected, the shooters came charging around the bus, never taking the time to see if they had hit their target. Kahllah was waiting for them. Her gun spit, dropping two of them, but there were still three more coming. No longer able to use the bus for cover she was a sitting duck. Kahllah reasoned that a good run was better than a bad stand and made to get out of there. She backpedaled, firing her gun to keep them off her back while she made her escape. Kahllah had her pursuers by at least half a block. There was an apartment complex on the next street and she was sure she could lose them between the buildings.

She had just made it to the corner and could taste freedom when something knocked it out of her mouth. Between Kahllah's momentum and the punch, she lost her balance and fell. She was trying to get up when someone grabbed her by her hair and lifted her off her feet with the ease of a parent hoisting a small child. Fighting against the pain in her skull, she twisted her head and found herself face to face with a monstrous, yet familiar face.

"Bastille," she rasped.

*

Bastille stood easily six foot six with a jaw that looked like it had been carved from the side of a mountain and shoulders wide enough to block out the moonlight. His smashed-in nose and badly scarred face told the tale of the many battles he'd seen. He was second in command of the Black Hand and the Brotherhood of Blood's chief executioner. At one time, Kahllah and her attacker had been friends, but now they stood on two different sides of a coin.

Bastille pulled Kahllah in closer, so close that she could taste his foul breath in her mouth when he spoke. "It has been a long time, Lotus. Had these circumstances been different I would have come to welcome you to the District and offered that we share a drink." With his free hand he reached into the scabbard slung across his back and removed a large flat blade, which resembled an oversized meat cleaver. "But instead I must offer you death."

"If it's all the same to you, I'll pass," Kahllah told him before drawing the blade she had lifted from the young man earlier and stabbed Bastille in the forearm. The big man's grip slacked enough for Kahllah to rip her head free, and put some distance between herself and the executioner.

Bastille plucked the knife from his skin as if it was little more than a thorn and tossed it away. When he looked at Kahllah, his eyes were almost remorseful. "I should've known you would make this harder than it needed to be," he tossed the big blade from one hand to the other playfully.

Kahllah took a defensive stance and the two combatants began circling each other. Kahllah was good, but Bastille's combat skills were the stuff of legends. He had killed at least fifty men, and those were only the kills that she knew of. "Have you strayed so far from the path of honor that you would slaughter an unarmed woman?"

Bastille gave a throaty laugh. "You ceased to be looked upon as man or woman when you took the oath. Like the rest of us, you are merely a weapon of the Brotherhood. Though you have disgraced yourself and the Brotherhood, out of respect for who you once were, I will allow you to die with a weapon in your hand." He pulled a dagger from his belt and tossed it on the floor between them.

Kahllah looked down at the blade suspiciously. "Go ahead, pick it up," he taunted her.

Kahllah dove for the blade, and just as she knew he would, Bastille attacked. His blade sparked off the ground a split second after Kahllah had rolled to her right. She came up just in time to use the dagger to block his next strike. The force of the blow sent a shockwave down her arm and almost caused her to lose the grip on the dagger. Bastille blindsided her when he caught Kahllah in the jaw with an elbow and put her on her back.

Bastille loomed over Kahllah, shaking his head sadly. "You have spent so much time away from the order that it has dulled your skills, Lotus."

"And you have spent so much time giving Kahn hand-jobs that it's made you cocky!" She drove the dagger into his foot, pinning it to the ground. Kahllah used the small window the dagger had provided her to launch everything she had at him. She delivered a combination of punches and kicks to his legs and chest, but they had little effect. Bastille's skin was like armor, and his bones like oak. In desperation, she fired her fingers at his eyes in an attempt to blind him, but it turned out to be a mistake.

Bastille grabbed her two fingers in his thick hand and squeezed. "I had intended to make your death swift, but now

I think I'll make you suffer before I allow you to die," he flicked his wrist and dislocated her fingers, before slinging her head first into a parked car.

Kahllah lay on the floor trying to make the world stop spinning. She tried to will herself to get up, but couldn't seem to get her body to cooperate with her brain. She was running on fumes and with hardly any sleep. She watched helplessly as he pulled the knife from his foot and limped over to her. He grabbed her by the front of her shirt and propped her into a sitting position against the car. He took his time angling his blade for the perfect strike. Bastille was toying with her. He wanted Kahllah to beg for her life, but she would not. No matter what false claims Kahn had laid against her, in her heart she was still a member of the Brotherhood and would die with the honor that came with her position.

"I'm surprised at you Bastille. I've always known you to be one of the few who held the good of the Brotherhood above the ambitions of a single man. Yet here you are to do Kahn's dirty work," Kahllah said.

"And I am surprised that someone as feared as the Black Lotus would be taken down so easily. Make no mistake that no matter who gives the orders, my blade only swings when it's for the good of the Brotherhood, and your death is

what's good for the Brotherhood and the future of our most sacred of orders. You have allowed yourself to be corrupted and the corrupt are weak. The weak will never have a place amongst the strong," he raised his blade high above his head.

As she looked up into the cold eyes of the executioner, she couldn't help but to think that Bastille was right. She was off her game and because of it she was about to pay the ultimate price. Kahllah would not close her eyes or turn away. If death was coming for her, she would meet it head-on.

Something sailed through the air and burst when it hit Bastille's shoulder. It looked like a water balloon but when the smell hit her Kahllah realized that it wasn't water that now soaked Bastille's arm. She rolled under the car just as someone tossed an emergency flare at Bastille and set him ablaze. Kahllah had known Bastille for many years and had never once seen him show pain or cry out; but that night as the fire licked up his arm, his shrieks could be heard for blocks.

Someone grabbed Kahllah's legs and dragged her from her hiding place beneath the car. She kicked and clawed as multiple pairs of hands worked to hold her down. There were two of them, both wearing hoods and blue bandanas

covering the lower halves of their faces. There was something familiar about the eyes of the one who was struggling to still her flailing hands.

"We don't have time for this," he shook her to her senses. "You can come with us and live to fight another day or stay here and see if the rumors about the executioner being invincible are true or not."

Kahllah was suspicious, but the men in the masks seemed to be the lesser of the two evils so she went along. The one who had spoken to her led them down the street, where there was a third man standing outside an SUV. In his hands arms he cradled an AR15, with his fingers drumming on the barrel nervously. When they reached the SUV, he tossed his machine gun into the back seat and jumped behind the wheel. The two masked men hopped in the car, but Kahllah stopped short.

"We have to go," the masked man urged.

"I appreciate your help back there, but I'm not jumping into a car blindly. Who are you?" Kahllah asked.

The masked man removed the bandana and revealed a face that Kahllah thought she would never see again. "A young student still holding onto the crush he had on the teacher. Now I'm going to need you to get your ass in the car before we get locked up or killed."

Without further question, Kahllah jumped into the back of the SUV. As they peeled off, she looked out the back window and saw Bastille literally rising from the ashes. Even at that distance, she could feel his murderous glare latch onto her. From that point no matter how things went with Kahn or the men under the mountain, there would have to be a reckoning between them. Bastille's pride wouldn't allow anything less, and neither would hers.

CHAPTER 11

Tasha Grady cruised down the FDR fighting to keep her heavy eyelids from shutting. She had just worked a double shift and found herself running into a third because she had taken some of her work home with her. She spared a glance over at the passenger seat, where her purse rested, and took a mental count of the folders stuffed inside. There were five of them in total; five murders, five motives, and five mothers who would be burying their children.

The files were open cases that the department had been hitting a wall trying to solve so Grady decided to take a crack at them. She was better than most at solving riddles; that's part of why she was able to climb from beat-walker to sergeant so quickly, though some in the department speculated her speedy rise had been due to more than just good police work. Over the last couple of years, her name had been attached to some suspect cases and even more suspect individuals. Before joining the NYPD, she was a girl from the projects with known criminal ties, which some on the force felt like she had never truly let go. Being a woman in a male-dominated field made things difficult enough, but being a Black woman with a shaky background, ensured that Tasha had to work five times as hard as anyone else in the department to prove herself. This is why instead of getting some much-needed sleep when she got home, she'd be working on the five unsolved cases.

By the time Tasha pulled into the underground parking garage of her building, she felt like she was out on her feet. Listlessly, she collected her files and her service weapon from the glove box. The Glock felt like a lead weight when she dropped it into her purse. Her heels clacked loudly on the floor of the empty garage as she walked towards the elevator. At that hour, most of the other tenants in the luxury high rise were fast asleep. They were mostly older people and business types who kept decent hours. It was a far cry from the heavy traffic and constant noise of the apartment buildings she had lived in while growing up. That was one of the reasons she'd purchased an apartment in that building. She needed a change.

She stepped from the elevator and walked to her apartment, which was at the far end of the hall. As she fished around in her purse for her keys, she felt the hairs on the backs of her arms stand up. Instinctively, her hand slipped around the Glock at the bottom of the bag. A split second later, one of the apartment doors down the hall opened. An elderly white woman, named Mrs. Kravitz, was taking out her trash. Tasha offered a warm smile in greeting, and was met with a distasteful stare. Mrs. Kravitz had never been a big fan of the young Black girl who lived at the end of the hall and as far as Tasha was concerned, the feeling was mutual. Ignoring the bitter old woman, Tasha stepped inside her apartment and slammed the door loud enough to irritate her neighbors.

Spending so much of her time between the precinct

and the streets, Tasha was rarely home and sometimes forgot how nice her apartment was. It was a plush two bedroom, with one and a half baths, a modernized kitchen, and a large balcony that gave her a view of the city that made the hefty price she'd paid for the apartment well worth it. Those rare occasions that she was home, Tasha would sit out on her balcony, drinking coffee and watching the sunrise.

After putting her bag down on the coffee table and shrugging out of her jacket, Tasha did something she had wanted to do for two days, reached under her shirt, and snatched her bra off. After being incarcerated in a prison of cotton and underwire for so long, her breasts were beyond grateful for the pardon. She scratched under them and it was such a good feeling that she wanted to bust out into song. Times like those she envied men because they'd never know the irritation that came with carrying around a set of D-cups in a bra that was made more for fashion than comfort.

She went into the kitchen and snatched the refrigerator open. The inside of her fridge was almost as tragic a sight as the overflow of cases on her desk at work. There was a carton of curdled milk, a half-eaten sandwich that was starting to grow hair, and a bottle of merlot. She grabbed the wine and placed it on the counter while she went about the task of finding a clean glass. Tash was just about to pour some wine into the Mason jar she had found in the back of the cabinet when a tickle of cold air crossed the back of her neck. It was coming from the open window. She wouldn't have paid it any attention except Tash never left the kitchen window open. She'd stopped leaving it open after a pigeon had flown in through it and she damn near had to shoot it to get rid of it. Someone had been in her apartment.

Carrying on as if nothing was wrong, Tasha continued

pouring her wine. She sipped from the jar, glancing around from the corners of her eyes to see if she could spot anything else out of place. She didn't see anything or anyone, but had the feeling that she wasn't alone. Her gaze drifted over to her couch where she had tossed her purse and thought of the gun inside. It was a long shot, but still her best and only chance. Casually, she sat the jar down on the counter then lunged for the purse.

Tasha had almost made it across the living room and to the purse when a hand grabbed her by the arm. Instead of pulling away, she went with the momentum and came around with a left hook to the jaw of whoever had grabbed her. When she felt the grip slacken, she jerked free and made a second attempt for bag. This time she was successful. As quickly as she could, she dumped the contents of the bag onto the couch. The hands had grabbed her again, pulling her away from the couch. When Tasha turned to face her attacker, she was now armed with her Glock 17. Her finger had just caressed the trigger, ready to fire, when suddenly she paused.

"What the fuck?" Tasha was stunned.

"Damn, baby. You plan on shooting the best piece of dick you ever had?" Animal smirked at her playfully, as if she hadn't almost blown his head off.

Of all the people she had expected to run into that night, Animal would've fallen to last on that list. Their improper relationship went back to when Tasha was still walking a beat and Animal was a teenager running with Tech. Back then, he had been her boy-toy, that piece of young dick she could call when she didn't feel like making love and wanted to be fucked. It had been a while since she'd last seen him and having him in her living room stirred old feelings that she'd thought were long gone.

"Animal what are you doing here? And how the hell did

you get into my house?" Tasha asked angrily. She was still holding the gun but no longer pointing it at him.

"I'm here because I needed to see you, and I got in through the window." He nodded towards the open kitchen window.

"Bullshit, I live on the fourteenth floor. What did you do, scale the building like Spiderman?"

"No, I just crossed the ledge from your neighbor's house."

"What did you do to the Gordon's?" Tasha asked, fearing the worst.

"Relax, Tash. I didn't hurt them; just tied them up nice and tight. I told that sweet old couple that I was from maintenance and had come to check on a complaint about a leak from the apartment below them and they let me right in. This is a nice building you live in, but the residents are far too trusting. I suspect that come tomorrow morning the entire security staff will be unemployed," Animal said in a disappointed tone.

"You know there are easier ways to set up meetings with me than tying up old people and breaking into homes, like a telephone. You weren't in prison long enough to forget how to use them," Tash scolded him.

"You'll have to excuse my dramatic entrance, Tash, but I'm in some serious shit here and I really need your help," Animal told her.

Tasha frowned. "I should have known. It's like the only time you come around is when you need something. The last time I did you a favor I almost lost my job and went to prison."

She was referring to the elaborate hoax she had helped Animal pull off that spared him a life sentence.

"But instead you got a promotion and from the looks of this apartment a nice raise," Animal shot back.

"Look, don't come up in my place trying to be no score keeper, because I think the scales would tip in my favor," she waggled her finger in his face. "After I put my ass on the line to save yours, you get out of prison and blow town without even so much as a goodbye. But I'm not mad at you for that, I'm mad at myself for expecting different."

"Tasha... "

"No, don't try and cut me off so you can spin some more of that smooth poetic bullshit like you always do, because I ain't trying to hear it!" she jabbed her finger in his face. "You know when we went our separate ways and decided to just be friends, it was hard for me, but I accepted it. You'd made your choice and I am by no means a hater, but you have no idea how complicated you make things every time you come back into my life. When you got out of prison and wrote me off it was actually a good thing because then I was able to officially write you off too and I was just starting to heal, and now here you come again!"

"Tasha... "

"Guys like you are a trip, Animal." She ignored him. "You've got everything you said you wanted out of life, even if you didn't get them with me, yet you still want more. So what is it now? You got bored with the life of being a husband and father in your big house on the beach and now you're back here slumming for some excitement? Your precious Gucci not holding your attention anymore?" she asked sarcastically.

"No, she's dead." Animal was finally able to get a word in. Tasha's face went slack.

"My wife has been murdered and my children kidnapped." Animal went on to tell Tasha the tragic story of what had happened to him over the last few days. By the time he was done with his tale, she was in tears.

"I'm so sorry," she said sincerely, feeling horrible about the way she'd treated him.

"Not your fault, you didn't kill her, I did. Maybe not literally, but I might as well have been behind the trigger, because I brought this down on our family."

"You can't blame yourself, Animal."

"Sure I can. Had I stayed my ass at home where I belonged then none of this would've happened. Can't turn back the clock and change anything at this point, but I can make it right. Tasha, I know you've done a lot for me already, and if I had any other choice I wouldn't be here asking you for more, but I've got nowhere else to turn."

"Say no more. Whatever you need, I got you," Tasha vowed.

"I need to know where I can find this boat," Animal handed her the manifest.

Tasha looked it over. She recognized the name of the boat from an investigation that had come across her desk a few months prior. By the time they got around to following up on it, the case had been squashed and filed under never happened. "Do I wanna know why you're looking for this boat?"

Animal thought on the question. "Probably not. To be honest with you, I'm still not sure why I'm looking for it. I just know a man was willing to die rather than reveal its location."

"Well I'm not sure how hard you looked before you came to me, but the time of arrival and destination are right here," she pointed at a series of numbers printed across the top of the manifest.

Animal squinted. "How the hell are some random ass numbers gonna help me find the boat?"

Tasha shook her head. "For as worldly of a young man as you are there's still so much about the world that your young ass brain has yet to get hipped to." She grabbed her laptop from the coffee table and fired it up. "You have to remember when dealing with boat or planes they don't use addresses to get from points A to B."

Her fingers floated across the keys punching the proper sequence on the Google Maps page and a location popped up.

"These numbers aren't random, they're coordinates," she said and tapped the red marker on the screen.

"Port of Newark," Animal read it out loud over her shoulder.

"If the information on the manifest is up to date, the ship is scheduled to pull into port at 5 am," she told him.

Animal checked the time on his watch. He still had a few hours before the Red Widow arrived. "Thank you, Tasha," he kissed her on the forehead. "I really appreciate your help... again."

"Just don't make me regret it... again."

"I can't make any promises, but I'll do my best." He was about to leave, but she stopped him.

"I know you well enough to where I don't have to guess what you'll do when you find the ones responsible for all this, but is there any chance that I can get you to just tell me what you know and let the police handle it?"

Animal gave her a look. "If you know me as well as you claim then you should understand why that's impossible." "And you should understand that if this turns into a mess

I won't be able to clean this one up," she shot back. "I've already betrayed my badge once in the name of love, and I can't do it again. Regardless of my personal feelings, I took an oath."

Animal nodded. "As did I, an oath to protect my family by any means necessary. I won't ask you to put yourself at risk on this one, but I would ask that you stay out of my way."

Tasha crossed the room, closing the distance between them. She hadn't meant to, but she reached up and twirled a lock of his curly black hair around her finger like she had done on so many nights she had spent with him. "And if our paths should cross in the line of our respective duties?"

Animal gently removed her hand from his hair and kissed the inside of her wrist. "Then I pray you don't hesitate because I won't," he released her hand. "Take care of yourself, Detective Grady."

Long after Animal had gone Tasha could still feel him in the room. She had told herself a long time ago that she was done with the young outlaw and had shut the door on whatever it was they had, but she couldn't help but to open it again every time he knocked. She and Animal had been playing that game for years, but when he left that night, it felt different. It was as if somewhere in her heart she knew that would be the last time she ever saw him.

*

For a time after Animal had left Tasha's apartment, he lingered in the hallway. It had been a long time since he had seen Tasha Grady, and she was right to be cross with him after the way he'd left things. He had genuine love for her, but things in his life had gotten crazy and he had to prioritize things, and his family came first. In truth, he owed Tasha at least a visit or a phone call, after all she'd done for him. There were a few times when he contemplated reaching out, but decided against it. There were feelings involved between them and he couldn't chance having a moment of weakness. Tasha was a good girl, but she wasn't Gucci and never would be, so he made a clean break.

Still, even after all he'd done to her, she still rose to the occasion when he needed help. For that, he would always respect her.

Animal pressed his forehead against the glass window, looking out at the east river. It was the first time he'd gotten to take a breath all night. He had endured so much in the last couple of days that he felt like he barely had the strength to move, let alone follow another lead. He was tired, but he had to keep going. He turned his attention back to the incoming cargo ship, and what it would take to pull off what he was planning. This was going to be a big job, and though Animal was good, he wasn't pompous enough to think he could pull it off on his own. It was time to call in the team.

He composed himself and made his way to the elevators. Animal tapped the button feverishly, looking at his watch. They only had a few hours before the Red Widow docked and there were still preparations to make. There were two elevators on Tasha's floor, both arriving within a few seconds of each other. Animal stepped onto the first one as the second one was opening. The doors were just closing as he got a glimpse of who was stepping off the elevator, and

he had to blink to make sure his eyes weren't playing tricks on him.

*

Tasha went back to her abandoned jar of wine, and filled it to the point where it spilled over the rim and onto her hands when she tried to move it. She licked the excess off her knuckles, before tipping the jar up and taking a deep sip. Seeing Animal always complicated things, and that random appearance was no different. She'd tried hard to get him out of her system, but remnants of him would always remain.

A knock at her door delayed the pity party she was contemplating throwing herself. A slither of hope crept into her heart. Maybe he had reconsidered. Crossing the living room, she wiped away the mist that had formed under her eyes and ran her fingers through her hair. She felt a mess, but that didn't mean she had to look it. Taking a deep breath, she opened the door with a smart remark pursed on her lips, but swallowed it when she saw who was on the other side.

"Evening, Detective Grady," Detective Brown greeted her with a sly smile. Detective Alvarez stood behind him, wearing a sour expression on his face. "Apologies for popping up unannounced, but we need to have a word with you about an old acquaintance of yours."

CHAPTER 12

Lilith Angelino-Suarez, better known by the moniker Tiger Lily, sat in the den of the expansive Westchester, N.Y. mansion she'd had built to her specifications a few years prior. She rarely visited New York unless it was to go shopping, and even on those occasions, she never stayed for more than a day or so. They only reason she'd had the mansion built was because she hated hotels. She was a woman who valued her privacy, and rightfully so, considering she had so many secrets.

She had been born to a dirt poor family in a small in a part of Cuba called Pedro Betancourt and migrated with her mother to Florida in the early eighties. They had moved to America for better opportunities than Cuba had to offer, but quickly found out that life in America was nothing like it seemed on television. The American ghettos weren't as dangerous as the ones in Cuba, but still dangerous nonetheless. Her mother made sure she learned the art of survival at an early age, among other things.

Lilith's mother had been a botanist in Cuba, but had been reduced to whipping up bathtub elixirs for those who didn't have the money or proper documentation to go to a regular hospital. Between that and whatever odd jobs she could

find, they made ends meet as best they could. When she could find it, Lilith's mother did honest work, but when things got bad, she did what she had to do to keep them from starving.

Her mother proved as good at playing on the desires of men as she was at making potions. She mostly targeted rich men who weren't very attractive or suffered from some type of physical defect, as they were easier to manipulate. She would bleed them for whatever wealth or influence she could before moving on to the next. It didn't set the best example for her young daughter, but it taught her to do what she had to do in the name of survival by any means necessary. The lessons taught to her by her mother would be what shaped Lilith into the young woman she would grow into. Lilith was cold-blooded with the way she would play men like guitar strings until one night she hit a sour note.

One night she'd met a rich man while trolling the bars and underworld dives of South Beach. He was older, almost fifteen years her senior, but he attracted younger women like flies to honey, Lilith included. There was something dashing about him, with his deeply tan skin, and silver hair. Before Lilith even realized it, she was at his table sharing a bottle of wine with him. She had learned that his name was Victor, or at least that what he was calling himself at the time, and he was in Miami on business. It wouldn't be until much later that Lilith would find out what that business actually was.

Later Victor extended an invitation to his hotel room for a nightcap, which Lilith happily accepted. He had a suite in one of the finest hotels in all of Miami. They went through another bottle of wine before having knockdown, drag out sex. For an older man, Victor had skills, and plenty of stamina. A few times during their romp, Lilith thought she would pass out from the sheer pleasure of it all. She was somewhere between relieved and sad when he finally fell asleep suddenly. It took longer for the tranquilizer she had put in his drink to take affect than she had expected. She genuinely liked Victor and hated what she was about to do to him, but he had it to spare and she didn't.

Lilith climbed out of the bed and slipped back into her dress. After checking Victor to make sure he was still sleeping soundly, she went about the task of looting his hotel suite. She had taken him for his money, credit cards, and even the gold watch he'd put on the nightstand before they had sex. She was just about to tiptoe from the room when a voice stopped her.

"You forgot to steal the pinky ring I left on the bathroom sink."

Lilith spun and couldn't believe her eyes when she saw Victor propped against the pillows on the bed. Lilith made to run for the door when she heard a snapping sound behind her. Something that felt like a belt snaked around her neck, cutting off her oxygen. As she struggled, she turned around and saw Victor holding the other end of the bullwhip that was threatening to suffocate her. The whole time Lilith felt herself being dragged across the floor and back to the bed all she could think was how? She had given Victor enough tranquilizer to damn near kill him, and he didn't even look drowsy.

"From the shocked expression on your face I gather you're wondering why the little additive you slipped into my drink doesn't have me sleeping soundlessly right now," he said as if reading her mind. "I've been working with poisons and tranquilizers for longer than you've been on this earth, little girl, so you'll have to excuse me if my body has built up somewhat of an immunity to most." He jerked the whip and sent her spinning across the room like a top.

Lilith was so dizzy that she tripped over her own feet and fell on her ass. When she tried to get up, Victor was on her again, kicking her in the stomach and knocking the wind out of her. There was no way he should've been able to move that fast, yet there he was. She'd thought he was going to

kick her again when Victor turned and walked back over to the nightstand near the bed. When he turned, he was holding a syringe. As he stalked towards her, a twisted look was on his face. The dashing older man she'd come back to the room with was gone, and in his place was a monster.

"Victor, please don't. I'm sorry," she pleaded. "Don't be, sweetie. This is the most fun I've had in

months and the party is just getting started," he squirted a bit of the fluid from the tip of the syringe to clear it of air bubbles. "I'm going to show you why I'm called the Master of Poisons."

He laughed before sticking her with the needle and everything went black.

When Lilith awoke two days later, she found herself in the place that would serve as her home for the next few years. For her first few months as his hostage, Lilith was subjected to all kinds of mental and physical tortures by the man she had set out to rob. There were nights she prayed for death, and she had even tried to kill herself once, but he wouldn't let her die. Once he had thoroughly broken her mind, he started what he called her reconditioning. She would later find out that his name wasn't Victor at all, but Nicodemus. He was a part of something he referred to as the Brotherhood, which at the time Lilith was ignorant to, but she would learn all about it the longer she stayed with him.

Over the years, Lilith had overcome her hatred for the man who had stolen her from her old life, but eventually she came to admire and even love him for the things he had taught her. He was the first one who let her taste the rush of real power, which was command over life and death.

In time, Lilith and he would become lovers, and elevate through the ranks of the Brotherhood together, eventually both becoming elders. As Nicodemus got older, he became more withdrawn, and became more interested in studying his venoms than he was pulling the puppet strings of the order. Lilith, on the other hand, became more entrenched. She was a forward thinker, and saw great profit earning potential in using the Brotherhood's expansive networks to branch out into more lucrative schemes instead of murder for hire, primarily drugs. Cocaine was still a booming business and the age of designer drugs like LSD were making a comeback. With the reach that the Brotherhood of Blood commanded, they could control a huge chunk of the global narcotics market. The elders who sat at the table at the time were set in their ways and had no interest in revealing more of their order than necessary. They were a secret order of assassins, not drug dealers. When it became obvious that the elders would never back her, Lilith left the order she had served faithfully for so many years, and set out on her own. If the current ruling body of the Brotherhood turned a blind eye to her vision, she would show them the light.

Her travels took her to and from several different continents, making connections and gaining allies along the way. Lilith found herself keeping company with some of the most dangerous men in the world, one of which would be responsible for introducing her to her future husband and benefactor.

While visiting her native Cuba, she had attended a gala being thrown by an old-money gangster named Poppito. He was a big time cartel boss who operated out of Old San Juan, Puerto Rico. The fact that he was a foreigner able to throw a party in Cuba told Lilith that he had clout, but she didn't understand the true measure of his power until she saw that the who's-who of the underworld from several continents had shown up. In Poppito and his cartel, Lilith saw a foundation, which she could build her dream on.

For as powerful as a man as Poppito might've been, he was weak for Lilith, and that would prove to be his undoing. When he left Cuba and went back to Puerto Rico, Lilith was by his side. Within six months, they were married, and within a year, she was running his business. Slowly but surely, she began pushing his men out and replacing them with those loyal to only her. With an army and a vast drug network at her command, Lilith was finally ready to set the wheels in motion to unseat the council and take control of the Brotherhood. After years of careful planning and scheming, her time was finally at hand, and then Sonja came along and everything went to shit.

From the time she was introduced to Poppito's only daughter, it was obvious that she and his new wife wouldn't be friends. They both had aspirations to rule Poppito's kingdom by any means necessary. Sonja was a bigger manipulator than Lilith was and more larcenous than just about anyone she'd ever met. The older woman couldn't stand her, but Lilith had fallen in love with her young daughter, Celeste. She was the child of two notorious killers, so she had the genetics, and was still young enough for Lilith to mold her into a weapon just as she had done with her adopted daughter Ophelia. She would be the perfect vessel to usher in a new era of the Brotherhood under Lilith's command, but first she had to get her mother out of the way.

Removing Red Sonja from the equation should've been a relatively easy thing. Lilith held sway over the cartel's soldiers, and Poppito was dying slowly from the daily poison regiment Lilith had him on. She had cut Sonja off from all resources and allies, leaving her helpless and at Lilith's mercy, or so she thought. In all her scheming there was one thing, Lilith had never factored in, Celeste's father Animal.

Sonja had gone to him and convinced the killer that his child was in imminent danger, and Animal reacted as any parent would, he came out with guns blazing. Sonja had Animal so blinded by rage over someone trying to harm his daughter that he was beyond reasoning with and as a result backed Lilith into a very uncomfortable corner. By bringing Animal and those loyal to him into the fight, Sonja showed Lilith just how dangerously cunning she could be. She had a new appreciation for her enemy, but it changed nothing between them. For Lilith's rule over the cartel to be solidi-fied, she had to get rid of Poppito's only remaining heir.

For the last few days, she had watched from a distance as Sonja's daughter's father cut down members of her cartel in the name of protecting his child. Lilith had been content to watch from the compound in Puerto Rico while the little war played itself out, until her son George was taken hostage. George was not a soldier like her other son Peter, but he played the game and knew the risks that came with it. Still, he was her baby boy and Lilith couldn't sit by and wait for news of his fate; she had to take action. As soon as she had gotten word of George being taken she secretly boarded a private jet and flew into New York.

With thoughts of her latest problem and how best to solve it, Lilith's eyes were fixed on the small monitor in front of her. It was a live video feed from a camera in one of the bedrooms. On the screen, there were two children, a boy and a girl, and one of Lilith's handmaids. After a few hours of being in the house, the boy had stopped crying when the handmaid had given him some McDonalds and a few toys. He sat in the middle of the room fiddling with a race car and munching French fries, finally seeming at ease. The girl was a different story. The three-year-old girl was like a wild animal, attacking any and everyone who tried to get near her, including Lilith. When she bit one of the handmaids, almost taking off her finger, Lilith made the decision to have the girl sedated. She now slept in the corner of the room. Even at such a young age, she proved to be extremely strong of will and it wouldn't be easy to break her, but Lilith had her ways. In time, she would come to embrace her destiny, just as Lilith had when Nicodemus reconditioned her.

There was a soft knock on the door tearing Lilith's eyes away from the monitor. "Enter," she called out. A few seconds later, in walked Ophelia.

Of all her children, Ophelia was the least troublesome. She was obedient, intelligent, and lethal. She loved Ophelia just as much, if not more, than she loved her sons even though Ophelia had not come from her womb. She had come into possession of the girl over a decade earlier in a small town in the Midwest. She was a child prostitute owned by some low level pimps. They had quite a few girls and boys in their stable but Ophelia stood out to Lilith because of her eyes. They were the saddest, emptiest eyes she had ever seen on a living person. The girl seemed somewhat dimwitted, and rarely spoke unless she was ordered to. What the pimps did wasn't Lilith's business. She was there for the sole purpose of recruiting several girls to use as mules, but she couldn't get her mind off the girl.

Lilith was no angel, but she was no monster either. The thought of girls barely into their teens forced to perform sex acts for money sickened her and against her better judgment, she decided to intervene on behalf of the children. Several days after Lilith's visit, the pimp's bodies were discovered in the rundown motel they forced the girls to turn tricks out of. Lilith did what she could to reunite most of the girls with their families, but the one with the sad eyes she kept for herself. She would raise her as the daughter she never had and mold her in her own image. In addition to a new life, Lilith also gave her a new name, Ophelia, after the character in Hamlet.

"Mother, your guests are here. They're waiting downstairs in the living room," Ophelia said in her soft voice.

"Thank you, I'll be right down," Lilith told her. She was about to dismiss Ophelia when she noticed that instead of her normal robes or long dresses, she was wearing jeans and boots. "Did you go out?"

"Yes, I was doing recon on our enemies," Ophelia said with her eyes lowered.

Lilith rose and crossed the room to stand before her daughter. She lifted her chin and forced Ophelia to look her in the eyes. "Where did you really go?" she asked, knowing immediately that her daughter was lying.

"I went to do what is required of me for the betterment of the Brotherhood and kill our enemies," Ophelia admitted.

This surprised Lilith. Ophelia was usually very obedient and hardly ever acted without her mother's approval, so it was interesting to hear that she had ventured out on her own. "And were you successful in your mission?"

"No," Ophelia said shamefully.

Lilith backhanded the girl with so much force that she bounced off the far wall of the room. In one long stride, she closed the distance between them and gripped Ophelia's face in her hand. "What is the penalty for failure, my child?"

"Stop it, Mother! You're hurting me!" Ophelia whimpered. Lilith's grip was so strong that she feared her mother would crush her jaws.

"Pain is a part of life. It was one of the first lessons I taught you when I rescued you from your slavers. Now answer my question!" Lilith commanded, applying more pressure.

"The penalty for failure is death!" Ophelia screamed.

"Then tell me, why is it that those you were hunting still have their lives but you stand before me about to lose yours?" Lilith demanded.

"His face!"

Lilith released her daughter from her grip. "What do you mean?"

"His face," Ophelia repeated, massaging her jaw. "I've seen it before, sometimes in my dreams. I feel like I should know him from my past, but I'm unsure. Everything prior to you adopting me has become foggy. Even during my

meditations I can't seem to penetrate the veil and see into my past."

Lilith knew that this was due to her reconditioning. In addition to training Lilith to be a skilled fighter, Nicodemus had also bestowed upon her his knowledge of potions and poisons. During Lilith's early days with Ophelia, she kept the girl heavily drugged, in part to numb the pain and help her forget what she'd suffered through, but also so that she would be easy to manipulate.

"Did he say anything to you?" Lilith asked. Ophelia remained silent.

"It's okay to tell me. I won't get angry with you again," Lilith said sincerely.

"He said that we were family."

"Your enemies will often try and confuse or mislead you with tricks and lies. This is why we have to be as strong of mind as we are of body," Lilith explained.

"Yes, I know, but this didn't feel like a lie. He seemed to truly believe what he was saying. Mother, you have always been honest with me when I ask you questions about my past, and I beg of you to be honest with me now. Is this man my brother?"

Lilith had been dreading this day since Animal and his crew came into the picture. She had known all along that

Ophelia was speaking about Ashanti. When she found out he was one of the young men loyal to Animal's cause she feared it would present a problem with Ophelia, which is why Lilith had tried to keep their paths from crossing. Ophelia was bound securely to Lilith, but there was no telling what kind of damage Ashanti could do to her hold over the young girl. Lilith thought of lying to Ophelia and dismissing Ashanti's claim, but she knew the girl would keep digging until she found out the truth, so Lilith gave Ophelia her own variation of it.

"Yes, he is your brother, but he is not your family," Lilith began. "In the beginning I sought to reunite you with your family as I had done with the other girls. I found them in New York City, your parents and two other children, one of which being this Ashanti. Your father was a man of great wealth and had your family living in a big house. I thought they would be happy to be reunited with their lost daughter after so long, but they were not. They had a new baby, a girl, who filled the void you had left. As far as they were concerned, you were really dead to them." It was a cruel, but necessary twist to her tale.

Ophelia broke down in tears when she heard this. It

was the first time Lilith could remember seeing her cry since their first nights together.

Lilith hugged Ophelia to her. "I wanted to tell you, truly I did, but I didn't want to hurt you."

"How could they? Am I that flawed and wretched that even my own parents can cast me away like trash?" Ophelia sobbed. "Nonsense, child. You are the most beautiful creature I've ever laid eyes on. You are my Belladonna... my Nightshade," she called her by her Brotherhood moniker. "You cannot punish yourself for the things your parents did. They are fools for casting you away, but I am not. Just know that regardless of what has happened and what will happen, that I love you more than anything and will never leave you like they did." She wiped the tears from Ophelia's eyes.

"I hate them," Ophelia croaked. "I hate them all for abandoning me and I will make them pay."

"Of this I am sure, my child," Lilith beamed. "Now compose yourself and get dressed. I can't have my guest see my favorite flower wilting."

*

Ten minutes later, Lilith had changed into something more fitting of receiving guests, a pantsuit and flat shoes, and was making her way down the spiral staircase into the living room. Following closely behind her was Ophelia. She had traded her jeans and boots for a one-piece camouflage body suit and thigh high green boots. Covering her face was a mask, similar to those worn by Tiger Lily and the Black Lotus. Carved in the center was a replica of a nightshade plant painted in green and gold.

There were four men in the living room, including Lilith's son Peter and two of his minions. When the guests spotted them, they all stood as a sign of respect, except Peter. He sat on the couch, picking under his fingernails. As usual, he wore fatigues and heavy boots. His head was shaved close to his skin, showing off the two devil horns tattooed on either side. They made him look like every bit the evil demon that he was.

This was the first time she had seen him since he'd gotten back from California and she had some choice words for him that would have to wait until after her meeting.

"Sorry to keep you waiting, gentlemen," Lilith said apologetically.

"No worries, your son Peter has been keeping us entertained," K-Dawg said, taking Lilith's hand and kissing the back of it.

"Is that right?" Lilith raised her eyebrow and looked to Peter.

"Yeah, I was just telling K-Dawg some old war stories," Peter said with a smug grin on his face.

Lilith wanted to slap him, but she held her composure.

"Where's your ever-present shadow?" she asked K-Dawg.

She was speaking of Justice.

"He had some other things to attend to, but sends his apologies for not being able to come," K-Dawg lied. In truth, he wasn't sure how Justice would react to being in the same room with the woman responsible for ordering his niece and nephew kidnapped, and the man who had murdered his sister- in-law. Though Justice claimed to be done with Animal, K- Dawg had a hard time believing him. He knew how close Justice and Animal were while growing up, and love like that didn't die easily, even if it was for someone who tried to kill you.

"A pity," Lilith said as if she gave a shit.

"Speaking of missing persons, where has that beautiful daughter of yours gotten off to? She and I were having such an interesting conversation about history," K-Dawg said slyly.

From the minute, he walked in the house and saw her; he knew who she was. K-Dawg had come up in the same hood as Ashanti and Animal, so he had known Angela since she was a kid. Everybody had always assumed she was dead, so it came as quite a shock when she answered Lilith's front door. What K-Dawg couldn't seem to figure out was how she ended up with Lilith, and didn't seem to have any memories of him or who she was.

"I'm afraid she too had other things to attend to," Lilith replied. "But enough small talk, how are things progressing? Is Shai with us?"

"Grudgingly, yes," K-Dawg confirmed. "He's just a little unnerved by the small hiccup in the road we've run into."

"You call a man murdering several of my people, costing me untold sums of money, and kidnapping my favorite son a hiccup?" From the corner of her eye, she saw Peter flinch when she called George her favorite. She had said it to insult him.

"No, I would never try and downplay such a tragedy. Kidnapping is a nasty business, but I'm sure I don't have to tell you that do I? On another note, everything in Puerto Rico went smoothly. The Red Widow should arrive sometime tonight with the cargo you requested. I trust the messenger got the package to you safely?"

"Package?" Lilith was confused.

"I had one of your runners deliver the documents you requested from your vault at the compound along with the shipping manifest for tonight. Didn't you get it?"

Lilith looked to Ophelia.

"About twenty minutes ago, one of our sources on the

police force informed me that one of our runners had committed suicide. He jumped out the window of a place called Original Sin," she informed her.

Lilith shook her head. "I'm disappointed with you, Nightshade," she used Ophelia's codename so as not to reveal her in front of K-Dawg. "Information such as this should have been brought to my attention immediately."

"I'd intended to, but we got... sidetracked. I didn't know what the runner was carrying; only that he was one of ours."

"Did the source say whether the police had recovered the package or not?" Lilith asked hopefully.

Nightshade shook her head. "No, the only thing they found at the scene was Luther Graham's body. Also, the runner wasn't the only casualty. Several other people were also found dead on the scene."

"Did they jump out of windows too?" Lilith asked sarcastically.

"No, they were shot."

"Just what we need, another crew poking their noses where they don't belong," Peter added.

"This wasn't a crew. According to the source this was all done by one man," Nightshade revealed.

"That's bullshit," Peter capped. "I've been to Original Sin and their security is tight. There is no way that one man could've done all that and escaped with his life."

"Unless it wasn't a man at all, but an animal," K-Dawg added. "I warned you against poking your stick in that cage, Lilith. With all due respect, Animal is a headache that none of us want right now."

"He's also a headache that we wouldn't have if my orders had been followed." Lilith cut her eyes at Peter, who was no longer smiling. The realization of what kind of monster he'd brought down on their heads was finally starting to set in.

"If Animal has gotten ahold of that package it could present a set of unforeseen circumstances that could compromise our plans."

Lilith began pacing the room. She was a ball of rage and needed to walk the anger out before she struck someone in the room. "That parcel contained some very sensitive information, Information that could tear out the foundation of everything I've worked so hard to build. I can't have that." She was thinking of the sheet of notebook paper. The documents naming her a shareholder in NYAK were important, but replaceable. It was the information on the notebook paper that was priceless. It was the only copy of it she owned and the chemist who had drafted it was dead.

"I'll make some phone calls and get in the streets and see if they're talking. In the meantime, I suggest you beef up security around this place. Once Animal tastes blood, he'll keep drinking until he's had his fill and then some," K-Dawg warned.

"Thank you for your concern. Peter, please see our guest out," Lilith dismissed him.

Peter rose and walked K-Dawg to the front door. The two men exchanged hushed words before K-Dawg left and went to his car. When Peter closed the door, he was surprised when he turned around and found his mother standing directly behind him. He opened his mouth to say something and she slapped him so hard that his lip split and blood trickled down his chin.

"Stupid, stupid boy! Do you see what you've done?"'Lilith snarled, raining spittle in his face.

"All I did was follow your orders, Mother," Peter said, wiping his mouth.

"My orders were for you to bring Celeste to me, not

storm into a man's home and rape and murder his wife!" Lilith shouted back. "Animal will come for any and all responsible for this. If he hurts my George because of what you've done, you will answer for it."

"Relax Mother. So long as we've still got his kids, we've got the upper hand. I'll bet if we send start sending him little fingers and toes in the mail he'll back off," Peter said smugly.

Lilith grabbed him by the throat and lifted Peter from his feet. For an older woman, she was surprisingly strong. "If you lay one hand on those children, either of them, you won't have to worry about Animal because I'll kill you myself, do you understand?" He nodded and she let him go. "Children are innocent and I will not punish them for the sins of their parents. We are soldiers, not savages. You've opened Pandora's Box and I expect you to close it."

"I'll go into the city and track down this Animal person-ally," Peter vowed.

"You'll do nothing, but ready your men and await further orders," Lilith told him.

"As you wish, Mother," Peter said, feeling slighted. He knew he had fucked up and trying to plead his case further was not only pointless, but potentially dangerous. He had seen his mother in murderous rages before and wanted no parts of it. He motioned to his two minions that it was time for them to go, but Lilith stopped them.

"Tell me, which of these men is your best soldier?" Lilith asked.

"That would be Angel," Peter said. A man with long black hair and wearing similar fatigues as Peter's stepped forward. "I have been in over a dozen firefights with him and he has never faltered. He is hands down the best man in my unit."

"Is that right?" Lilith regarded Angel. Though he was

frightened of the woman, he did his best to look brave. Unexpectedly, Lilith tapped his chest with the tips of her fingers in a complex pattern. "You have roughly twenty seconds left to live, Angel. Use them wisely," she turned and headed back towards the steps leaving Peter and his men standing there in wide-eyed shock. Nightshade fell in step behind her.

"Shall I go out in search of Animal and retrieve the package?" Nightshade asked as they ascended the stairs.

"No, I need you with me. I'm hopeful that Animal will be so focused on trying to use the NYAK documents against me that he'll overlook the real prize. We'll continue according to plan for now. But to be on the safe side I want extra eyes on the port. I want to know the minute the Red Widow and my cargo arrives, do you understand?"

"Yes, Mother. I won't fail you again," she promised and went off to do Tiger Lily's bidding.

"For your sake, I hope not," Lilith said to the space her daughter had occupied a few seconds prior. As she was continuing up the stairs, she heard something heavy hit the floor in the living room. For the first time that night, Lilith smiled.

CHAPTER 13

R affa Kahn sat behind his desk in the corner office of the accounting firm he'd co-founded, stroking his thick black goatee as he often did when he was deep in thought. Behind him, a large glass window took up almost the entire wall. On clear nights, he had a picturesque view of downtown Washington, D.C. Sometimes he would stand in the window, looking out at the city, and pinch himself just to remind himself that it was real. Sometimes, it was hard to tell one reality from another when you walked in two worlds. As far as the government was concerned, Kahn was an overpriced accountant who handled accounts for some of the largest companies in the eastern United States, but those who really knew him knew that what he made as an accountant was a drop in the bucket when weighed against the type of money he collected at his real job. All in all, no matter which life you looked at, he had done extremely well for a kid who had vanished from the world at the tender age of fourteen.

Kahn was a man who was no stranger to the triumphs and tragedies of life. In fact, it had been the tragedies suffered throughout his life that drove him to be more than what society had expected. He'd gone from a dirt poor kid,

stealing and selling drugs in the streets of Cuba, to a man of stature and power who had amassed more wealth than he ever thought possible. Everything he had, he had worked incredibly hard for, no handouts or assistance. He was self-made and prided himself on that more than anything. Kahn had learned from an early age that when opportunity knocked you didn't just open the door, you pulled it inside and held it hostage. This is what he did nearly twenty years prior when a stolen necklace would forever change his life.

Kahn had been out robbing one night with some friends that he shared an abandoned house with. Everyone else in the group had managed to finagle something and they were about ready to call it a night, but Kahn's pockets were still empty. When his friends had decided to call it a night, Kahn continued trolling the streets in hopes that his luck would change. It did when he wandered into an affluent section of Santiago de Cuba. He spied a Hispanic woman wearing expensive clothes, with diamonds accenting her hands and neck coming out of a shopping center carrying lots of bags. From her pale skin to her expensive clothes, you could tell that she wasn't a local; likely one of the rich tourists who sometimes frequented the country. Kahn hated to take things from women, unless they were white, but he was desperate that night. From just her necklace alone, he could feed his entire house for months. After much internal debate, Kahn decided to make his move.

He stalked the woman as she crossed the parking lot and made her way towards a silver BMW. She was so busy chatting on her cell phone that she didn't even notice him behind her. When she sat her purse atop her car, Kahn swooped in. He grabbed the woman roughly by the shoulder, spinning her around, and scaring the daylights out of her. "Your money or your life," he commanded, waving the raggedy .22 he was carrying at her.

When the woman saw that the person who was attempting to rob her was just a scruffy looking boy, the fear faded from her face, replaced with a look akin to amusement. "Little one, you're about to make a mistake that you'll regret later. If it's money you're looking for, I'll gladly give you a few dollars, but you won't be taking anything from me," she said calmly. The woman reached for her purse to hand Kahn a few dollars when he shoved her against the car.

"Bitch, you willing to die over them jewels and whatever you got in that purse?" Kahn shoved the gun in her face. His hand trembled nervously. Back then, he had still been a virgin to death.

Seeing how unstable the kid was, the smile faded from the woman's face. "Fine, take what you want, just be mindful with that gun."

Kahn grabbed her purse then snatched her cell phone too and stuck it inside. "Run that necklace too!" he ordered.

"Son, you've already taken my money and I'm more than willing to let you have it, but this necklace was a gift from my late husband," she explained.

"I don't give a fuck who gave it to you, it's mine now," Kahn snatched the necklace from her neck. He'd thought about taking her car too, but back then he didn't know how to drive, so he settled for her money and jewelry and took off on foot. As he exited the parking lot, he spared a glance over his shoulder and found the woman watching him with an amused expression on her face.

Between the cash he'd found in the purse and what he'd gotten from fencing the necklace Kahn felt like a kid on

Christmas. The take wasn't for more than a few thousand dollars, but to a kid who had nothing it was like hitting the lotto. He was the man of the hour when he got back to the house he was squatting in and told his fellow robbers about his successful mission. Of course, some of them wanted to share in his fortune, but Kahn hoarded it all for himself. None of them offered to share with him when they had broken lucky and he hadn't. He went out and bought new sneakers, clothes, and gorged himself on fine food from the local markets. Kahn felt like he'd pulled off the most successful lick of his young life, until a few days later when karma paid a call on him.

Kahn had been sleeping upstairs on the dirty mattress that served as his bed when he awoke with a start. He wasn't sure what had awakened him, but he felt like something was wrong. He slipped into his new Nikes and ventured out of his room. The house was unusually silent that night. Normally in the house full of unruly teenagers there was always some kind of commotion, but that night the house was as still as the grave. He tip-toed down the stairs, looking for signs of one of his fellow thieves, but found none. That was until he tripped over something at the bottom of the stairs and fell on his face.

When Kahn pushed himself into a sitting position, he noticed that his hands and knees were covered in something wet and sticky. At first he thought one of the other kids had spilled something and neglected to clean it up, but upon closer inspection he realized that it was blood. His eyes immediately darted to the stairs, where he had fallen, and it was then he spotted his friend Juan lying at the bottom of them. His eyes stared off aimlessly, but the life had long ago fled them. Across his throat, were several gashes as if some sort of animal had attacked him.

Kahn scrambled to his feet and ran as fast as he could

for the front door. It didn't even matter that he was covered in blood, and only wearing his sneakers and underwear. He needed to get out of the house before whatever had gotten to Juan mauled him too. He had almost made it to the front door when he slammed into something very solid. His path had been clear only seconds prior, but now there was a black wall standing between him and freedom. As his eyes traveled the length of it, he realized that it wasn't a wall at all, but a man. He was dressed in black from head to toe and wearing a mask crafted of silver, polished to a high shine.

Young Kahn tried to run back the way he had come, but the man in the silver mask had grabbed him by the back of his neck and lifted him off the feet. The next thing Kahn knew, he was sailing across the room, crashing into the wall hard enough to put a hole in it. He sat on the floor, dazed and with his head spinning as the man in the silver mask stalked towards him. Kahn watched in shock as he drew a large axe from a scabbard on his back and raised it to deliver the killing strike.

"No," a voice called from somewhere in the next room. "Bring him here, Nicodemus. I have something I want to show our young thief."

The masked man, who had been called Nicodemus, pulled Kahn by his arm to his feet and dragged him into the next room. When they were inside, he shoved Kahn so hard that he lost his balance and fell. Instead of hitting the floor, Kahn landed on something soft and lumpy. When he rose up and looked down, he realized that he was lying on a pile of bodies. They were all dead, the murdered children and young adults that occupied the house they squatted in. All of them bore the same animal like slashes that he had seen on Juan's throat. Kahn's stomach lurched and he threw up everything he had eaten that day.

"I'm disappointed in you, little one. You have the stomach to steal from a woman, but not to look upon death?" a voice slightly familiar to him mocked.

He looked up and saw another masked figure. This one was a female, he could tell from the curve of her breasts in the black jumpsuit she wore. Unlike Nicodemus, who wore a plain silver mask, hers was the color of burnt copper with what looked like tiger stripes etched across the cheeks. An orange flower with black specks was carved in the center of her mask, just over the tinted eyeholes. Choked in the crook of her arm was another one of the boys who squatted in the house, Pablo. He was their leader and resident tough guy, but at that moment, he looked like every bit of the frightened child that he was.

"Why did you kill my friends? We haven't done anything to you. This isn't right," Kahn said. He wasn't sure why he said it, or even if it mattered. He just needed to hear his own voice to be sure it was really happening and that he wasn't caught in a nightmare.

"Isn't it?" she stepped forward, dragging Pablo with her. She regarded him from behind her mask. "Several days ago, you took something from a woman that didn't belong to you, was that right?"

Kahn could've shit himself when she mentioned the woman he'd robbed in the parking lot. He should've known from the expensive necklace and fancy car that she had the means to send killers after him for what he'd done. It was probably just his luck that he robbed the wife of some big time drug dealer or rich businessman.

"Please, I'm sorry. I don't have all of the money, but I still have some of it and I'd be more than willing to give it back if you let us go free," Kahn pleaded.

"This isn't about the value of material things, it's about

karma. Tell me, what do you know of karma?" the woman asked.

"Nothing," Kahn admitted. He was familiar with the word but didn't truly understand it's meaning.

"Karma is a fickle mistress, but one thing that is consistent about her is that she always comes back to claim what is owed to her. Sometimes it affects the offender directly," she raised her hand and for the first time Kahn saw the metallic looking claw covering it. "And sometimes it spills over to those closest to us." She brought the claw down and tore out Pablo's throat, before tossing his body onto the pile with the others.

Khan stood there, watching Pablo bleed out onto the pile of other young boys. Of all the people who stayed in the house, he and Pablo were the closest. They had spent many nights staying up until the wee hours, talking about their dreams of escaping Cuba and going to America where they would make their fortunes. Seeing his friend Pablo slaughtered like a dog filled Khan with so much rage that his body began to tremble. He turned his hateful eyes towards the killer, and though he tried to hold it back, a lone tear rolled down his cheek.

"I know that look," the woman moved closer. "Hatred is the one emotion that we can't mask, no matter how hard we try. It's because unlike some of the others, hatred is something born from the heart and not the head. Right now, you're probably thinking that if you had a weapon, you'd do to me exactly what I've done to your friends. Isn't that right?"

Kahn didn't reply.

"I'm a sporting woman," she selected one of several blades that were strapped to her thighs and tossed it at Kahn's feet. "Take up the blade and avenge your friend. Strike me down for killing your comrade."

Kahn hesitated. He figured it had to be some kind of trick. Even if he did manage to make it to the blade and kill the woman, Nicodemus would likely strike him down shortly after. Still, if he was to die with his friends, at least he would take Pablo's killer with him. The minute Kahn reached for the blade, pain exploded in his back when the woman slashed him with her claws. It burned as if someone had opened his skin and poured alcohol inside of it. Kahn was in so much pain that all he could do was lie on the floor and whimper.

"The first rule of battle is to never take your eyes off your opponent," the woman told him, wiping her blood stained claws clean on the dirty sheet they had hung over the window as a curtain. She looked down at Kahn and shook her head. "A pity, because I'd had high hopes for you. Kill him and meet me outside, Nicodemus," she ordered and started for the door.

Behind her there was a feral growling, like a wounded animal sending out a warning to someone who had strayed too close. She turned around just in time to see Kahn streaking at her with the blade she'd offered him. He was faster than she'd expected, but untrained, and it took little to no effort to deflect his strikes with her metallic claws. She moved her arms in a circular motion, disarming Kahn and leaving him exposed. With a flick of her hands, she pierced both of Kahn's shoulders to the wall with the index fingers of her claws.

Kahn howled as he felt muscles and tendons ripping. He had experienced pain in his life but never on that level. A few minutes prior he wanted nothing more than to live, but at that point he was praying for death if it meant the pain would stop. Just as he was about to black out, she removed the claws and let him fall to the ground. Kahn lay there, bleeding like a stuck pig while the woman knelt over him. She raised one of her bloodied claws and removed her mask and he was shocked at who he saw behind it. "You?" he gasped.

"I tried to warn you when you were robbing me that you were making a mistake you'd regret later." She smirked at him. "You're street trash, but you have potential. I can respect a man who is willing to fight until the end. For this, you get to keep your life."

"So you're not going to kill me?" Kahn asked, both surprised and relieved.

"No, but by the time I'm done you may wish that I had," she stood, removing her claws and hooking them to either side of the utility belt she was wearing. "Bring him then burn this place and its secrets to the ground," she told Nicodemus before leaving the room.

*

That was the last night Kahn ever had to steal or go hungry. The woman who had entered the house as his executioner turned out to be his savior, and later on his mentor. Her name was Lilith, but she went by Tiger Lily and was an elder in what would become his new family, the Brotherhood of Blood. For years, Kahn had studied under Tiger Lily, learning from her and soaking up everything she taught him. Of all the lessons she taught him, the one she was the most animate about was that failure was unacceptable. This is what made it so hard for Kahn to digest what his second in command, Bastille, was standing in his office telling him.

Bastille was one of the most, if not the most, dangerous men in the Brotherhood. Him being named the order's official executioner was not by chance, but because he was amongst the best at what he did, which was deliver swift and merciless death. In all the years Kahn had known him, Bastille had never lost a battle, but at that moment, he looked like a whipped dog. His clothes stank of gasoline and there were fresh burns on the side of his face and his neck. It was a grotesque sight and he needed obvious medical attention, but Bastille wouldn't hear it. For as bad shape as he was in physically, his pride was hurt worse than his body.

"I'm telling you, Khan, I had the bitch beaten. I would've taken her head if those other guys hadn't shown up!" Bastille fumed.

"And who were these men who were able to best the Brotherhood's executioner and make off with the prize?" Kahn asked.

"I don't know; they were wearing bandanas to cover their faces. At first I thought they were gang bangers, but the way they moved was too organized for them to be common thugs. They've had training, likely some of those band of misfits she's taken to running with," Bastille suggested.

"I doubt that. Ashanti and his bunch were all accounted for the last time I checked, except Animal," Kahn told him. He'd had eyes on them almost the whole time they were in New York. Animal had managed to slip past his watchers and no one was quite sure where he'd gotten off to. Though his face didn't show it, this troubled Kahn greatly. Animal was only one man, but an extremely dangerous one. Losing track of him was like having your pet poisonous snake escape in your house and wondering if you would catch it before it snuck up on you and bit you.

"Then maybe it was Animal who saved her."

"I'd thought about that, but had it been Animal who got the drop on you, you'd be dead instead of burned," Khan said seriously. Animal's affiliation with Kahllah made them enemies, but he still respected his skills as a killer.

"I don't care who it was, but when I find them I'm going to skin them all alive and wear their pelts like a winter coat!" Bastille slammed his meaty fist onto Kahn's desk, almost knocking over the picture of him and President Obama at the last Inaugural Ball.

"My old friend, you are as gifted with words as you are with a blade," Khan said good-naturedly. "Fear not, I'm sure you'll have a second chance at the Black Lotus sooner than later. If she's in the D.C. area it doesn't take a lot of thought to figure out where she's headed."

"To the Mountain," Bastille voiced what Kahn was thinking.

"Yes, in a futile attempt to plead for her life no doubt," Kahn said in disgust.

"Well if that's the case, she'll be marching into her own death. Since you've revealed her traitorous plans to over-throw the order all doors have been closed to her. I made it clear to other brothers and initiates that anyone who is caught aiding the Black Lotus will meet the end of my blade. I promise you, there is no one foolish enough to lend help to that turncoat."

"If that were true then you wouldn't be standing here looking like Freddy Kruger and it'd be her head on my desk instead of your fist prints," Khan shot back.

"On my honor and my title of executioner, I swear to you that the next time we meet I will crush the Black Lotus under my boot as easily as the flower she was named after,"

Bastille promised. He hated to be made to look inferior, especially in the eyes of Khan. He was the leader of the Black Hand and his opinion carried a great deal of weight.

"I'm sure you will. Had there been any doubt in my mind about your abilities your head would complement hers on my trophy wall," Khan said seriously. "I'm concerned about the Black Lotus being here, but I'm more concerned about those who helped her and what they mean to our plans for the future." He got up from behind his desk and began pacing his office.

"They were probably just mercenaries or something. You know the Black Lotus has a great many friends from all different walks of life," Bastille said.

"No, these weren't mercenaries. Whoever helped her knew exactly when and where to intervene, which was information known only to those with access to Brotherhood networks. There is a snake in our midst."

"Kahn, it's as I've said; all the Brothers know the penalty for helping her. Who would be foolish enough to risk excommunication and certain death for a traitor?"

Kahn stopped his pacing, and stroked his goatee absently. His eyes were still fixed on the city outside his window. "Who indeed?"

CHAPTER 14

K ahllah sat at the card table in the middle of the dimly lit garage, with her hands wrapped around a hot cup of tea. The heat coming through the glass soothed her sore fingers. It had been quite painful popping them back into place after Bastille had dislocated them, but Kahllah was no stranger to pain or dislocated bones. Until that moment, she had never really appreciated the simple things, such as a cup of tea or the temporary quiet of having survived almost being killed. Kahllah's mind kept replaying the look on Bastille's face as he prepared to take her head, and the feeling of helplessness as she watched. She had been on death's door many times, but each time she always had options. Not that night. She was so mentally and physically exhausted that her body betrayed her. Bastille had been right when he said she was slipping. She'd become so involved in the problems of others that she'd taken her eye off the ball and it almost cost her. Thanks to the mercies of the young man sitting across from her she'd have a chance to correct her mistakes.

He was hunched over, speaking in a hushed tone on his

cell phone. His silky black hair was longer than she remembered; now spilling down freely past his shoulders. His handsome sandblasted face was still relatively the same, except for the five o'clock shadow he now sported. She liked it on him, because it didn't take away from his boyish good looks, but it did give him more of an edgy look. It had been years since she had seen Anwar and back then, he had been barely a boy, but he was a man now. After giving a few last minute directions to whomever he was speaking to, Anwar ended the call and turned his attention to Kahllah.

"Things are a little crazy tonight and require a bit more attention than usual," Anwar said apologetically.

"No need to explain. If anything I owe you a debt for saving me from the executioner's blade," Kahllah said. "For a minute, I thought I was being abducted by gang bangers." She was speaking of the bandanas they'd used to cover their faces.

Anwar laughed. "That was to throw off Bastille and his men. All members of the Brotherhood have been forbidden to provide you with assistance under the threat of death."

This surprised Kahllah. "I didn't realize I was so popular these days."

"Popular isn't quite the word I'd use, but you're definitely a hot topic right now. I'm pretty sure my head would wind up on the chopping block if word ever got out that I helped you, but it's the least I could do, especially after all you've done for me."

"There are no debts between us," Kahllah said dismissively. "As always, you are too modest Black Lotus. I am forever, and gratefully, in the debt of the woman who gave me a second life," Anwar declared.

When Anwar had come into the Brotherhood, he was slightly older than the age they usually took on initiates, but an exception was made due to the special circumstances under which he had brought himself to the order's attention. Back then, Anwar was known as the Child-Prince because he was merely a teenager, but held sway over a small army. They called themselves the Al-Mukalla, which was the city Anwar and his family hailed from. They had come to America in search of good fortune and they found it in the heroin trade.

Kahllah and Anwar's paths crossed when the youngster found himself on a Brotherhood hit list. It was discovered that monies that Anwar had been sending back home to the Middle East to take care of friends and family were being used to finance a terrorist cell, which was behind the deaths of several American citizens. Anwar wasn't involved and had no knowledge of what the money had been used for, but it didn't matter when the bag was dropped and his head was declared the prize.

Kahllah was given the task of executing him, and she would've had it not been for the divine intervention of a mutual friend who worked for Anwar named Sharif. Sharif had been an assassin in service to the Al-Mukalla and a longtime acquaintance of the Black Lotus. Sharif had been in possession of something that had been long sought by the Brotherhood and agreed to allow Kahllah access to it in exchange for sparing Anwar. A secret bargain was struck between the two killers, and Anwar would be allowed to keep his life, but it would be spent in the service of the Brotherhood of Blood as Kahllah's first and last apprentice.

"You flatter me, Anwar, but I'm not so sure I'm completely deserving of your praises. I knew from the first time I saw you that a young soldier like you would make a welcome addition to my order. My decision to recruit you was based on what was best for the Brotherhood," Kahllah told him.

Anwar gave him a disbelieving look. "Possibly, but if

that was the case how come you never shared Sharif's gift to you with the elders?"

Kahllah didn't answer.

"Just as I thought," Anwar continued. "But enough about the past, let's get back to the present and your set of problems, like Bastille trying to collect your head."

"Had you not shown up when you did, he'd have probably succeeded. Speaking of that, how is it that you knew I was in the city let alone where to find me?" Kahllah asked suspiciously. Anwar had been inducted into the Brotherhood under her, but it had been some time since they'd last seen each other. She had seen firsthand how easily old friends could become new rivals so her guard was still up.

"The same way everyone else knew. You're on a quite a few watch lists so you were flagged the minute you landed in D.C.," Anwar told her.

"Impossible. I took all the necessary precautions and used none of the Brotherhood channels."

"With all due respect, Lotus, you need to think about stepping into the new millennia one of these days. Fake I.D.'s aren't as foolproof as they once were when you have things like facial recognition software. The Brotherhood has made quite a few strides in the technology we now use since last you spent time amongst us."

"It was like pulling teeth to finally get the elders to relent to accept something as simple as Wi-Fi, and now they're going all *Mission Impossible*." She shook her head in disbelief. Though most of the order had long ago embraced technology and the advantages that came with it, the elders hadn't been so easily accepting. They guarded the secrets under the Mountain fiercely and didn't trust machines within the sacred halls they occupied.

"New leadership often brings new ideals. The days of old are coming to an end and we're about to usher in a new era of the Brotherhood. I'm still not sure if that's a good or bad thing," Anwar said.

"No doubt this new era is being guided by Khan's hand," Kahllah spat.

"Yes, the leader of the Black Hand has had the loudest voice, but he isn't alone in his thinking. Some of the Brothers, especially the younger ones, are tired of living their lives in servitude and secret. I was a little older when you brought me in so I was fortunate enough to have already sampled life as a free man, but some of the others weren't as fortunate. The Brotherhood recruits its members as children and until they're adults they never know anything except service to the Brotherhood. Can you imagine what it must be like for a twenty-one year old to have never sampled the flesh of a woman, or known the pain of a hangover? I do not envy them."

"You sound like you agree with Khan's arguments about how the order is run," Kahllah accused.

"I don't necessarily agree, but I don't wholeheartedly disagree either. I understand why our order moves the way it does, and why we sacrifice lands and titles when we take the oath, but I wouldn't mind being able to reap some of the fruits of my labor."

"Surely by now you've earned the right to live independently of the order," Kahllah said.

"Yes, I have a nice house in Oxon Hills and own two stores, but I am still at the beck and call of the Brotherhood. That isn't true freedom, just a longer leash," Anwar said honestly.

"And how do Sol and the others feel about these changes Kahn is trying to implement?" Kahllah asked.

"Sol doesn't say much of anything anymore, and on those rare occasions when he does speak, it is with Kahn's voice."

Kahllah shook her head. "Sol has always been more interested in counting coins and wallowing with his whores, but I can't imagine that the rest of the elders would sit idle while Kahn corrupts the order. What of the others?"

"Harron has been M.I.A for nearly a month now. He and his captains were dispatched to Prague to investigate reports of a rogue sect looking to seize control of our European chapter. About a week into his trip all communications ceased. We fear that Harron and his men are dead, and Prague has fallen. I personally petitioned to be allowed to fly to Europe to find out what happened, but I was denied. The Black Hand felt like with all that's going on we needed to consolidate our forces under the Mountain and couldn't risk losing."

"More of Kahn's manipulation," Kahllah spat. "And Nicodemus?"

"Nicodemus sleeps," he said solemnly. "A few days ago Nicodemus was discovered in his laboratory, unconscious. Apparently he was bitten by one of the snakes he uses to make his poisons. They say there was no antidote."

"The Poison Master has been handling snakes longer than you and I have been alive and he's extremely careful in his work. Nicodemus has been bitten more than a few times, but he would never house any venomous creature without having an antidote for their bite," Kahllah said suspiciously.

"They've ruled it an accident, but there are whispers that it was an assassination attempt. The last I heard he was still alive, but I'm not sure of his condition. He's being kept in his quarters and under heavy guard. No one but Kahn and the healers have been allowed to see him."

Kahllah frowned. "This whole thing stinks to high hell and I refuse to sit around acting like I can't smell it! I need to get inside the Mountain and see Nicodemus."

"Weren't you listening when I said he's being kept in his quarters under guard? Better still, have you forgotten the manhunt launched in your honor? Every available eye is peeled for the Black Lotus. They'd cut you down before you made it through the front gates."

"You're right, which is why we aren't going in the front," Kahllah announced. "The Mountain holds many secrets, secrets only known to a select few. I'll take care of our entry into the Mountain. Once we're inside, I'll just need you and your men to buy me a few minutes while I speak with Nicodemus."

"As I've told you, Nicodemus is near death and barely lucid. Unless you have the antidote for the poison that's ravaging his body, I fear this will be a wasted trip and unnecessary risk."

Kahllah thumbed the gold necklace around her neck and her fingers came to rest on the cylindrical pendant hanging from the end of it. "Not an antidote, but a gift."

PART 4

WAR READY

CHAPTER 15

The first thing Ashanti heard when he stepped off the elevator was shouting. It sounded like World War III had broken out in Abel's apartment. There were several raised voices, but Sonja's was the loudest. After the night he'd had, the last thing he wanted to do was have to go in and break up a fight.

Abel must've sensed him in the hallway because he opened the door before Ashanti had a chance to knock. His eyes looked tired, and so did the rest of him. Ashanti knew he had been leaning heavily on Abel lately, and hoped he wasn't putting too much on him.

"Fuck is all that noise?" Ashanti asked when he stepped through the door. Now that he was inside the voices seemed much louder.

"My brother is tripping. When he came home and found out that Animal was gone and nobody knew where he was, he lost it," Abel told him. His brother Cain had become extremely fond of Animal. Even before he'd met the man he followed his exploits in the streets. Most kids looked up to athletes and entertainers, but Cain looked up to mass murderers.

"What happened to your face?" He noticed the knot on Ashanti's head and his busted lip.

"It's a long story," Ashanti said and continued past him. He walked into the kitchen to find a scene that he could've only described as comical. Cain and Red Sonja arguing, while Brasco sat at the table breaking some weed up. He watched the exchange with an amused expression on his face. Zo-Pound sat in a folding chair shaking his head in disgust as the two of them went at it. Ashanti noticed that Zo was wearing a t-shirt that looked at least a full size too small.

"I'm sorry, I just can't understand how a house full of so-called competent people can lose track of an entire person," Cain was saying.

"For the hundredth time, we didn't lose him, he left," Sonja shot back.

"Same shit, the point I'm making is it shouldn't have happened. Even only having one eye I was able to see he wasn't in his right frame of mind when he left. If something happens to Animal then all this and the sacrifices made will have been for nothing," Cain looked at his brother Abel when he said this.

It was the elephant in the room that they had yet to address. When they'd run down on George at the club, they ended up having to shoot their way out. In the process, Abel laid a cop. Killing a law enforcement agent wasn't like dropping some common street nigga that nobody would miss. It was a capital offense, and if it ever came back on Abel he was going to get the needle. Abel had downplayed it as if he wasn't on his mind, but they all knew that wasn't true. Ever since it'd happened he'd been acting different. Abel had always been fun, loving, and warm, but he'd become distant and quiet. Cain was worried about his twin and truth be told, so was Ashanti.

Cain stopped his ranting when he noticed Ashanti standing in the doorway of the kitchen. "Our fearless leader has returned," he said sarcastically.

"Not now, Cain. I ain't in the mood for another one of your temper tantrums," Ashanti warned as he walked past him to get to Zo-Pound.

"Thanks for coming," he gave Zo dap.

"You already know," Zo told him.

Ashanti looked down at the tight shirt his friend was wearing and smirked. "Nice shirt."

"Fuck you," Zo said good-naturedly. "Mine had blood on it so Cain let me borrow one of his."

Ashanti got serious. "You good?"

"Wasn't my blood, it belonged to the janky little fucker who tried to off me. Apparently there's a price on my head big enough to have niggas trying to bite the hand that was feeding them," Zo said angrily.

"Join the club. Some dudes tried to off me too," Ashanti pointed to his busted lip. "Two of us almost dying in one night ain't no coincidence. Before Cain dropped that ungrateful ass nigga Ocho he told me somebody dropped a bag on my head. My guess is everybody in this room is a walking payday." Zo said.

"It was probably that cartel bitch," Brasco added.

"I doubt it," Sonja spoke up. "Lilith wouldn't have used thugs, she'd have used hired assassins and the both of you would be dead."

"I forgot you're the resident authority on all things related to Lilith," Ashanti said. "You know it's like the deeper we dig into this the more it stinks, and quite frankly so do you."

"And what's that supposed to mean?" Sonja asked defensively.

"It means that after that stunt you pulled with not telling us about the flash drive, I can't help but to wonder if there's anything else you're keeping from us."

Sonja rolled her eyes. "I told you that I didn't know what was on the flash drive!"

"I find that hard to believe," a voice startled them. All eyes in the kitchen turned to the hall just outside the entrance. Animal stood looming in the shadows. He'd slipped back into the apartment just as quietly as he'd slipped out.

"I've never known you to touch a situation without first knowing it inside and out," he stepped into the kitchen. In the light they could all see the blood and dirt on his clothes. Slung across his back was a messenger bag.

"Oh my God, we've been so worried about you! Where've you been?" Sonja asked.

Animal gave her a look that was so cold you could felt the temperature drop in the room. He stepped around her, nodding at everyone in the room in greeting. When he got to Brasco, his face softened. Brasco stood and they shared a manly embrace. "Been a long time."

"Too long, my nigga," Brasco said emotionally. "I just wished that we'd have met again under different circumstances. Listen, I'm sorry to hear about—"

"I know, I was able to hear you in there," Animal cut him off. "I was lost, not dead. Thank you for your kind words old friend, but right now the sound of your gun will give me more comfort than your condolences. We'll mourn my wife after I've assassinated her killers and brought my kids home."

"That's the Animal I was waiting for to make an appearance!" Red Sonja said proudly.

"Shut up," Animal said to Sonja and everyone else's surprise.

"Excuse me?" she was taken aback.

"I said shut your troublesome ass up. You brought this shit to my door," Animal said harshly.

"Animal, my daughter has been taken too, why are you acting like you're the only victim in this?" Sonja's eyes welled up with tears.

"Nah, baby. I ain't the only victim, just the only fool. You played me Sonja... you played us all."

"Animal, I don't appreciate how you're coming at me. I know you're upset about what happened to your little girlfriend, but —" Red Sonja never got a chance to finish her sentence.

Animal swooped in and grabbed Red Sonja by the throat, forcing her against the wall so hard that the plaster splintered. There was a wild look in his eyes and his words were quick and sharp. "Her name was Gucci!" he rained spittle into her face. "And she wasn't my girlfriend, she was my wife... my everything! You might not have respected her in life, but you're sure as hell going to respect her memory. Do you understand me, Sonja?"

"Just be cool, Blood," Ashanti laid his hand gently on Animal's shoulder. He was rewarded by Animal shoving him so hard that he crashed into the refrigerator.

"I asked you a muthafucking question," Animal squeezed Sonja's throat a little tighter. "Do-you-understand?"

"Yes, Tayshawn! Yes!" Sonja gasped. She had seen Animal angry before, but never like he was at that moment. When Animal finally released her, she slid down to the floor, clutching her throat. She had pushed him to his limit and gotten away with it many times over the years, but for the first time she was afraid that he actually might kill her.

"By now, you're probably all wondering where the hell I've been," Animal addressed the room.

"It had crossed our minds," Ashanti said looking down at the blood on his Converse.

"On a fact finding mission," Animal took off the messenger bag and placed it on the counter. He took the papers from it and held them up for Sonja to see. "I'm going to assume you know what these are."

"They look like bank statements to me," Sonja said as if she didn't know where he was going with it.

"Why don't you look a little closer," Animal pushed the papers into her face. "These are bank statements for a Ms. L. Angelino. Stop me when any of this starts to sound familiar," he told her. Sonja remained silent.

"Who is L. Angelino?" Abel asked. He'd been so quiet they'd almost forgotten he was in the room.

"L. Angelino is a shareholder in a chemical company called NYAK. I don't expect you to recognize the name since we've all come to know her as Tiger Lily," Animal revealed, much to everyone's surprise except Sonja's.

Brasco looked confused. "Blood, you said this chick is a drug dealer. What would she be doing breaking bread with a chemical company?"

"I was hoping she could tell us." Animal turned to Red Sonja. "From the time you showed up on my doorstep you've been jerking my strings, I was just too blinded by my love for that little girl to see through it. You knew how deep this rabbit hole with Lilith went and you let me crawl into it blindly anyhow. If that's how you treat the niggas you claim to love, I'd hate to see how you do the ones you hate."

"Animal, it's not like that," Sonja tried to telling him. "Save that shit for someone who doesn't know you, Red Sonja. In all the years I've known you, you've never gone at any enemy without knowing them; their strengths, their weaknesses, their vices... I'd be a fool to think that the same doesn't hold true with this situation. You might've dressed it up as being about your father, but I believe it's been about Lilith all along. No more lies, Sonja. If you've ever truly loved me then now is the time to prove it by being honest for a change."

Sonja's mind reeled. A million lies sprang to her tongue, but she couldn't manage to put them into words. Lying was something she did better than most, but with Animal, she found herself at a loss. Red Sonja had known from the moment Animal left Puerto Rico to rush to Gucci's side that Gucci was his one true love, but there was a part of her heart that still held onto the foolish hope. Staring into his eyes... eyes that used to look at her lovingly, and seeing nothing but emptiness and pain staring back at her. If he hadn't been before, he was truly lost to her now. His soul had died with his lover, and it was all Sonja's fault.

"I never meant for any of this to happen," Sonja said after a long pause. "In the beginning, I thought Lilith was exactly who she presented herself to be; an overly ambitious old whore. She wasn't the first who had tried to sleep their way into my father's cartel and she wouldn't be the last. Daddy seemed happy enough for the time being, so I left him to enjoy his new toy, waiting for the time to come when he got bored and threw her in the trash like the rest, and that proved to be a fatal mistake. Lilith was nothing like the others and it didn't take long for her to show it. Within her first year in our home Lilith had all but totally usurped my father's authority and infected his cartel with agents of the Brotherhood."

"So you knew Lilith was a part of the Brotherhood?" Ashanti asked.

Sonja shook her head. "No, not at first. I didn't learn that until later on. After Lilith had been with us long enough to get her hooks into my father, several mysterious men showed up at the compound. Not long after, there was a rash of unexplained deaths occurring amongst both our soldiers and the soldiers of our enemies. I knew that these guests of Lilith's had a hand in it."

"How did you know they were Brotherhood and not just some mercenaries on Lilith's payroll?" Animal asked.

"I've been around mercenaries all my life and these men were no freelancers. They moved like cats, skulking around in the shadows of the compound, always watching and whispering amongst each other. They hardly said two words to anyone outside of their group except Lilith. From the time they showed up, I knew there was more to them than what met the eye. Unfortunately, I didn't find out who they really were and why they'd come until it was too late."

Animal measured her words. "That still doesn't make them Brotherhood. Outside of Kahllah and my father, I've never met another member, so I'm no authority, but from what I've heard, it's an order that prides itself on secrecy. The only way to positively I.D. a member of the Brotherhood is to have someone on the inside."

Sonja lowered her eyes. "I developed a friendship with one of the men."

Animal snorted. "That's just a nice way of saying you were fucking him. I don't know why I'm surprised. You've always been good at using that gaping hole between your legs to get what you want."

Moving as fast as lightening, Sonja slapped Animal's face. It was more of a reaction to his sharp words than something she intended to do, but it conveyed her feelings about what he'd said. "How dare you! Animal, I don't give a damn whether I'm right or wrong, I will not allow you or anybody else to disrespect me, ever!"

Animal took a step towards Sonja, but Brasco moved

between them. Their eyes met and for a few seconds there was a battle of wills. Animal was the leader of their group, but it had been Brasco and his uncles who turned Animal onto the streets, before Gladiator had made him a killer.

Brasco was the one person in his life who had never changed and Animal had a great deal of respect for him. He was in a volatile state, but going upside Sonja's head wouldn't help the situation. Animal spared a last hateful glance at Sonja before backing away.

"His name was Ethan; at least that's what I knew him by. While the others who Lilith had brought in were secretive and kept themselves separate from everyone else, Ethan was slightly more approachable," Sonja continued. "I later learned that this was because he was new to the order and still had a touch of the streets in him. Unlike some of the others who had been brought into the order as children, Ethan was already an adult when Lilith recruited him to serve in her new regime. He was a good dude, but he had a tender heart and a big mouth. I'd only bedded him twice before he was he was whispering all his dirty little secrets in my ear. For all his faults, Ethan was still special to me, and next to you, one of the most beautiful men I'd ever laid eyes on."

"I'm flattered," Animal said with an edge of sarcasm to his voice.

Sonja ignored him and continued her story. "We kept our romance a secret but it wasn't long before Lilith found out and she didn't take it well. She'd tried to bed him before but he refused her, so it was like a slap in the face when she found out that we had been together. To punish us, she used those claws of her to scar my Ethan's beautiful face. She thought by making him ugly that I wouldn't want him, but it only made me love him harder. After what she'd done to Ethan's face he hated her just as much as I did, and this is when we began to conspire against her. Ethan and I were planning on running away together, but he was killed helping me escape with Celeste."

Animal's wheels began to spin as he processed the new information. "If your father was a target of the Brotherhood he'd have been long dead before any of you even realized they were amongst you. Why go through all the trouble of marrying him then quietly infiltrating unless killing Poppito was never the objective." He was finally starting to figure it out.

"Because she never wanted his life, she wanted his business," Sonja revealed.

"The Brotherhood sells death, not drugs," Ashanti chimed in.

"As I'm sure we've all learned by now, Lilith isn't like a typical Brotherhood member," Sonja pointed out. "Unlike someone like Kahllah who follows of code of honor, Lilith knows no such codes. She's a power hungry bitch whose only concerns are money and power. She wants to corner the drug market using a combination of her connections within the Brotherhood and my father's supply line."

"And let me guess, she's been moving drugs back and forth using ships," Animal said.

"How'd you know?" Sonja asked in surprise.

"Because of this," Animal pulled another sheet of paper from the bag. "As you were talking I was putting the missing pieces of this puzzle together and it got me to thinking: if I wanted to flood the country with drugs and had the connections Lilith does, what would be the most effective way to go about it? Planes are out of the question and moving them by land could present too many unnecessary risks, but a cargo ship would satisfy all my needs. The Brotherhood has agents in pretty much every division of law enforcement so why not Customs? What I'm holding is a shipping manifest for a boat called The Red Widow that's coming into the port of Newark tonight."

"If we intercept that shipment, it'll give us the upper hand in this," Ashanti said.

"As usual, we're on the same page," Animal said proudly.

"If that boat is coming in tonight we don't have much time. We need to arm up and get moving," Zo said.

"Agreed, but before we head out, there's just one more thing that's nagging at me." Animal turned to Sonja. The way he was looking at her told her that she wasn't prepared to answer whatever he was about to ask. "How did Lilith manage to get her hooks into NYAK?"

Sonja's tongue suddenly got very dry. She opened her mouth to speak, still not sure how she would answer when she was saved by what sounded like a ringing phone.

Abel reached in his pocket and pulled out what looked like a car stereo remote. He looked at the flashing red light at the end of it and frowned.

"What the hell is that?" Ashanti asked.

"Motion detector. It's part of the security system I had installed when Cain and me moved in here. It's how I knew you were outside the door before you knocked," Abel explained. "I shut it off after you came in, but re-set it once our friend here managed to pick our front door lock," he nodded at Animal. "Cain, pull the feed up."

Cain hit a button on the television remote and the screen flipped from the news station to an AUX channel. It was a live video feed that showed them the front door and part of the hallway. There was a man standing outside their apartment door wearing a blue and white delivery uniform and holding a large pizza box in his hand. A hat was pulled down snugly over his head making it hard to see his face. He stood there for a while, as if he was trying to decide if he had the right apartment or not.

"I'm glad one of y'all ordered some food, because I was in this bitch starving," Brasco said greedily. He hopped up and went to get the door with the blunt he'd just rolled dangling from his mouth.

Sonja moved closer to the screen and stared up at it. There was something familiar about the delivery man that she couldn't put her finger on. When he tilted his head, she was able to see his face, and her eyes nearly popped out of her head. "That's no fucking delivery. Brasco, don't open that door!" she shouted, running to stop him. But it was too late.

CHAPTER 16

After his meeting with Lilith, K-Dawg stopped by his secret apartment to change his clothes. He traded his suit and tie for a pair of jeans, a hoodie, and Timberland boots. He stood in front of the full length mirror and couldn't help but to smile. For the first time in a long time, he was feeling like his old self, so now it was time to get back to his old tricks.

He jumped in his whip and made a beeline for the heart of the city, Harlem. He crept through the familiar blocks with his window cracked just a taste, inhaling the stale air. It had been a long time since he had cruised the streets of the city he had once loved so much. Much of it had changed, with fancy cafés and new high rises replacing some of the old dope spots and bodegas. Years ago, K-Dawg had sold more than a little bit of cocaine on those very same streets. He was the king of kings during the era when dope money was plentiful and snitching was a no-no, but those days were long gone and he was a different man. However, the plan was still the same... the penthouse or the morgue.

He navigated his car across several avenues and the projects came into view. The tall brown buildings seemed to loom over the city like a grim warning to those who weren't from the hood to stay out of the hood. To that day, the sight of them still sent chills down K-Dawg's spine. The hood held both good and bad memories for him, mostly bad though. They were a constant reminder of what he came from and never wanted to go back to.

K-Dawg was one of a set of twins, born to a mother who loved him and a stepfather who couldn't stand the sight of him. Mr. Wilson went out of his way to be cruel to K-Dawg every chance he got. It was hard to imagine a man despising an innocent child, but his step-father hated him. It wasn't because of anything K-Dawg had done, but because of what he represented. He and his twin sister were the only children in the house who didn't belong to Mr. Wilson. They were the products of a vicious rape, and the family's darkest secrets.

His mother had been home from work on the night it happened. She generally took the bus from her job to the house she shared with her husband and children, but that night she was tired and decided to hail a taxi. The driver was a white man with red hair, green eyes, and a warm smile. She gave him her address and settled into the back-seat. At some point, she must've fallen asleep and when she woke up, she was in a place she didn't recognize. She questioned the driver as to her location, but he didn't answer. When she tried to get out of the taxi, she realized that the doors wouldn't open from the inside. When the driver turned to her, his warm smile had faded and there was a look of hatred plastered across his face.

The driver spent the next few hours beating and having his way with K-Dawg's mother. The whole time he was violating her all she could remember were his jade green eyes hovering over her. When he was done he left her on the street for dead, but luckily someone had found her and called an ambulance. When K-Dawg's mother next awoke, she was in the hospital. She and her husband kept the secret of her rape from everyone, including their friends and family, but secrets never stayed secrets for long. A few weeks after the rape, K-Dawg's mother discovered she was pregnant. She prayed to God that the two lives growing inside her were from her husband's seed and not the wicked taxi driver; but when the twins were born and she looked into their green eyes, her worst fears were recognized.

It was hard for K-Dawg's mother at first, but over time, she had learned to love her children. The same could not be said for her husband. Every time he looked at the children, especially the boy, he was reminded of what had happened to his wife. He tolerated the girl, but would have nothing to do with the boy. K-Dawg's mother knew that her husband hated her son, but she wouldn't realize how deep that hatred ran until the day she got the call at work that her daughter

was dead. Apparently, Mr. Wilson had been trying to poison young K-Dawg by lacing a cup of juice with antifreeze, but the girl had gotten to it by accident. By the time the ambulance arrived, it was too late. It wouldn't be until years later that karma would catch up with Mr. Wilson for what he had done, but it wouldn't come from the justice system, it came from the barrel of K-Dawg's pistol. For the killing of his father, K-Dawg was sent to prison where he served five years for manslaughter. It was within the walls of state prison that the young teenager's mind would become corrupted and start him on the path of darkness he now walked.

As he neared the projects, he saw a man standing on

the corner, wearing a hood on his head and trying his best to look inconspicuous. He shifted his weight from one leg to the other, looking up and down the street nervously. K-Dawg pulled his car into a parking spot a few yards away and flashed his high beams twice. The man in the hoodie walked towards him looking around cautiously as if he was afraid he was being watched. He made to get in on the passenger side, but K-Dawg motioned for him to come around to the driver's side window.

"Sup, Jewels?" K-Dawg greeted him through the open window.

"Ain't shit, out here waiting on you and trying not to freeze my ass off. I was expecting you a half hour ago," Jewels said. He was a light-skinned dude with a sunken face that looked like there wasn't enough meat in his cheeks.

"My fault. I had to do something that took a little longer than I expected. Don't worry though, I'll make the wait worth it. You've been a big help to me Jewels."

"Yeah, I just hope helping you doesn't get me killed. When I turned you onto those shooters, I told you that everybody was a-go except Zo. Lakim was pissed when he heard somebody tried to smoke his little brother," Jewels said angrily. Lakim was King James' second in command and the man Jewels answered to directly. He was a low level member of their crew and a sneaky cat who was always looking for a come up. A friend of his had told him about someone who was offering up big money for some bodies that needed dropping and Jewels offered to help. He was hesitant when he heard that Ashanti was one of the men on the list because they knew each other from when Ashanti was working with their crew. He and Ashanti had never been friends, but he was good to Jewels. When Jewels heard how much money K-Dawg was offering, loyalty went out the window and he did what he had to do.

"Sorry about that. Zo almost getting killed wasn't part of the plan, but you know sometimes these young boys get overzealous," K-Dawg lied. He had given specific instructions that everyone loyal to Animal be taken out, including Zo.

"Whatever, man. Just give me my money so I can get the fuck up out of here," Jewels said.

K-Dawg grabbed an envelope out of the glove box and extended it to Jewels. When the young man reached for it, he snatched it back. "You know this is only half, right?"

"Fuck you mean half? We agreed on a set price!" Jewels argued.

"Yes, a price based on the success of your people. As I'm sure you've heard, their targets are still alive," K-Dawg informed him.

"Man, you can't blame me for that."

"Indeed I can, Jewels. You were the broker for this little deal. Look I ain't trying to argue with you, lil' nigga. You can either take what I'm giving you or go fuck yourself." K-Dawg pretended he was going to put the money back.

"Okay," Jewels relented, as K-Dawg knew he would. When he went to open the envelope to count the money, K-Dawg stopped him.

"Don't count it out here, too many eyes. Unless you don't trust me?"

"Nah, I trust you, K-Dawg," Jewels assured him while stuffing the envelope into his back pocket. It was a lie, he was really too afraid of K-Dawg to raise a real stink over it. Even if K-Dawg did burn him, there wasn't shit Jewels would be able to do about it.

"Say, Jewels, you didn't tell anybody about this did you?" K-Dawg asked.

"Hell no, man! I could get clipped for going against the

grain. This is a secret I'm taking to my grave," Jewels promised.

"Indeed you will," K-Dawg said, before raising the gun he'd been hiding and shooting Jewels in the face. By the time Jewels' body hit the ground, K-Dawg was long gone. He wasn't worried about doubling back to retrieve the envelope because there was no money in it, only cut up scraps of paper. Jewels was a dead man the minute he agreed to aid K-Dawg in his scheme.

K-Dawg waited until he had put a bit of distance between himself and the crime scene before slowing his vehicle down. He coasted near the curb and tossed the gun out the window into a nearby trashcan. Two things he had learned from experience were that you didn't keep dirty burners or leave loose ends. Jewels was a loose end. The men who had tried to kill Ashanti and Zo were dead, leaving Jewels as the only remaining link between K-Dawg and the assassination attempts so he had to go. It was very possible that Jewels might've actually kept his mouth shut, but K-Dawg figured why risk it? K-Dawg wasn't so much worried about Jewels running his mouth to the police, but he didn't want King James to catch wind of it. The young gorilla learning of K-Dawg being back in the States was a card he wasn't ready to play just yet.

K-Dawg's cell phone chirped on the passenger seat. He didn't recognize the number, so he was hesitant about answering, but he did anyway. When he heard who was on the other end of the phone, a broad smile spread across his face. "Of course, I'd be willing to help you," he responded to the question that was asked. "Do you have a pen so you can write it down?" After making the caller read back the information K-Dawg had just given him to make sure there was no confusion, he ended the call. All K-Dawg could do was laugh when he thought about the predictability of certain types of people. The universe had just thrown him a way to kill two birds with one stone, literally.

CHAPTER 17

Peter had been drinking heavily since he'd seen his mother earlier that night. He was angry at her for the way she had spoken to him at the house. Peter was a general and commander of her army, but she scolded him as if he was an unruly child in front of his men. To make matters worse, she had killed Angel. Angel was not only one of Peter's best soldiers, but also a good friend.

He couldn't understand why she was so upset with him. Granted, his mother hadn't ordered him to murder Animal's wife, but he reasoned she had it coming. Had she had just cooperated things would've have gone smoothly, but she pulled a gun and turned a kidnapping into a multiple homicide. The only regrets that Peter had about that day was that he'd only gotten to fuck Gucci once before he killed her.

To him, it seemed like his mother was more concerned about the wrath of the man called Animal than the woman he'd killed. In all the years, he'd been privy to his mother's secret life; he'd never seen anything that remotely resembled fear in her eyes until this business with Animal. It disgusted him the way his mother and the others spoke about Animal as if he was some type of god of death. Peter had seen his work and respected him as a killer, but he was still just a man and therefore not invincible. If he could bleed, he could die. If he could present his mother with the young killer's head, it would put him back in her good graces. With this in mind, Peter went against his mother's wishes and set out to prove her wrong about him and Animal.

Finding Animal proved to be tricky. He knew his mother had spies watching Animal and his crew, but those spies were loyal only to her and he doubted they'd share the information with him without tipping her off to what he was planning. Not being able get what he needed from them, he took a stab in the dark and reached out to the only other person who might have an idea where to find him. He'd expected some resistance or at the very least a bunch of questions, but K-Dawg proved to be quite forthcoming. He not only gave Peter the address of the building they were rumored to be held up in, but he also provided him with the apartment number. Peter had never really cared for K-Dawg, but in light of how helpful he'd been, he thought maybe he had judged him too harshly.

Peter and his men had been watching the building for the last hour or so and so far had only seen the twins come or go and a man who he didn't know. Their presence confirmed that K-Dawg's information was good, but there was still no sign of the prize. This changed about ten minutes prior to that point when Animal finally showed up at the building. Peter started to move on him as he was entering the building, but decided to wait until after he entered the apartment. He would wipe them all out at the same time.

Peter donning the delivery uniform had been a result of

him having to improvise to get into the secure building. He could've just shot the security guard on duty in the lobby, but the sounds of gunfire might've alerted his enemies. He spotted a delivery man chaining his bike up outside and had a brilliant idea. The security guard hardly paid any attention to him when Peter came in wearing the uniform and carrying the box. He didn't become fully aware of his presence until Peter grabbed him from behind the desk and strangled him to death. With the security guard out of the way, Peter's men were able to get into the building undetected.

Peter got off the elevator on Cain and Abel's floor. The whole ride up his heart thudded in his chest in anticipation. By the time he got to the door, his adrenaline was pumping so hard that it began to sober him up and the realization of what he was about to do set in. A part of him began to wonder if it was the best course of action. Maybe his mother had a point and he should wait. When he heard footfalls nearing the door from the other side, he knew it was too late to turn back. "Fuck it," he said before removing the machine gun he'd been hiding in the box and shooting through the door.

*

Brasco could feel his insides shift as he neared the door. He was a big man and needed at least three square meals per day to keep his strength up. Animal and the others were welcome to keep scheming on empty stomachs if they wanted to, but he was about to tear off into that pizza.

He heard Sonja shout something at him from the kitchen, but couldn't quite make it out. He called back for her to repeat what she'd said and dropped his blunt on the floor. No sooner than Brasco bent down to pick it up, a bullet whizzed over his head.

"We got company!" Brasco shouted a warning to his comrades, scrambling back down the hall on his hands and knees as the high powered machine gun punched holes in the door. He pinned his back against the living room couch, protecting his head from the spray of glass and plaster from the bullets shredding everything they struck.

Sonja was the first one to emerge from the kitchen. She made it to the living room just as Peter became visible in the doorway. When their eyes locked, there was a spark of something that passed between them. The momentary pause allowed Sonja enough time to dive out of the way just before he let off another burst from the machine gun. She crawled across the floor and took cover next to Brasco.

"Please tell me that isn't another one of your crazy ex-boyfriends," Brasco said, sucking a piece of wood when a bullet struck the arm of the couch.

"I wouldn't fuck that psycho with your dick," Sonja said in disgust. "He's not an ex, but a rival," she added, snatching the cushions off the couch. Brasco watched her, wondering what she was doing, until he saw the stash of guns hidden in a secret compartment of the couch. She remembered Abel showing it to her when they'd first arrived.

"That's what the fuck I'm talking about," Brasco said excitedly, grabbing a Tech-9 from the stash. Sonja selected a baby 9mm. Brasco waited until he heard a pause in the gunfire before popping up from behind the couch. "Now I'm ready to play!" he yelled before cutting loose with the Tech-9.

Peter was barely able to hit the floor and get out of the way of the Tech's bullets when they came speeding at him.

Two of his men weren't quite as lucky. Peter watched

from a crouching position as their bodies danced like puppets on strings before finally hitting the floor. Peter returned fire, scooting back through the door, and the first wave of his men forward.

At the other end of the hall, Peter saw the prize emerge from the kitchen. Bullets and debris flew all around Animal, but he barely seemed to notice. His lips were pulled back into a fierce sneer as he calmly picked off Peter's soldiers. From his vantage point, crouched in the doorway of the apartment, Peter had a clear shot at Animal. As if he felt the pending danger, Animal's eyes landed on Peter. That was a split second before Peter tapped the trigger of his machine gun, with intentions on sending Animal to his final reward.

*

Everyone in the kitchen jumped when they heard the gunshots. Sonja was out first, shouting at Brasco, with Ashanti and Cain on her heels. She had just made it through the kitchen door and Ashanti was about to step out, when Cain grabbed him by the back of his shirt. Cain pulled him back just as a wave of bullets ate up the doorframe of the kitchen, narrowly missing Ashanti's face.

"What the fuck is going on out there?" Zo asked, getting low. In his hand, he clutched his trusty .357.

"We're being invaded," Abel pointed at the television screen. Just outside their door they could see more than half a dozen heavily armed men dressed in black.

Animal was standing with his back against the kitchen wall. From that angle, he could see Brasco and Sonja crouching behind the sofa and taking heavy fire. From the way pieces of fabric and wood were flying from the sofa, he knew the couch wouldn't hold up much longer. Seeing the mother of his daughter and one of his best friends in the line of fire reminded Animal of Gucci, Noki, Kastro, and everyone else dear to him whose deaths he hadn't been able to prevent. He couldn't sit idle and watch it happen again. Before anyone could stop him, Animal had stepped out into the living room and started shooting.

"Animal, no!" Ashanti tried to go after him, but Cain kept him pinned.

"Not like that, Ashanti. There's too many of them," Cain told him. He waited until he was sure Ashanti wouldn't do anything stupid before letting him up.

"We can't just hide in here and wait for them to come and kill us!" Ashanti said angrily.

"If you know anything about me, it should be; the beast hides from no one," Cain said. He began rummaging for something under the kitchen sink and came up holding two shotguns, one of which he tossed to his brother. They locked eyes and communicated silently as only twins could. Abel took up a position near the kitchen door, while Cain opened a small panel in the wall on the side of the refrigerator that housed a dumbwaiter. With the shotgun tucked to his chest, he climbed inside. "Wait for my signal and then I want every muthafucka in this kitchen to come out hitting."

"Wait, how are we supposed to know what your signal is?" Zo asked.

"Trust me, you'll know it when you hear it," Cain told him before sliding the panel back down and disappearing.

"I sure hope your brother has a sound plan," Zo said to Abel.

Abel didn't even respond. He just clutched his shotgun and waited.

*

What happened next seemed to take place in slow motion. Animal was firing his pistol trying to back his attackers up long enough for Brasco and Sonja to get clear.

He was locked in a fire fight with two men trying to flank him, when he spotted another man in a crouch by the door. It was the fake pizza delivery guy. He had Animal dead to rights. The gun barked, and the bullets seemed to trickle out, heading in Animal's direction. He was too far away from the kitchen entrance to turn back, and not close enough to the couch to take cover. In short... he was dead.

A blur of motion drew Animal's attention. Suddenly there was something between him and the man in the pizza delivery uniform. No, not something... someone. Brasco tackled Animal just as the bullets that had been meant for him tore through his friend's body. They both collapsed to the floor with Brasco landing on top of Animal pinning him.

Animal frantically tried to push Brasco off him, but he was too heavy. He felt like dead weight. Animal feared the worst, but he could feel his friend's heart still beating so there was hope. From beneath Brasco's body, Animal couldn't see what was going on, but he spied shadows of the men in black on the wall, drawing closer. They were coming for him. Animal had just managed to free his shooting arm and was about to fire blindly when he heard what sounded like thunder coming from the hallway.

*

Peter couldn't believe how rotten his luck had turned. He had Animal right where he wanted him and had his fat friend not gotten in the way; he'd be presenting the young killer's corpse to his mother. No matter, he still had time to finish the job. He was on his hand radio about to order the second wave of shooters to rush the house when he saw the stairwell at the other end of the hallway open and out stepped a man with a head full of long braids and the face of a monster.

"Can I have your attention please?" Cain shouted from down the hall. Instinctively, the shooters turned. "Thank you," he said before letting loose with the shotgun.

Peter was familiar with the inner workings of nearly one hundred types of guns and their ammunition, but whatever the shotgun was packing was like nothing he'd seen before. The bullets tore cantaloupe-sized holes in his men, burning away their skin and clothes where they struck.

"Dragon-Mouth rounds," Cain said answering the question plastered across Peter's face. "Very exclusive and very messy," he said before letting off another burst.

Peter looked on in horror as the scarred young man advanced on them, laughing maniacally and cutting through his men. Just when he thought things couldn't get any worse, they did. Animal's crew had regrouped and gone on the offensive, coming out of the kitchen blasting with guns of different shapes and sizes. He knew when he was beaten and figured a good run beat a bad stand, so he took off running towards the other staircase. He had just made it to the door when one of the Dragon-Mouth rounds struck the wall near his head sending burning embers flying into his face. As he staggered down the stairs, half-blinded by the embers, he thought of what his mother would do when she found out about his latest blunder.

After dispatching the last of Peter's men, Cain stepped into the apartment to rejoin his friends. He surveyed the ruined apartment and shook his head sadly. "There's no way in the hell we're getting our security deposit back after this."

*

With some help from Zo-Pound, Animal was finally able to get Brasco off him and rolled onto his back. Animal knelt over his friend and checked the extent of his injuries.

Because he'd been shot in the back, Animal could only see the wounds that had managed to exit through his chest.

From the amount of blood pooling beneath him, Animal knew it was bad.

"Fool ass nigga, why would you jump in front of a bullet like that?" Animal asked angrily.

"Blood, you've been jumping in front of bullets for me for years. It was the least I could do. Besides, you're the star of our little soap opera. I couldn't let them write you out of the script just yet," Brasco joked. He was trying to be strong but couldn't hide the pain in his face. His breathing was heavy and his eyes rolled around in his head as if he were having trouble focusing.

Ashanti came to kneel beside them. He didn't have to see Brasco's injuries to know how badly he was hurt. The dark expression on Animal's face told him all he needed to know. They were about to lose another solider. Brasco and Animal had been instrumental in Ashanti's life growing up. They'd always taken care of him like he was their little brother. Knowing that Brasco was about to die was too much. He tried to fight it, but couldn't stop the tears from welling in his eyes.

"Lil' nigga, if you start crying I swear on the set I'm gonna get up from here and knock you the fuck out," Brasco warned Ashanti.

"I wasn't about to cry. I got something in my eye," Ashanti lied.

Sonja came over and joined them on the floor beside Brasco. She reached out to touch him but the murderous look Animal shot her gave her pause. "Animal, you know I've got medical training. Let me help."

Brasco turned to Sonja and mustered a weak smile. "I appreciate it, little lady, but I wouldn't waste my time if I were you. I've been shot enough times to know when I ain't got it in me to get up no more. Hey, Ashanti."

"Yeah," Ashanti answered, trying to swallow the frog in his throat.

"Let me see your hammer," Brasco tried to raise his arm, but didn't have the strength. Ashanti placed his gun into Brasco's hand and closed his fingers around the handle. This seemed to please Brasco. "That's what I'm talking about. We die the same way we lived, with pistols in our grip. Ain't that right, Animal?"

"Yes, a soldier's death," Animal said, thinking of the mantra Gladiator had taught him and he in-turn had taught to each member of the Dog Pound.

"Can I ask you something, Animal?"

"Anything, Brasco."

Brasco paused as if he was trying to organize his thoughts. "Why'd that bitch ass nigga have to shoot me in the back? I'd have liked to have seen it coming," he said, before taking one last breath and then going still.

"We gotta get out of here. With all that shooting I'm pretty sure one of the neighbors has called the police already," Sonja said.

"Then that means when we vanish it has to be without a trace," Cain said. He looked to his brother. "You know what to do."

Abel nodded and disappeared into the kitchen. They could hear the ticking of the stove, followed by the pungent odor of gas spreading through the house. A few seconds later, Abel came out of the kitchen holding the messenger bag. "We're all set. Let's move."

"I can't leave him here like this. He was my brother and deserves better," Animal said, still kneeling over Brasco's body.

Cain placed a hand on Animal's shoulder. "I don't like it either, but he's dead and there's nothing the living can do for the dead except honor their memories. If you want to make sure his memory lives on then when we get your kids back you make sure you tell them what kind of man their Uncle Brasco was. Honor him that way."

After a while, Animal allowed Ashanti and Cain to help him to his feet and steer him through the sea of dead bodies and out of the apartment. Using the elevator was out of the question so they took the stairs and exited the building through the underground garage. They had made it roughly two blocks before they heard the explosion. The band of outlaws stood on the sidewalk looking up at the flames that spilled from what used to be the twins' balcony. Cain wasn't lying when he said they had to disappear without a trace. The apartment wasn't in either of the twins' names and any evidence that could connect them to it would be devoured by the fire.

Ashanti and Animal stood shoulder to shoulder watching the fire and paying silent homage to their fallen comrade. For a long few moments, neither of them spoke. It was Animal who eventually broke the eerie silence.

"Ashanti, I remember you once telling me about a man that you used on a job, One-Eye Jack. Do you know how to get in contact with him?"

Ashanti gave him a strange look. "Yes, but if we're planning on robbing Lilith's boat what good is that crazy old pyromaniac gonna do."

"We're not going to rob The Red Widow... we're going to sink it."

CHAPTER 18

When most heard stories about the infamous Mountain occupied by the Brotherhood of Blood, thoughts came into mind of some dreary fortress carved into the side of some mountain in a far off region. Nothing could've been further from the truth. It was actually a compound nestled in the Blue Ridge Mountains of Bluemont, V.A.

The Brotherhood's stronghold was located beneath a place called Mount Weather, which was a government facility that was controlled by the Department of Defense. It was said to be the center of operations for F.E.M.A, but that was only to hide its real purpose. Mount Weather was a facility where the top people in the government were to be relocated to in the case of a national disaster. Occupying 434 acres of mountain area, it was said to be one of the largest and safest facilities in the world. You couldn't get within pissing distance of Mount Weather without having the government crawling up your ass. It made the perfect hiding place for the order of assassins.

Kahllah rode in the back of an unmarked van with

Anwar and his men from D.C. to Bluemont, Virginia. The distance was only forty-eight miles, so the ride wasn't a long one, but it felt like it. She could tell by the expressions on the faces of the young souls gathered that they were trying to brave, but were actually nervous. She couldn't say that she blamed them. They'd just been asked to accompany a woman they didn't know by anything other than reputation on a suicide mission.

"Are you sure about this Kahllah?" Anwar asked from the passenger seat where he was riding. "There's still time to turn back."

"Not for me there isn't," Kahllah said. If she tried to run, she knew that Khan and his agents would hunt her for the rest of her life. The only way to solve her problem was to face it head on.

They drove the van as close to the mountain as they dared before pulling off the road. The closer they got, the greater the risk of being detected by one of Mount Weather's security patrols. They were extremely diligent in their job of making sure no one got too close to the facility without being intercepted. Kahllah and Anwar would have to hike the last few miles on foot. Kahllah grabbed the backpacks that contained the things they would need for

their mission while Anwar gave last minute instructions to his men. They were to return to the spot where they'd dropped them off every three hours for the next twelve hours. If Kahllah and Anwar hadn't returned by then, the men should assume they were dead and abort the mission.

The first couple of miles through the woods leading to the Mountain were spent in silence. Kahllah was preparing herself mentally for what was to come. Getting into the Mountain would be easy enough; it's what she had to do once she was inside that would present the real problem. There was no way to know for sure if she would be able to rouse Nicodemus, and even if she was lucky enough to wake him, who was to say that he would be sympathetic to her plight? Nicodemus was fiercely loyal to the Brotherhood and quite fond of Lilith. It was a very real possibility that they'd been able to turn Anwar against her and he could've been walking her to her death. Still, she didn't have much other choice. She had exhausted all other options and now all she had was faith to go on.

Times like those, she missed her father. If Priest were still alive, he'd have not only stood up for her, but also taken the lives of those who sought to harm her. He had always been her biggest supporter when it came to pursing her dreams, and her biggest disciplinarian when she found herself straying from the path. Sometimes the things he did seemed cruel, but it was just his way of showing her that he cared. Priest had never been the most conventional parent, but what he lacked in parental skills, he made up for in love. She questioned a great many things about her father, but how much he loved her was never one of them.

"Is it true?" Anwar asked, breaking the silence.

"Is what true?"

"The things they're saying, about you straying from the path," he elaborated.

"What do you think, Anwar?"

"The fact that I'm cutting through the woods with you in the middle of the night should tell you what I think. I know you're no traitor, Kahllah, but I also know how easily things from the world outside ours can sway us from the path the elders have laid for us. I've had my fair share of second thoughts as to whether or not me remaining with the Brotherhood was the best thing for me."

Kahllah nodded in understanding. "I don't know if it's

accurate to say that I've strayed from the path. It's more like the path has strayed from me. There was a time in my life when I lived solely for the purpose of serving my order, but now I'm not so sure we share the same ideals. Things are changing and I'm not sure where or if I fit in with these changes."

"I can respect that," Anwar said. He could tell she really didn't want to talk about it so he let it drop.

They hiked through about three more miles of wood until they came upon a tall rock face. From the overgrown vegetation under their feet and snaking its way up the wall, you could tell that the path hadn't been used in ages.

"Have we taken a wrong turn?" Anwar asked, studying the wall. It seemed to stretch infinitely upward. Anwar was a skilled climber, but not that skilled.

"No," Kahllah stepped forward and began running her hands along the wall as if she was looking for something.

There was the sound of something moving through the brush a few yards away. Anwar removed a pair of small, night vision binoculars from his pack and scanned the woods. In the distance, he could see several men wearing masks moving through the trees. They were fanned out and searching for something, likely them. Anwar wasn't sure if his men had betrayed him, or just dumb luck, but they had been found out.

"Lotus, in about thirty seconds we're going to have company and I don't think they're bringing wine to have with dinner. If you've got something planned, please do it now before we die in these woods."

"Be quiet and let me think," she continued searching the rock face. She finally found what she was looking for, a small notch carved into the rock. It wasn't very large, only big enough for her to slip her pinky into.

"Almost... almost... " she continued wriggling her finger

around in the hole, looking for the release. Finally, there was the whoosh of air and the rock face slid back, allowing enough space for her to slip through. Without a word, she grabbed Anwar and pulled him through behind her. Once they were inside, the rock face slid back into place as if it had never been disturbed.

They found themselves within a dark and stale smelling tunnel. Kahllah removed one of the glow sticks she was carrying, and snapped it, releasing the chemicals that caused the soft white glow inside.

"I had no idea that was there," Anwar said, looking at the wall in amazement.

"Of course you didn't. You're not old enough or of a high enough rank," Kahllah told him. She wasn't trying to slight him, just being honest. "This is a secret known to only the eldest and most trusted of our order. There are entrances like these all over the mountain. They were created so that in the event that the Mountain was ever breached by our enemies, the elders wouldn't be trapped."

"And do you care to tell me how you know about these doors if they're secrets only for the elders?" Anwar asked.

"My dad showed it to me and his dad showed it to him. Our roots in the Brotherhood are three generations strong... technically four now." She thought of Animal's children.

This surprised Anwar. "I didn't know you were a legacy."

"Neither did I until recently. Enough talking, voices carry far too easily in these tunnels and we don't want to get caught," she told him before walking off.

It was so dark that Anwar couldn't see how far the tunnel stretched, but it seemed to go on forever. They had been walking for nearly twenty minutes when he felt the ground start to slope downward. They were headed deeper into the Mountain and into the heart of their stronghold.

"Hold this." Kahllah handed him the glow stick and walked slightly ahead of him where it was too dark to see. Anwar could hear her rummaging around inside her pack. When Kahllah reemerged from the darkness she had changed her clothes. She was now wearing a long white robe with billowing sleeves. A white hijab covered her hair and the lower half of her face.

"What do you think, could I pass for a healer," she twirled so he could get a good look at the whole outfit.

Anwar admired her curves pressing against the thin white material. "I don't know, but I'd let you lay hands on me any day," he joked.

"Let's see how witty you'll be if we get caught and Khan cuts out your tongue," she scolded him.

"Lighten up, sheesh. Where did you stash your blades?" he asked.

Kahllah rolled up her sleeves and showed him the two long daggers she had strapped to each forearm. "They aren't my swords, but they'll have to do."

"Where to now?"

Kahllah pointed to several notches carved into the wall. "Up. There's a hatch just above us that should put us in the garden if I'm not mistaken. At this hour, it should be empty," she took the glow stick back from him.

"Unless someone has decided to take a late night stroll," Anwar said.

Kahllah ignored his comment and began climbing up the notches in the wall. Even with the glow stick clamped between her teeth, partially lighting their way, it was still hard to see what was above her. She had to take her time to make sure she didn't crack her head. When she got to the top, she used one hand to hold firmly to one of the notches while using the other to push the hatch in the ceiling. It hadn't been used in a while, so it was stuck and she had to give it a good push to get it to move. She accidentally pushed a little too hard and sent it flipping open, making a slapping sound when it connected with the floor overhead. Both Kahllah and Anwar froze, listening for any signs that someone had heard the noise. Only when she was sure that all was clear, did she climb out into the garden.

The Mountain's indoor garden was one of the only things in the entire compound that sported any real colors. There were almost two hundred different species of flowers, plants, and weeds; some of which you could no longer find anywhere on the planet except the Brotherhood's garden. Sunlight was fed through the large halogen lamps that covered almost the entire ceiling, and they were watered by time-released sprinklers. Kahllah had spent countless hours roaming the two-acre indoor jungle and studying the different types of plants. It was that very garden that inspired her name Black Lotus, and taught her the skills to change the color of the normally white flower to black. Ironically enough, it was Tiger Lily who had taught it to her.

For all their differences, they shared a love and vast knowledge of plant life. After helping Anwar through the hole, they began the trek to Nicodemus's quarters.

Walking the halls of the Mountain felt strange to Kahllah. She had grown up in the cold gray halls, yet now they felt alien. It was just another sign the growing distance between she and the order. As they were strolling down a long corridor, they noticed two of the brothers coming in their direction. Kahllah knew their faces, but not their names. They had been chatting amongst themselves, but when they spotted Anwar and Kahllah, they focused their attention on them. Kahllah's heart raced and her armpits sweated. She tucked her hands into the sleeves of the robe, clutching her blades. If they were stopped, there would be no negotiation. She was going to end them before they had a chance to sound the alarm.

They were within mere feet of the two brothers when something akin to recognition crossed one of their faces. She began easing her blades from their sheaths in anticipation of battle. Kahllah was just about to strike when the brothers nodded in greeting and kept walking. "That was close," she sighed.

"Tell me about it. I think I shit my pants," Anwar said, half-jokingly. "Let's get this over with quickly."

Nicodemus didn't occupy the same wing of the mountain as the other elders. His quarters were the east wing. When they rounded the final corner to get to Nicodemus' room, they spied two guards standing outside his door, armed with tall spears. They were dressed in all black with masks covering their faces, one red and one blue. When they spotted Anwar and the woman in white coming their way, they stood at attention and gripped their spears a bit tighter.

"Evening, brothers," Anwar greeted them warmly. "I've brought a healer to give the elder his treatment."

The one in the blue mask cocked his head and regarded Kahllah. "Nicodemus has already had his second session for the day and we weren't notified about a third."

"I'm afraid this was kind of short notice. We'd gotten word that Nicodemus' condition is worsening, so we had one of our most skilled healers flown in from Spain. I've only just now picked her up from the airport," Anwar lied. He was surprisingly quick on his feet when it came to bending the truth.

Red Mask and Blue Mask exchanged glances. "We'll have to clear it with Khan or Bastille first," Red Mask said.

Anwar sighed. "I guess you've got to do what you've got to do, but I warn you that if something happens to Nicodemus because I didn't get her to him in time you'll be the one to explain it to Khan."

This seemed to get their attention. Red Mask and Blue Mask stepped to the side to confer. After some debate they returned to their positions. "She may go inside, but you'll have to wait out here," Blue Mask told him.

"Of course," Anwar stepped to the side so she could pass. He waited until she had disappeared inside before releasing the breath he was holding. "It's all up to you now Lotus," he whispered to himself.

*

Nicodemus' sleeping quarters were on the small side, barely big enough to hold his bookshelf, bed, and writing table. On the shelves, and stacked wherever there was space, were books about world history, war, and of course poisons. He had always been a very well-read man.

She smelled him before her eyes landed on him in the darkened room. The scent of death and sickness hung thick in the air. Moving as soundlessly as possible, she crossed the room to his bedside and cut on the small reading lamp. Hanging from the headboard of his bed was his trusty bull-whip. Nicodemus was so skilled with it that he could strike with deadly accuracy. She had once seen him knock a cigarette from a man's mouth from halfway across the room because he refused to stop smoking while they were having dinner at a restaurant. She ran her fingers along the with-ered leather remembering happier times under the Mountain, when she felt a sharp pain that made her snatch her hand back. Blood welled on the tip of her thumb from whatever she had pricked her finger on. She looked closer at the whip and saw the sparkle of diamond dust braided into it. That was a new addition.

Her eyes traveled from the whip to the man lying in the bed and when she took stock of him, her heart sank. His once vibrant and thick silver hair was now thin and dull. His cheeks looked sunken and dark circles rung his closed eyes. This feeble thing lying in the bed before her was not the man she remembered. "What have they done to you?" she stroked his hair lovingly. Nicodemus stirred fitfully in his sleep, but he did not wake.

Kahllah pulled off her hijab and sat it to the side. She knew she didn't have much time before the guards got suspicious and came to check on her. She pulled the gold necklace from inside her robe and popped the cylindrical pendent from her neck. She held it in her hands, feeling the warmth radiating from it. The true purpose of the pendent was something that she had never shared with another soul, including her father. It was the price Sharif had paid for Anwar's life; his blood. Carefully, she twisted the cylinder between her two fingers and opened it. Most dismissed the stories of the children of the damned as myths, but Kahllah knew better. She had trafficked with the house of the Gehenna assassins and had seen first hand what the cursed blood could do. She had always thought she'd save Sharif's gift for herself to use during dire times, but it didn't get direr than what had become of Nicodemus. If she planned to live, she needed Nicodemus to wake up and the blood was her longest and best shot.

Using her thumb, she gently pried open Nicodemus's dried and cracked lips. The stench of his breath was equal to, if not greater than, the smell in the room. She tilted the cylinder, pouring the thick red liquid into his mouth. She saw his tongue move as if he could taste it and became hopeful, until he went still again. It must not have been enough! Her shoulders sagged in defeat. The contents of her pendent had been her best and last hope. Now that it hadn't worked, she had to figure out what to do next. Her thoughts were disturbed by a loud shriek coming from the hall.

*

Kahllah had only been gone for five minutes, but to Anwar it felt like an hour. He tried to engage the guards in small talk, but they were more concerned with their posts than anything Anwar had to say. In an attempt to keep his mind busy, he started counting the cracks in the floor.

From down the hall he could hear footsteps drawing nearer. Someone was coming. He looked back at the door nervously, wondering what the hell was taking Kahllah so long. When Anwar saw who was coming, his heart dropped from his chest and landed in his stomach.

Bastille's huge form came into view. His big sword slapped against his back as he moved. On one side of his face he sported bandages, no doubt as a result of Anwar trying to set him on fire. When Bastille spotted the third man with the two guards he'd posted outside Nicodemus' room, his face soured. "What is he doing here? I gave strict orders that no one was allowed anywhere near this room without clearing it with Khan or myself," he addressed the masked men.

"Just chatting it up with my fellow brothers," Anwar smirked.

"Shut your mouth, worm. I wasn't talking to you," Bastille snapped. He turned his attention back to the guards. "Well?"

"He said Khan sent him to escort the new healer to Nicodemus," Red Mask told him.

"And now that I've done my job, I'll be leaving." Anwar started backing away.

"You're going nowhere," Bastille grabbed him by the front of his shirt and shook him like a rag doll. "Who did you send into that room?"

"Your mother," Anwar replied before digging his nail into the bandage on Bastille's face, re-opening the wound. Once he was free of the big man's grip, he took off running down the hall. Anwar felt bad about leaving Kahllah, but he could not avenge her pending death if he died too. He'd made it halfway down the hall when pain exploded in his thigh and he collapsed. He recoiled in horror when he saw the spear Red mask had thrown jutting from his thigh.

Bastille stalked towards the downed Anwar, blood running from the wound on his face, and his sword in hand. He pressed his heavy boot onto the wound, causing Anwar to yell out in pain. "Who is in that room with Nicodemus?"

Anwar remained silent, staring up at Bastille hatefully. Bastille pulled Anwar to his feet and propped him against the wall, placing the sharp end of his sword to his throat. "You will talk or you will die."

"Fuck you," Anwar snarled. He would be defiant to the end.

"No!" a feminine voice cried from the doorway of the room.

Bastille was shocked to see Kahllah standing there. Kahn had said she would try for the Mountain, but Bastille never expected her to be able to breach it. He turned his empty eyes back to Anwar.

"I was wondering who helped the traitor and did this to my face," he turned his head to one side so Anwar could get a good look at the damage. "I'm trying to figure out whose death with be sweetest, yours or that cunt's."

"Better to die as a free man than to die in bondage," Anwar spat in his face.

Bastille wiped the spit from his face with the back of his hand. "You've got heart... I like that. I wonder how it'll taste sautéed with peppers and onions," he swung his blade around and impaled Anwar on the end of it. Bastille pulled his sword from Anwar's chest and licked the blood off the edge. "Sweet indeed."

Seeing her pupil and friend laying at the feet of the executioner reduced Kahllah to tears. Anwar had been the second death in less than forty-eight hours that she had failed to prevent. Now his blood was on her hands along with Gucci's. At that moment, something inside her snapped and she charged.

Red Mask and Blue Mask moved to stop her, which was a mistake. Without breaking her stride, she drew two of her hidden blades and buried one in each of their chests. She didn't even look back to see the bodies drop. With sadness in her heart and rage in her eyes, she drew her final two blades and attacked Bastille.

The two daggers striking his big sword sent sparks flying in the hallway. Bastille had expected her to be slow and distracted as she had been in D.C., but who he faced was the Black Lotus of old. She moved as swiftly as the wind launching a series of attacks with the long daggers, opening gashes. Bastille managed to catch her with an uppercut, snapping her head back and busting open her lip. He tried to press her, but she was far quicker than he remembered and she managed to land several cuts on his arms and shoulders. He tried an overhand strike, which she dodged and stabbed him in the side. She made a sharp motion and broke the tip of one of the daggers off while it was still inside him. Bastille staggered backward, fighting to catch his breath. The two combatants circled each other in the narrow hallway, both bloodied and breathing heavily.

Kahllah broke the dance first, launching a roundhouse kick at his head. Bastille caught her by the ankle in mid-air and swung her into the wall, knocking the wind out of her. He struck again with his blade, but connected only with the stone floor. Kahllah was back on her feet and moving on him again with the dagger. She faked high then went low, plunging her remaining dagger into his broad chest.

"This is for the blood of all the innocent souls you've spilled in the name of the order," Kahllah told him, driving the dagger deeper into his chest.

Pain shot through Bastille's body causing him to drop his sword. He was disarmed, but still had another trick up his sleeve.

Kahllah heard the crackling sound just before electricity shot through her body. She dropped to one knee and Bastille kicked her in the face hard enough to snap her head back.

He kicked her over and over again until she ceased to move. As Kahllah lay on the floor, fighting to stay conscious, she couldn't help but to wonder how he had managed to beat her. When she saw the small stun gun in his hand she had her answer. He had won the duel by cheating.

Bastille retrieved his sword and limped in Kahllah's direction, dragging the blade behind him and dripping blood.

"You have no idea how long I've waited to have you at my feet like this. The mighty Black Lotus, crushed. It's over now. The old ways of the Brotherhood are dead and a new foundation will be built on top of the rotting corpses of people like you," he hoisted his sword.

"Before you kill me, I just need to know one thing,"

Kahllah rasped. Her ribs felt broken and she was having trouble breathing. "What really happened to Nicodemus?"

Bastille paused. "If you must know, Khan poisoned him. It was just shit luck that he had built up such a tolerance to where the poison didn't kill him, only put him in a coma. But if it'll make you feel better, I plan on putting him out of his misery as soon as I'm done with you."

"Thank you for the warning," a voice called from somewhere around Bastille.

Kahllah heard a sharp crack right before Bastille's body went stiff. His thick fingers clutched at something around his neck as he gasped for air. There was what sounded like a slicing sound before blood squired onto Kahllah's face. The last thing she remembered was seeing Bastille's lifeless eyes when his severed head rolled to a stop next to her. Then everything went dark.

CHAPTER 19

The Port of Newark was relatively quiet that night, which suited Customs officer Tony Jones just fine considering he hadn't wanted to work that night anyhow. He'd gotten a call from his co-worker Mike, who usually worked the night shift, saying that he wouldn't be able to make it in that day, but needed someone he could trust to do him a solid. If Tony agreed, Mike promised to split the under the table payment he was due to receive with Tony. Tony was hard up for cash so it was a no brainer.

Most of the boats that were scheduled to pull into the port that night had already arrived and were accounted for, but the one that had pulled in less than an hour ago wasn't on the schedule. In fact, everyone working the port that night was presented with a thick envelope full of cash to pretend they didn't even see it. It was a medium sized cargo ship with the words La Viuda Roja painted on the hull. The sight of the thing gave Tony the creeps and he wished the men dressed in black would hurry and finish unloading it so he didn't have to look at it anymore.

Tony decided to take a walk around the docks while he

snuck off to smoke the joint he had tucked in his pocket. The men in black had it under control so no one would miss him if he took a short break. He had just stepped behind one of the tall containers to fire up his weed, when he spotted a man sleeping on a sheet of cardboard. Tony let out a heavy sigh. He was constantly having to chase off vagrants who would slip into the port looking for somewhere to sleep for the night.

"Move it along, buddy. You can't sleep back here," Tony called to the man, but he didn't reply. Now irritated, he slipped on his black leather gloves and prepared to move the man physically. "I said, get the fuck up," he rolled the man over and recoiled when he saw the milky white eye staring up at him from behind a horribly burned face.

Cain grabbed Tony by the neck and pulled him down, sliding a blade up through his chin and into his mouth. He laid Tony down as gently as if he were putting a child to bed, before stepping from behind the canister and signaled his friends.

*

"That's the signal," Abel said looking through the scope of the sniper rifle he had mounted on the top of a car just outside the fence of the port. Cain waved his arm back and forth letting him know that it was all clear.

"We're up," Animal said, snatching the knapsack he was carrying from the floor and putting it on his back.

"You might want to be a little more careful with that thing," Ashanti warned, taking a cautionary step back. He knew exactly what was in the bag and what it could do.

Animal ignored him and went about the task of checking the clips of the two he had on him. In addition to the care package he planned to leave Lilith with, they had also scored some guns from One-Eyed Jack. The two Rugers weren't his Pretty Bitches, but they would do.

"Everybody clear on what they're supposed to be doing?"

"Yep," Zo said spinning the cylinder on one revolver then the other. One-Eyed Jack had offered him an automatic, but Zo felt more comfortable going in with guns he was already familiar with. "Seems almost a sin to sink all that coke to the bottom of the ocean. Do you know how much money we could've made on the streets from this shit?"

"We ain't drug dealers tonight, Zo. We're saboteurs," Animal told him.

"Animal, I still don't see why you don't let me go in with y'all. You know I know how to handle myself," Sonja pouted.

"I've already told you why, Sonja. I've already lost one child's mother so God forbid if something goes wrong and we don't make it out I don't want both my kids growing up orphans. Someone has to be here to tell Celeste and T.J. who their father was and why he died," Animal said sincerely.

Ashanti made a face and shook his head. After all Sonja had put Animal through, he was still trying to look out for her. Some people never learned. "Ain't nobody else dying tonight. That's on the set," Ashanti declared and started walking towards the fence. He still hadn't gotten over what happened to Brasco and couldn't stand to lose another one of his brothers.

"We'd better catch up with this crazy little nigga before he sets it off before we get there." Zo-Pound followed Ashanti.

Animal was about to join them when Sonja called after him. "Animal, before you go in there, there's something I need to tell you." There was a nervous edge to her voice.

"You can tell me when I come back," Animal smiled and went to join his crew.

*

The plan was for Abel to take out the customs officer who had been patrolling the dock and clear the way for Ashanti, Zo, and Animal, while Sonja and Abel stood back as their back-up. Abel would be tracking them through the scope on the gun and watching their backs. Cain would linger just outside the boat and watch for signs of trouble on the ground floor. He wasn't too pleased about not being able to board the boat and join in the murder, but Animal wouldn't let him. Cain was too unpredictable and the last thing he wanted to deal with was a raving killer complicating their plans. Once they had boarded the boat, it would be up to Ashanti and Zo to neutralize any threats while Animal went into the bowels of the ship to set the charges. Once the bomb was placed, they'd have roughly two minutes to get the hell out of dodge.

Animal, Zo, and Ashanti huddled behind a container just outside the gangplank that led to the deck of the Red Widow. Ashanti, being the shortest, was elected to peek out and see how many guards there were blocking their entrance. He looked back towards where he knew Abel was hiding and held up two fingers, then pointed to the boat. A few seconds later, there were two chirping sounds, followed by the splash of something hitting the water. With the way now clear, the three of them boarded the boat.

Once they were on the Red Widow, they split up. Ashanti and Zo would cover the upper decks, while Animal ventured into the bowels of the ship. He was making his way below deck when he smelled it. It was the same pungent odor he'd picked up on when he busted into Momo and Luther's room, only this time it was different... it was pure and didn't have the burned taint to it. Animal covered his nose and continued on his way.

Animal was just reaching the first landing when he spotted a man in black fatigues and wearing some kind of gas mask coming up the stairs. Luckily, Animal saw the man before he saw Animal and he put him down before he even realized that he wasn't alone. Above him, he heard the shuffling of feet, before something fell over the side of the boat and hit the water. He smiled, knowing that Ashanti and Zo-Pound were on their jobs.

When Animal reached the lower level, the smell became so pungent that he had to use one hand to cover his mouth to keep from gagging. His eyes began to sting and he knew he wouldn't be able to take it down there for much longer. It was like the whole ship was made of the stuff. As he rounded the corner, he literally bumped into another one of the black clad soldiers carrying a rifle. Animal tried to bring his gun into play, but this soldier was quicker than the last one. He slammed the butt of the rifle into Animal's wrist, dislodging the gun. Animal recovered quickly, and was on him before he could lift his rifle. They struggled and the rifle went off, riddling the floor was bullets. Animal managed to get behind him and grab him in a reverse choke-hold. With a quick turn of his bicep, he snapped the soldier's neck.

On the deck above him, Animal heard the sounds of shouting and heavy footfalls. The sound of gunfire had stolen the element of surprise from them and the clock was officially ticking. He had to move quickly. He darted into the cargo hull and found himself in a room full of round canisters. There were at least fifty of them, all standing four feet tall. That's where he would set the charges.

As Animal made his way to the center of the canisters, he noticed the smell was strongest there, almost overpowering. Letting his curiosity get the best of him, Animal popped one of the canisters open. He'd expected to find cocaine, but instead it was full of the the same blue crystals Momo and Luther had been smoking. Animal opened three more of the cans with the same results. Now he knew what Sonja wanted to tell him. There was never any coke on the boat to begin with. It had always been about the crystals.

"That rotten bitch!" Animal cursed. He felt like a total fool for letting Sonja dupe him again. He would settle up with her later, but right then, he had a job to do. Cocaine or not, he was going to sink Lilith's cargo. He scooped a handful of the blue crystals and put them in his pocket before placing the bomb on the floor. Animal had just set the timer on the bomb when he heard rushed footsteps behind him. He turned just in time to see another black clad soldier, wearing a gas mask, and charging him wielding a fire axe. Just as Animal ducked, the axe cut through the air nearly missing his head. He slammed his fist into the black clad soldier's face as hard as he could, but it didn't even seem to faze him. He could see his eyes through the visor of the gas mask and he had the same crazed look in his eyes as Momo.

Animal rolled across the floor, drawing his remaining gun at the same time. He fired blindly, hitting the soldier in the shoulder and it didn't even slow him down. Animal scampered out of the way just as the axe came down again. His eyes went to the digital timer on the bomb and saw that he had just over a minute to escape. He hated running from a fight, but he hated dying in a fireball even more, so he bolted. He had just cleared the door, when the crazed soldier grabbed him by the ankle, tripping him up. Animal pitched forward, face first, hitting his head on the rail and losing the gun over the side.

Animal had regained his senses in time to see the axe speeding towards his face. He rolled out of the way and kicked the man in his knee hard enough to make it buckle. When he had him down, Animal took off, but the soldier was right behind him. He had made it as far as the first landing, where he'd left the first soldier he'd killed, when the mad man caught up with him. He tried to swing the axe, but it ended up getting stuck between the rails of the cramped stairwell. Animal kicked him in the face, cracking the gas mask and sending glass shards into the soldier's eyes. When the soldier removed the gas mask, Animal saw the tiger slashes crisscrossing his face and knew it had to be the same man Sonja claimed had given his life to help her escape. "Ethan?"

Hearing his name seemed to give the mad man pause, but the moment of sanity only lasted for a second before he was back to trying to kill Animal. They were struggling on the stairs when there was an explosion that rocked the ship with enough force to send them both spilling down the stairs. The ocean rushed into the stairwell and within seconds, Animal found himself knee deep in salt water. The ship was sinking, but much faster than he had anticipated. If he had any hope of surviving, he had to get above deck.

Using the railing to pull himself forward, Animal began making his climb up the stairs. He'd cleared the landing when he felt something beneath the water grab his leg. "You can't be fucking serious," Animal sighed before he was pulled under the water.

Animal and Ethan struggled for dear life beneath the

water. Animal had never been the best swimmer, and fighting someone underwater was a first for him. His thoughts were on survival, but Ethan was holding onto his leg for dear life. Cutting or beating Animal to death was no longer good enough; he was trying to drown him. Animal's lungs burned as he tried desperately to hold his breath while he freed himself. Water seeped into his mouth and he could feel himself begin to gag. Laying on the stairs, Animal spotted the gun the other soldier had dropped when he killed him. He clawed desperately at it and by sheer will alone; he was able to grab it. Using his last bit of strength, he turned the gun on Ethan and pulled the trigger.

Animal swam through blood and brains trying to make it to higher ground. The entire staircase was flooded now and he had a hard time determining which way was up. Follow the bubbles, he repeated over and over in his head. He was able to swim to the top of the stairs only to find that his way had been blocked by one of the canisters that had slid in front of the door when the ship started to go down. His last chance was to try and reach the small hatch just above him. He kicked as hard as he could, but he felt himself weakening. His lungs felt like they were about to explode. When he felt himself blacking out he knew it was over. He would never see his children again, but he gained some measure of peace knowing he and Gucci would soon be reunited.

*

Animal thought he was dreaming when he felt hands pressing up and down on his chest. He opened his eyes just in time to see Cain leaning in about to give him mouth to mouth. The unexpected sight scared him so badly that he snapped bolt upright and the two knocked heads. He broke into a fit of coughing, expelling the water that had made it to his lungs. He looked around and was surprised to see himself surrounded by Ashanti, Zo, and the twins.

"I'd say he's okay now," Cain said, rubbing his forehead where it had collided with Animal's.

"What the fuck happened?" Animal asked looking at the relieved faces. It was then that he realized Sonja was absent.

"We were hoping you could tell us," Ashanti said. "We heard the bomb go off then the ship started sinking. We tried to wait for you, but there were soldiers everywhere. We barely made it off the boat ourselves. For a minute, we thought we'd lost you."

"You know I'm harder to kill than most," Animal joked. He made to get to his feet and was overcome by a wave of dizziness.

"Take it easy, homie. You were in the drink for quite some time." Zo helped to steady him.

"How did I get off the boat?" Animal asked. He didn't remember much of anything after shooting Ethan.

Cain shrugged. "We've got no clue. We found you floating in the wreckage. The strange thing about it was that somebody saw fit to strap a life preserver on you first, before tossing you into the water."

"Sounds like you've got a guardian angel," Ashanti said.

"A guardian angel indeed," Animal said while trying to put the pieces back together in his head. "Where's Sonja?"

"Gone," Abel told him. "Sneaky bitch clocked me over the head and took off with the car and the messenger bag. Homie, I know that's your B.M. and all that, but the next time I see that broad it's on sight!"

"Don't worry. I have a feeling we haven't seen the last of

Red Sonja," Animal told him. Reflexively, he stuck his hand in his pocket and felt something soggy at the bottom of it.

When he removed his hand from his pocket, he noticed that it was completely blue.

"What's that?" Cain asked curiously.

Animal tried to wipe his hand on his pants, but only succeeded in making more of a mess. "I'm not entirely sure yet, but I have a feeling that whatever this is has a big part to play in all this."

"Well, we ain't got no car, no money, and a bunch of dirty guns on us. What should we do?" Ashanti asked.

Animal shrugged. "Start walking I guess."

The five young weary warriors started their long trek back to civilization. Their mission hadn't had the expected results, but it wasn't a complete loss. Lilith's shipment was fish food, Sonja had finally showed her true colors, and Animal had lived to continue the pursuit of his children and take revenge for his loved ones. No matter what happened, blood would answer for blood.

"What happened to your face?" Zo asked.

Animal touched his fingers to his cheek and they came away stained with blood. There was a thin cut along his jaw, just below his ear. Ironically it was the exact same spot as the scar he had given his brother Justice.

EPILOGUE

When Detectives Brown and Alvarez reported for work the next day, they felt like they had just stepped into the Twilight Zone. There were at least two dozen people crowded at the sergeant's desk, all trying to talk at the same time. The phones were ringing off the hook, and every able body available scrambled back and forth to try and get a hold on things.

From what they'd learned, the strange activity from the night before hadn't been just limited to the murders they were chasing, there had also been a gas explosion that wiped out an entire apartment on the Westside, and a boat had sank at the Port of Newark.

"Hey, Detective Brown, a fax came for you this morning from the lab in Brooklyn," a thin cop whose name escaped him called.

"Man, sure hope they got a hit on that blood sample," Detective Brown said excitedly, cutting across the room with his partner on his heels. He was so anxious that he grabbed the folder without bothering to say thank you. Hands trembling with hope, he opened it. They'd gotten lucky and the person who'd bled on that street was in the database for violent offenders. When he saw the accompanying picture all he could say was, "Holy shit!"

"What is it?" Detective Alvarez pressed. Detective Brown held the picture up for his partner to see, and he too was stunned. They were more than familiar with the second shooter because they'd been chasing him since he was in pampers. He was a young trigger man who went by the name Ashanti.

A SNEAK PEAK AT THE HIGHLY ANTICIPATED...

THE GOOD SON • A HOODLUM NOVEL

1

W ally tugged at the neck line of what had once been a fresh white-tee and his fingers came away damp. He was sweating like a runaway slave with the massa hot on his heels. It was ninety-three degrees outside, and the heat trapped in the two-bedroom project apartment made it feel like the temperature was on hell. The air conditioner was busted and all they had to work with were two dollar-store fans that only circulated the hot air. Between the heat and the fumes coming from the kitchen, Wally felt like he was going to fall out, but he reasoned it was all a part of the job.

In the kitchen, Melinda stood over the stove, whipping two pots like she was making Sunday dinner. She was auditioning for a job with the new crew who had set up shop, so she knew she had to bring her best whip game. A bead of sweat rolled down her butter colored cheek, and splashed on the mural she had tatted on her forearm in memory of her deceased brother True. Ambidextrously she worked the water around in both pots at the same time, watching the cocaine and baking soda take their marital vows before the drug gods and forge a union known as crack. When she was satisfied with the consistency, she whipped the pots around once more for good measure before taking them from the heat and sitting them on the dining room table.

One of the fiends they had at the spot to test the finished product danced too close to the pots and Melinda met him with a forearm the chest. "You can't taste the meal until it's done. When it cools, you'll get your blast."

"C'mon shorty, I can take my steak rare. Just let me wet my beak right quick." The fiend shuffled in place, scratching his arm and sucking up the drips hitting the back of his throat. There was no way to say for sure when he'd last fixed, but his extreme thirst made it seem like a while.

Melinda didn't like the desperate look in the fiend's eyes. Her hand swept across the table and inconspicuously picked up one of the razors they'd bought to cut the crack up. She hoped to God she wouldn't have to use it, but she was prepared to.

"Yo, why don't you be the fuck easy?" A slender light skinned dude stepped into the living room. He was dressed in a Nike jogging suit, with a gold chain and cross hanging down his chest. From the way everyone in the room perked up, you could tell he was the man in charge. "How we looking?" he asked Melinda.

"I just whipped the last two," Melinda nodded to the two pots.

The slim kid picked one of the pots up and examined it. Floating in the bottom of the cloudy water was a perfectly round cookie. "You got skills, kid," he told Melinda.

"Shit, I been in the kitchen since I was a kid. I told you I had the god-hand with it. Y'all need to stop fronting and put me on the payroll," Melinda said.

"Yeah, we might have a position to you," the slim kid cracked a smile. "Yo Wally, go find them other two young boys and have them come up here and help you cut this shit up. We about to flood the hood."

"I'm on it," Wally moved for the door. He had just undone the lock when the door burst open. He never got a good look at the person who had kicked the door open, but he had a great view of the stars that danced in front of his eyes when the baseball bat made contact with his head.

Two men rushed the pad, holding automatic weapons and wearing masks and ordering everyone to freeze. They were led by the young boy who had swung the bat. He wore his hair in box braids with red bandana tied around his head. He opted not to cover his face, because he wanted his victims to know exactly who they were dealing with. He saw Wally trying to get up and gave him another whack with the bat. He hit him and over and continued hitting Wally long after he'd stopped moving. Everyone in the room was horrified about Tech's display of brutality, which was just what he was shooting for. He wanted to leave no doubt in anyone's mind about how far he was willing to go in the streets.

"I think he's dead, so you can stop hitting him," Swann entered the apartment. He was a light skinned kid who looked more Hispanic than Black. His sandy hair was neatly braided into cornrows that hung to his shoulders. Physically, Swann was a pretty boy, but mentally he was as ugly as they came. His exploits in the streets had earned him a reputation as a killer, and a seat at the table of one of the most notorious crime families in the eastern United States, the Clarks.

"What the fuck is this about?" the slim kid asked as if he didn't already know what was up. He thought he would be able to fly under the radar and get his weight up a bit before he had to deal with the problem that he knew would come from opening up a crack spot in a hood that was claimed as property of the Clark family.

Swann looked at Tech, who stepped forward and smacked the slim kid. "Nigga, you know what it is. You been warned about this bullshit, but you still trying to violate so now you gonna get violated," Tech barked.

The slim kid looked like he wanted to try Tech, but he knew better. Tech was the alpha male in the Dog Pound, a crew of young hitters who were about the business of mayhem. None of them were old enough to drink, but they were old enough to kill. The slim kid figured he could probably take Tech in a fist fight, but whether he won or lost the end result would be the same. He would die.

The slim kind finally found his voice and addressed him. "I know you said we couldn't pump around here unless it was y'all work, so I was just trying to sell off what lil bit I had left so I can get up out your way."

Swann looked at the two fresh brewed pots on the counter. "And this is why you still cooking and bagging?" The slim kid looked at the paraphernalia on the table.

His lie was a weak one, and he knew it before he'd told it, but it didn't stop him. He had a feeling this was about to go poorly, so he tried to appeal to Swann's nostalgic side.

"Swann, you know what it is to be a young nigga struggling, you been there. Every kid in the hood has heard the stories of how you gave it up as a young outlaw trying to get to the top."

Swann's lips twisted into a scowl. "The fact that you know my history and you still tried this dumb shit only makes me feel more disrespected," Swann picked up one of the coffee pots with the crack cookies floating in them. "You lil niggaz always wanna throw that shit out there about how you like us, but you ain't like us. Y'all punks, out here stepping on toes, because you so thirsty to get noticed.

Well guess what, we see you now homie," he smashed the coffee pot against the slim kid's head. He looked at the slim kid, now on the floor crying, and shook his head in disgust. He turned to Tech. "Earn yo stripes, Blood, but leave nothing to chance. Everybody is aboard on this flight."

"Swann, you gotta be kidding leaving this young boy to clean up this mess. He ain't ready," one of the masked men said. He was the burlier of the two.

Swann looked at him. "And I was how old when you and Tommy used to give me guns to play with, Doc?" he asked. The burly masked man didn't have an answer.

"Exactly," Swann said and turned back to Tech. "When you done, toss the pad. All you find all you keep. Consider it a bonus."

"Say no more," Tech dropped the bat and drew a 9mm from his waistband.

"Wait, you gonna kill me over a few sales?" the slim kid asked in a frantic tone.

"Nah, I'm gonna kill you so the rest of these mutha-fuckas know what happens to clown ass niggaz who go against the grain," Tech told him before pulling the trigger. The bullet took the slim kid off his feet and slammed him into the window. Tech shot him twice more, painting the wall and table with blood. When he was done with the slim kid he turned his attention to Melinda.

Melinda threw her hands up defensively. "Wait, wait, wait, I ain't got nothing to do with this. I was just trying to make some extra money cooking up for some work. I don't even know these dudes like that."

"Next time, be smarter with the company you keep," Tech said and prepared to finish her.

"Hold on, youngster," Swann said. He was examining the remaining coffee pot. He turned his eyes to Melinda. "You got some skills, ma. You want a job?"

Melinda hesitated; making sure it wasn't a trick question. "Ah... yeah," she stammered.

"Cool, come see me tomorrow morning and I'm gonna put you to work. I don't think I have to tell you what'll happen if you ever breathe a word of what happened here, right?" Swann asked.

"Hell no, I ain't seen shit and I don't know shit," Melinda assured him.

Swann nodded.""Good answer. You start tomorrow morning at eleven."

"But wait, how will I find you?" Melinda asked.

"You won't have to, I'll send somebody to pick you up," Swann told her.

"But you don't even know where I live."

"I will by tomorrow morning," Swann winked. "Just some food for thought in case you get any big ideas, ma. The name is Swann. Ask anybody in the hood how I give it up." Swann turned and addressed his crew. "Let's make moves. Shai's function starts in a few hours and it'd be in poor taste for us to show up late."

OTHER NOVELS BY K'WAN

Gangsta
Road Dawgz
Street Dreams
Hoodlum
Eve
Gutter *(Gangsta Sequel)*
Blow
Diamonds & Pearl
The Diamond Empire
Lawless
Wrath

SHORTS/ANTHOLOGIES/NOVELLAS

The Game
Flirt
Flexin & Sexin *(Vol.1)*
From The Streets to the Sheets
From Harlem With Love
Love & Gunplay *(Animal Story)*
The Leak *(Animal Story)*
Purple Reign *(Vol. 1: Purple City Tales)*
Little Nikki Grind *(Vol. 2: Purple City Tales)*
The Life & Times of Slim Goodie *(Season 1)*
First & Fifteenth *(A Hood Rat Short)*
Black Lotus
Black Lotus 2: The Vow

HOOT RAT SERIES
(IN ORDER)

Hood Rat
Still Hood
Section 8
Welfare Wifeys
Eviction Notice
No Shade

ANIMAL SAGA
(IN ORDER)

Ghetto Bastard: The Beginning
Animal
Animal II: The Omen
Animal III: Revelations
Animal IV: Last Rites
Animal V: Executioner's Song

THE FIX SERIES
(IN ORDER)

The Fix
The Fix 2
The Fix 3